KU-385-530

GROUND ZERO

Also by Conor Cregan

With Extreme Prejudice
House of Fire
Valkyrie

GROUND ZERO

Conor Cregan

Hodder & Stoughton

Lines from *The Second Coming* taken from *Yeat's Poems*, edited and annotated
by A. Norman Jeffares, published by Gill and Macmillan are
reprinted with kind permission of A. P. Watt Ltd
on behalf of Michael Yeats.

First published in Great Britain in 1998 by
Hodder and Stoughton
a division of Hodder Headline PLC

The right of Conor Cregan to be identified as the author of
this work has been asserted by him in accordance with the
Copyright, Designs and Patents Act 1988.

10 9 8 7 6 5 4 3 2 1

A CIP catalogue record for this title is
available from the British Library
ISBN 0 340 68935 8

Typeset by Hewer Text Ltd, Edinburgh
Printed and bound in Great Britain by
Mackays of Chatham Plc, Chatham, Kent

Hodder and Stoughton
A division of Hodder Headline PLC
338 Euston Road
London NW1 3BH

To Angie

Author's Note

On 11 March, 1945 a team of German commandos landed in New Mexico, intent on stealing plutonium for an atom bomb. No mention of this incident appears on any official files, and most of those who know about the event still refuse to speak. Most of them, but not all of them.

Much of what follows is based on fact.

Things fall apart; the centre cannot hold;
Mere anarchy is loosed upon the world,
The blood-dimmed tide is loosed, and everywhere
The ceremony of innocence is drowned;
The best lack all conviction, while the worst
Are full of passionate intensity.

W.B. Yeats
The Second Coming

Each time Oskar Finger turned traitor, he maintained it was for the sake of peace. He passed German secrets to the French to try and prevent a war; French secrets to the Americans to help end the same war; and American secrets to the Russians to make sure another would not start.

By that time, Finger had a cocaine habit and a certain resentment of official power brought on by an inflated sense of his own worth as a physicist and years of isolation in the New Mexican desert. And he demanded money for his services.

He found his Russian controller very willing to pay. Oskar Finger was passing him the secrets of the atomic bomb.

It was a painfully cold February day in Washington, DC in 1945 when the controller adjusted his hat and pulled the scarf he wore against the biting wind below his chin. 'You're late!' was all he said to Oskar Finger, and he said it without moving his lips. Finger swung his eyes around the Lincoln Memorial and, when he had regained some dignity, concentrated on his controller.

The flip side of handsome – age had allied with bad luck and other things – the controller's facial skin sank like overwet plaster, giving him a bland countenance, while tiny lines gathered in abundance around the mouth and eyes, showing strain and fracture in equal amounts. And the eyes were watered over with a translucent cloak of sadness.

'Read the writing on the wall and talk to me,' he ordered Finger then.

Oskar Finger had once been handsome, but now he was losing that with the same rapidity he secretly suspected he was being pushed out of the first division of theoretical physics. Only good for administration and reportage now, and not a chance of a Nobel Prize.

Red-haired, slightly weak-chinned, wearing glasses and a tweed jacket, he could still vault the steps of the Lincoln Memorial, but none of the girls there ever looked at him any more. 'They have enough plutonium for a bomb,' he said.

Across the Potomac, where small slabs of ice jockeyed for position in the muddy flow of the river, the two men stopped before Arlington House and stared back across the water. Some premature spring foliage now threatened to curtain off sections of the American capital on the north side of the river, and the White House had a dull frozen look of dependable authority against the clear blue sky, while Old Glory stretched out to the clear air like a welcoming palm. Finger and his controller walked down to a secluded row of graves in the cemetery below and each man stood before a headstone.

'The bomb will be transferred by rail to the coast in two parts: plutonium in one, casing and the rest in the other,' Finger explained, 'then placed on board a ship and taken to England. I took a special risk stealing the details. It's all in this.' Finger knelt down, blessed himself and passed an envelope to his controller. 'Now, may I have my money? I have to go. I have to lecture some generals on all of this.'

'Will they use it on Germany?' his controller asked. The smell of onions and beer drifted from his mouth.

'I'm a scientist,' Finger insisted, 'not a strategist. Now, my money? I want to go. I do not wish to be electrocuted.'

Very slowly, the controller passed Finger a roll of twenty dollar notes.

'Do you have to be so public?' Finger said. 'FBI men

follow all of us. All the time. I'm taking a great risk being here.'

'The best place to hide a blade of grass is a green field. Take the long way back.' The controller raised his hat. The combination of manners and threat irritated Finger.

'When will Moscow have its bomb?' Finger said then, curiosity conquering any fear he had.

'When they have the explosive. You couldn't get us some of that plutonium, could you?'

'Don't joke. This war will be over soon. I want it to be the last. I risk myself for peace.'

'Of course,' the controller said. 'We'll be across the Oder by Hitler's birthday. And the Rhine? Do you hear anything at these lectures you give?'

'I told you, I'm a scientist,' Finger insisted. But his pomposity got the better of him. 'If you want a guess from what I pick up, I'd say three weeks. Perhaps a month. Perhaps they have been waiting for this bomb. End the European war with a bang, so to speak. Ten, maybe twenty, thousand tons of TNT. Not to mention radiation poisoning. It's quite a weapon. Frankly, there are some people down in New Mexico who think the atmosphere will catch fire. Then ... woosh!'

Oskar Finger's sudden confidence puzzled his controller. 'A war-winner, though,' the controller said.

'A war stopper,' Finger insisted. 'I do this to make Moscow an equal.'

'Moscow does appreciate you, Herr Finger,' the controller said.

An icy breeze passed them and rustled the trees around. Finger visibly shuddered and had to compose himself. 'I am no longer a German. I have not been one since the Nazis took power. Now, goodbye.'

The controller smiled and raised his hat one more time. The wind caught the few strands of hair he still had and held them erect until he had watched Oskar Finger disappear into the natural cover of the Virginian landscape.

The red-brick boarding house the controller always stayed at in Washington was a functional ragtime dwelling with a little too much taste and not enough cash to back it up.

The landlady was an attractive Appalachian woman with lumbago and very large breasts. Four hours after his meeting with the physicist, she caught Oskar Finger's controller trying to climb the staircase without making a sound.

'Evenin', M'ser Penny,' she said, 'heard you on the wood. You wasn't fixin' to leave 'out sayin' goodbye?'

He grinned and contemplated her imperfect teeth. Then he put his hands in his pockets and ambled upstairs. 'I have a lot of business, Mrs Abery. But I'll be back again. And you can call me Simon.'

'I'll make some coffee and call you a cab,' she said. 'And you must call me Violet.'

After exchanging a few more words with Violet Abery, Simon Penny went into a large bathroom and, out of habit, took a shallow bath. It took longer than it should have because one of the taps did not work properly. He was still drying his face and hair when he reached his own room. The gun made contact with his head as soon as he entered, the hammer click vibrating through his skin, the pressed steel digging into his temple, forcing him against the pastel wall. And Oskar Finger's hand was shaking.

'Who are you?' he demanded. 'This thing ... this thing' – he kicked a suitcase transmitter lying open on the floor behind the bed – 'it's German.' Then he threw some documents and codebooks across Penny's bed. 'None of this is Russian, it's all German.'

'So call the FBI,' Penny said.

Finger swung him round and on to the bed. He held the Colt automatic with two hands, trembling so much now Penny was more afraid he would be shot by accident than design.

Finger went over to the suitcases and began tossing things around the room. 'I've been feeding the Nazis the secrets to Armageddon,' he muttered to himself in a kind of self-pitying panic. He turned to Penny again with a pained pleading on his lips. 'Haven't I?'

'And been well paid,' Penny said.

Oskar Finger was sweating now, and continuously rubbing his stubbled face. 'You're a Nazi, you bastard.'

Penny raised his hands. 'I am neither. However, if you do choose to call the FBI, we'll both go to the electric chair. And, as you know, it is a particularly painful death, though I do have cyanide. But only enough for one.'

'I should kill you here.'

'Still probably means the chair for you.'

Finger shook his head and stepped back. 'Stay where you are. No, over there, against the wall, hands on your head.'

Penny obeyed. When he reached the wall again, he turned his head. 'No matter what you do, you'll fry without me. I'm your only hope. Now, if I were you I'd put the gun away, sit down, join me in a bourbon and help repack my luggage. I've a cab coming soon. I'd like to know how you got here.'

Finger paused before his next line. 'I need more money,' he said.

'And your meeting with the generals?' Penny asked.

'Rescheduled.'

'The little variables of espionage,' Penny said. 'Always expect cancellations. So, no one else knows you know about this bomb shipment?'

Finger wiped his brow again. Then he slammed his fist into Penny's kidneys, hurting himself more than his victim. Penny held his own pain and slid down the wall. Finger rubbed his aching fist before leaning down and grabbing Penny's long thin hair. 'I don't like you,' Finger said. There was a moment, just a moment, when Finger felt good again. 'I have never liked you. In a way, I'm glad you're a Nazi.

It means I was right about what I felt. That's good. Son of a bitch.'

Penny brought his elbow back into the physicist's stomach and slammed down on the hand holding the gun. Finger folded, and Penny took his head and dashed it on the wall. Then he lifted the scientist, dragged him over to the bed and opened the bedroom door.

'Mrs Abery, could you come up to my room?' he shouted.

CITY OF THE SUN

I

In the early hours of Monday, 5 February, 1945, after the main midnight situation conference had dispersed, a special meeting took place in the Führerbunker below the Reich Chancellery in Berlin.

Present at the meeting were Adolf Hitler; General Reinhard Gehlen, head of Foreign Armies East, the intelligence branch of all German armies fighting on the eastern front; and Walter Schellenberg, the head of SD Ausland, the foreign intelligence service of the Nazi party, and now Germany's main intelligence organisation.

Such was the secrecy of the meeting, no stenographer was required.

Waiting for Hitler in the stale atmosphere of the conference room, Schellenberg sat on one side of the long table which took up most of the floor space, his back to the filing cabinets and the situation map on the wall, biting his nails, while Reinhard Gehlen faced him, left hand drumming fingers next to a black telephone.

Schellenberg's face conveyed the struggle of years of duplicity and intriguing which had brought him to the rank of SS general by the age of thirty-three, his boyish looks now withering almost directly to old age under the strain of trying to appear loyal to his Führer and secretly work for a deal with the western allies at the same time.

Reinhard Gehlen just frowned. Schellenberg had been muscling in on his eastern front fiefdom for months now, using Hitler's refusal to accept gloomy Foreign Armies East intelligence summaries to shove its chief sideways. Gehlen's resentment came in parcels with every gesture he made.

A small man, very lean, with dark smooth hair giving way to a high forehead, Gehlen had the cold appearance of an academic functionary, or a priest perhaps. Only his lips gave any hint of emotion. His protruding blue eyes stared remorselessly at a point on the situation map to the right of Schellenberg's head. Something which upset the young SS General, as it was designed to do.

Adolf Hitler entered the room like a blast of air conditioning but did not shake hands with either general. He had damned so many of Reinhard Gehlen's intelligence reports in recent months that simply having the General in his presence was something of a humiliation, while Schellenberg's association with the increasingly marginalised Heinrich Himmler meant he was not a first choice on the guest list at the Führer's court at any time. Not that he wished to be. But Hitler, ever the street-fighter, was practical in matters of survival.

He walked over to the situation map on the wall and studied the map with a magnifying glass, holding one arm with the other hand, suety face somewhat less bloated than usual, eyes bloodshot but alive.

'Right, gentlemen, resume your seats, please,' he said. The respect in his voice puzzled Schellenberg. 'The situation is urgent,' Hitler continued. 'General Gehlen..?' The Führer of the ever-shrinking Greater German Reich then stood back against the wall with the map, with a slightly embarrassed look, folded his arms, and put one hand on his chin as if he was holding it up.

Gehlen passed Schellenberg a file with Chef Reichssache stamped on it. 'An atomic bomb,' he said. 'Obtained by bombarding unstable atoms of heavy elements – uranium, plutonium – and splitting these atoms. The energy released is fantastic. I will not dwell on our failures in this area. The Americans have been working on it since 1940.'

'Twenty thousand tons of TNT!' Schellenberg said then, 'that's incredible!' Any distress he had, multiplied.

'Yes,' Gehlen replied. 'Now, the point is, the Americans are already shipping adequate quantities of uranium and plutonium to this desert facility in New Mexico – Los Alamos. And they have enough plutonium for a bomb.'

'And guess where they plan to test it, Walter?' Hitler said. He stopped himself before his emotions took over.

'How did you ever get this, Reinhard?' Schellenberg asked.

'How did SD Ausland not?' Hitler barked, some of his pent-up frustration leaking out. 'Gehlen has penetrated Russian intelligence at the most valuable levels. There are those who say Stalin is one of his agents.'

'In some way or other, we are all working for General Gehlen, I suspect,' Schellenberg said, trying to dilute Hitler's emotion.

Reinhard Gehlen's frown divided and his blue eyes fixed on Schellenberg. 'The amount of plutonium needed for a blast equivalent to twenty thousand tonnes of TNT is about the size of an orange,' he said, demonstrating it with his hands.

'That's the beauty of it,' Hitler added, smiling. The mood-swing unnerved Schellenberg even more.

'Detonated by the implosion of shaped charges, a sub-critical mass of the substance is forced into a critical mass,' Gehlen added. 'A tamper of ordinary, stable uranium maximises the reaction and, thus, the destructive yield. We have ordinary uranium in significant amounts.'

'And we can implode,' Hitler said, not realising the irony of the phrase. 'All we need is the atomic explosive.'

Schellenberg inhaled and held his breath. His face changed colour. Like a man waiting for the drop to be opened.

'The Führer would like you to organise the seizure of a suitable amount of plutonium, for the purposes of using it in a weapon on the spearhead of Russian forces now gathering behind Kustrin on the Oder,' Gehlen said.

The formality sounded to Schellenberg like a sentence being read out. He almost swore but he had seen the results of too many flying courts martial along the roads of northern Germany, men hanging from lampposts and trees for trivial offences, to risk anything incriminating coming from his mouth.

'But how?' Schellenberg just could not contain himself any more. He flicked through the pages of the file but then gave up and waited for Reinhard Gehlen to give him the answer.

'Exactly three weeks from now,' Gehlen said, 'a shipment of plutonium – about seven kilos – in two hemispheres, will be put on a train in New Mexico and transported to Mobile in Alabama, placed on board a submarine, and shipped to Europe, where it will be loaded into a bomb casing.'

'Like stealing a piece of fruit, right Walter?' Hitler said. 'The use of such a wonderweapon would stagger mankind. I want this bomb. With it, we can send these Bolsheviks back to the Vistula, buy time, split the alliance and bounce back like Frederick the Great.' He glanced over at a portrait of the Prussian king.

Schellenberg just stared into space. 'Of course, my Führer,' he said.

The headquarters of SD Ausland in Berlin was a four-storey art deco former Jewish old-folks home on Berkaerstrasse. When Walter Schellenberg finally reached his office that morning, after a diversion out of the city to meet his boss and mentor, Heinrich Himmler, a large bomb fragment had lodged itself in the wall and several of the windows were smashed.

Schellenberg threw the file Reinhard Gehlen had given him on his desk and examined his face in the small mirror hanging over an enamel basin across his office. The mirror had cracked.

Outside, it was raining again. For once, the weather was on Germany's side. Operating from hard runways around Berlin, the Luftwaffe could hit Red Army supply lines bringing equipment up for the great Oder offensive everyone knew must come. But the Red Air Force could not get off the grass fields it used for runways on the other side of the river. Schellenberg's brief moment of confidence subsided. It was like trying to stop the tides, he thought.

He watched the rain fall and shivered. Then he picked up Gehlen's file and rang for coffee. When he had settled himself he pressed his buzzer again. 'Get me all the files from Operation Grief,' he said. 'And I'm not to be disturbed.'

When the files were brought in, Schellenberg opened a drawer and poured himself a drink. It was only after his third drink that he began to read the details of Operation Grief.

2

At almost the same moment in western Germany, somewhere between Aachen and the Rhine, on a narrow stone bridge covered in lichen, moss and fallen snow, a captain in American Ranger uniform watched a private in American paratrooper boots retying his bootlace while a gust of wind whipped up the falling snow and twisted it round the paratrooper's green combat trousers. Some of the snow clung to the young man's raw hand and he lost his grip. The lace fell from his fingers.

When Thomas Heuzer stepped forward from the veil of snow, the paratrooper dropped his lace again and fumbled with his rifle. The skin around his mouth, broken by the cold, cracked and he bled slightly. Heuzer's, tanned to a colour which made him look like he had been on a beach, gave him a Californian air to go with his accent. The paratrooper challenged him anyway.

'Evensong,' Heuzer replied.

The paratrooper hesitated, then lowered his rifle and almost came to attention.

'At ease,' Heuzer said. 'On your own?'

'No, Captain, my buddy's takin' a dump back there.' He gestured towards a copse on a hill about half a mile away. The snow had almost completely obscured it now. 'Got the shits somethin' terrible.'

Heuzer looked at the treeline. 'Well, he should be here with you,' he said. 'Outfit?'

'Hundred and First Airborne, sir,' the paratrooper said, turning his shoulder towards the officer. He looked at Heuzer's Ranger patch again and tried to make it out through the snow.

'Ninth Independents,' Heuzer said. 'Where you from, son?'

'Delaware, Ohio, sir.'

Heuzer nodded. 'Nice, friendly place?'

'We like to think so.'

'Well, don't be so friendly here. Password or no. Krauts have people dressed up as Americans all over this area. Met a few of them further up. Won't be meeting them again. I got three wounded in a hole about a mile that way. Where's your command post?'

The paratrooper lifted his rifle back up to waist level and pointed back down the winding road. 'It's a couple of miles. But there'll be a jeep along to relieve me and my buddy in about ten, maybe fifteen, minutes. I thought we were the furthest forward. They didn't tell me anyone'd be comin' back this way.' He coughed, shuffled, then he looked down at his bootlace.

'They didn't tell me either,' Heuzer said. 'Go on, tie your boot up. And I'll smoke.' He pulled out a packet of cigarettes. 'I'd offer you one only you're on duty.'

The paratrooper smiled and bent down to his lace. Heuzer lit a cigarette, drew on it twice, then put his hand over the young paratrooper's mouth, shoved his head forward and cut his throat.

Two more men in American Ranger uniforms crept out of the pines and moved either side of Heuzer.

'There's a second man up in those woods,' Heuzer shouted in German. 'Get him.'

A blond sergeant tugged Heuzer's arm. One of the sergeant's front teeth was missing and part of an earlobe, the result of a mine explosion in Russia. 'Herr Hauptmann ...'

The first of six Sherman tanks broke through the snow about five hundred metres away, slid on the ice, then almost tipped into a ditch. The commander yelled something at his driver, then the tank stopped, skidded again and stalled, before moving towards Heuzer.

'You're running into an ambush,' Heuzer said to the tank commander, a major with a birthmark on his face, when the first tank finally pulled up in front of him.

'Strength?' the major inquired.

'About ten.'

'Jesus!' The major rubbed his mouth. 'Tigers?'

'No, men,' Heuzer said.

The first bazooka rocket hit the American tank between the body and the turret on the left side, and Thomas Heuzer led the last ten surviving members of Operation Grief into action again.

Thomas Heuzer had once been turned down by the SS for having a filling in one of his molars. He joined the Wehrmacht instead, then the paratroopers. And when war broke out, a facility for languages – he could speak five with fluency – took him to the Brandenburg Regiment, the German special operations unit. One of its earlier leaders had promised the Brandenburgers would one day be able to fetch the devil from hell, an irony not lost on Thomas Heuzer who once commented that it was 'too easy a task in Germany'. The phrase was turned on him later.

In 1941, Heuzer was part of a team which laid the ground for the successful German assault on Crete. He was wounded at the gates of Moscow in December of the same year in support of an operation to kill Josef Stalin: his first exposure to the whim of Adolf Hitler, who called it off at the last moment.

After that Heuzer organised several raids behind Russian lines during the spring of 1942, and took command of an anti-partisan unit during the German drive on Stalingrad. Wounded again, he was transferred to military intelligence headquarters in Berlin, the Abwehr's famous Tirpitz Ufer building, winding up in Abwehr II, the sabotage and subversion department, which controlled the Brandenburgers, while the German Sixth Army was being annihilated on the Volga during the early months of 1943.

While at Abwehr II Heuzer became involved in two operations which were to dominate the remainder of his life as a serving officer: the Tod Programme of infiltrators and assassins, and the army plot to kill Adolf Hitler.

In 1944 both of these involvements came to a head when the Abwehr was absorbed by Walter Schellenberg's SD Ausland and Colonel Claus Von Stauffenberg put a bomb under Adolf Hitler's conference table in East Prussia.

What remained of the Tod Programme and Heuzer were merged with SD Ausland's Group S, a kind of licensed pirate crew cum department of dirty tricks run by Hitler's favourite commando, Otto Skorzeny, and the Gestapo began arresting Heuzer's old Abwehr superiors.

Heuzer should have been decorated: he had been supplying information on the anti-Hitler plot for two years. But such was the degree of involvement in the conspiracy by his own superiors that he found himself in Gestapo custody instead. He was saved from the noose by Walter Schellenberg, who had begun to use the infiltration specialties of the Tod Programme as a private courier service in his attempts to secure a separate peace with the western allies. Schellenberg claimed Heuzer had been his agent all along, brought Heinrich Himmler in on the case, and another man went to the gallows accused of negligence.

Meanwhile, Heuzer rejoined SD Ausland's Group S, and to re-establish his loyalty, set about organising the teams of English speakers who were infiltrated behind American lines dressed in American uniform during the Battle of the Bulge in the Ardennes.

Operation Grief had lived up to the English meaning of its name, but Walter Schellenberg could not be sure for whom. When he had finished reading Heuzer's file, he smiled to himself. 'Time for you to repay my generosity, Herr Hauptmann.'

✻   ✻   ✻

'And then there were five, Herr Hauptmann,' Karl Peiper said to Thomas Heuzer. The two men stood looking at the German dead near the moss-covered stone bridge east of Aachen.

Thomas Heuzer went among the wounded Americans, shooting each of them in the head with his pistol.

'There was another one, Karl,' he said to his sergeant. 'A second paratrooper.' He pointed to the copse on the hillside. The snow was obscuring it again. He started to walk towards it. Behind him, six burning tanks refracted the unreliable daylight and snowflakes turned to steam on the hot metal.

'Leave it, Herr Hauptmann,' Peiper said. 'It's over. Let's go home.' He grabbed Heuzer's arm and pointed to the German lines.

Fifteen minutes later, the American paratrooper who had watched Thomas Heuzer cut his friend's throat and the Germans in American uniform destroy six Sherman tanks and blow up the bridge he was supposed to be guarding, lifted himself from the copse where he had been hiding, waiting for relief that had not come, and walked towards the road.

He had been suffering with nerves for months and dysentery for three days now so he walked very slowly. The snow was dying and the body of his friend, the paratrooper from Ohio, whose throat Thomas Heuzer had cut, was jackknifed in a small shell-hole off the road. Away from the other American dead. Snow had gathered on the seat of the man's trousers.

The surviving paratrooper wandered along the line of smoking vehicles and dead men, stopping only at the body of his comrade. Then he picked up a weapon, placed it to the side of his abdomen, just above the hip, and pulled the trigger.

3

Heuzer was marked under the left eye, freshly shaved, sporting a fresh crew cut and holding a pencil when he entered Walter Schellenberg's office late that Monday afternoon. He came slightly to attention but only just enough to comply with protocol.

Schellenberg noticed the irritation on the captain's face more than anything, like a trapped animal, desperate to break free, but afraid of being set free. Heuzer's eyes looked beyond their immediate situation, to somewhere Schellenberg almost felt pulled to but was sure he did not wish to go. But the captain's face had a chameleon-like quality which made Schellenberg feel he was looking into a mirror.

'You look tired, Thomas,' Schellenberg said to interrupt the effect Heuzer was having on him.

'The roads were blocked,' Heuzer said. 'And we had difficulty getting an aircraft.'

'Well ... good to see you're safe,' Schellenberg said then. And he sat back from his desk as if he was afraid of what Heuzer would do to him. 'I have a problem, Herr Hauptmann. And when I have a problem, I like to share it.' He tossed the file Gehlen had given him at Heuzer. 'Now the Führer has given this to me and I'm giving it to you. Who's left of your team?'

'Just Sergeant Peiper and I. One of my lads stepped on a landmine five hours ago. Two others were too close.

Trying to get back to our lines in a rush. Urgent request, we were told.'

Schellenberg raised an eyebrow but said nothing. Heuzer began to read the papers in front of him.

'I've designated it Ground Zero for practical reasons,' Schellenberg said. And he began to relax. 'I was going to call it Blue Moon for poetic reasons. How are things on the Rhine?'

'We're just about holding them,' Heuzer said. He was now as relaxed as Schellenberg. 'But if they push ... like the Oder front. Germany is two rivers from ...'

'Destiny,' Schellenberg said. 'You know sometimes you are frank to the point of difficulty, Thomas. It's a character flaw. And I will not always be able to protect you from your character flaws.'

'Apologies. Sometimes I dispute myself. A desire to please, perhaps.'

Schellenberg grinned. 'Or assert yourself,' he said. 'At least, you are your own man.'

When Heuzer had read four or five pages of the Ground Zero file, Schellenberg leaned over his desk. 'Reichsführer Himmler and I would like you to bury this operation. I don't care how and I don't care what excuses you use, just bury it. As a favour to me.' Some of Schellenberg's colour returned. He pulled open a drawer and took out a small bottle of clear alcohol. 'Reinhard Gehlen is trying to have me killed. He wants to be the only one left for the British and Americans to deal with when they arrive. I need a plan like this like a hole in the head. Here I am trying to sell the Americans on peace with terms and the Führer wants me to steal their most precious weapon. God, this is a shit life I lead. Look, all you have to do is delay it long enough for the Allies to arrive and make it irrelevant. So plenty of wonderful ideas that will not work, Thomas. Cheers.'

'And if I am questioned by General Gehlen or whomever the Führer sends ...?' Heuzer asked.

'That's your lookout,' Schellenberg replied. 'You're a dab hand at espionage, you deal with it. I haven't got an endless string of men to replace you on the gallows. And remember, Thomas, when your resentment builds, all I have to do is give the Gestapo what I have on you, and you will join your old bosses dancing on air, suspended by piano wire.' The ruthlessness of his statement shocked Schellenberg. 'Thank God Otto Skorzeny's on the eastern front, or I'd have a real problem. The Führer loves him and he's too keen for my liking. It's really his bloody fault Gehlen's annoyed with us. He keeps stealing the General's special operations. So what do you think?'

Heuzer raised his eyes from the file. 'Interesting.'

Schellenberg poured him a drink. 'Yes,' he said. 'That's what it is considering our situation. That old joke about being able to take a street car from the eastern to the western front is fast becoming a reality.'

'Such a weapon exists?' Heuzer asked. 'An atom bomb?'

Schellenberg nodded. 'Apparently so. And all you have to do is come up with a reason why a plan to steal the explosive is out of the question.'

'It is a tall order,' Heuzer said.

'You have the Führer's complete confidence,' Schellenberg said. He grinned. 'It might have been fun under different circumstances. It's a pity Alfred Naujocks had to go and desert to the Americans. This is right up his street. God, the acts of criminality we used to perform for Heydrich during the good old days when they were a fast track to fame and future. Now they will probably result in jail or the gallows. Naujocks's treason didn't do me any good, I'll tell you. Selfish bastard. Probably living it up in some American whore house. Always knew when to cut his losses, Alfred. I'm just too loyal, myself. There's champagne over there. Get it.'

Heuzer obeyed. And as Schellenberg became more upbeat he noticed the captain's character was changing again, with his own mood.

'Of course, we do not have an aircraft capable of such distance,' Schellenberg said then. 'Not the return flight, anyway. See, we've found a reason to scupper it already. But ask for things all the same. Anything you want. Hell, you can have a regiment for all the good it'll do. I don't care. I'm only interested in saving my own neck. And with my neck is your neck, Thomas.' Schellenberg contemplated something awful for a while and there was silence.

Heuzer did not take the delight in Schellenberg's distress that he might have, but he smiled and poured the champagne. He drank a glass and read on.

Schellenberg moved things around his desk and smoked a few cigarettes. Then he examined pictures of his wife and children.

'Of course, you should make preparations of your own, Thomas,' he said, 'for the future. Just in case. Have you made plans?'

'I have not the wherewithal. In life, the only thing of value is time, I have found. And sooner or later the price is too high or there is none left for sale.'

'You're a clever one, Thomas. You might even be an idealist. Or want to be one. You know, I think I envy you. Look at us, Thomas. I'm two years younger and yet I look ten years older than you. I fear for my kids, you know, not for myself. That business about price, you might have something there.'

'The fine print on the contract,' Heuzer said.

'If I can last until the British or Americans get here, then I'm safe. I'm valuable. As long as the Russians don't get me, then I'm going to be safe. But I'll probably write my memoirs in prison.'

'So you figure all is lost?' Heuzer asked.

Schellenberg broke into laughter and laughed so much it brought tears to his eyes. 'Jesus Christ, Thomas, we lost this war the day we started it. I should know, I was there then. With old Alfred Naujocks, the traitorous bastard. I've served

Germany well and I'll probably suffer for it. All I ever wanted was a job. I bet Stauffenberg never had to worry about a job. Bloody queer.'

'I didn't know you knew him that well,' Heuzer said.

'Not as well as you. They were all queer, all that mob who hung around that poet George – Stefan George. Are you queer? I think I'm getting drunk.'

'You should now perhaps show more discretion, sir,' Heuzer said.

'Don't worry, this office is swept clean. I have a deal with Göring and the *Forschungsamt*. I give him artwork, he keeps the ears away from me. And the Gestapo's private listeners are amateurs. Look, just do as you're told. And don't bother me with it till you're ready to present a concrete argument why it cannot succeed. You have carte blanche, okay? I'm going up north to my friend and protector, the Reichsführer, for a few days. I don't feel safe in Berlin any more. If the Führer asks for me, say I'm commanding a tank regiment with Army Group Vistula. Personal orders of the Reichsführer. That should impress him.'

Karl Peiper was lying on a couch in the small office Heuzer used at Berkaerstrasse when the captain came back from his meeting with Schellenberg.

'Jesus, Herr Hauptmann, you look like you've just seen a ghost.'

Heuzer sat down and unbuttoned his tunic before taking a cigarette from a packet he had stolen from one of the Americans they had killed that morning. He did not light the cigarette, merely turned it in his fingers. He threw the packet to Peiper.

'I think I've just been sentenced to death,' he said.

Peiper vaulted over the arm of the couch and came close enough to see the anger in Heuzer's eyes. And it made the sergeant step back.

'No,' Heuzer said then. 'No.' He shook his head violently and crushed the cigarette in his hand.

4

If a sudden belt of warm air had not hit Washington, DC that Tuesday, perhaps the FBI might not have found Oskar Finger's body for several more days. As it was, Agent Jeff Francis had to hold a handkerchief over his mouth and nose while examining the body of the scientist.

Then, staring at the single bed in room 4 of Violet Abery's Washington boarding house, he finally lowered the handkerchief and touched the wounds on the landlady's body.

'He shot her, then himself. They were up to some strange stuff, all right. Look at his wrists. He's been bound, too.' He touched Oskar Finger's skin. 'He sure messed her up.'

The man beside Francis grimaced then turned his head away. 'Come on, let's get outta here,' he said. 'I got a stomach I'm tryin' to hold on to.'

Francis grabbed his partner's arm. 'Losing your touch, Manny?' he said. 'Just pinch your nose and don't swallow.'

Manny Rivera allowed his vulnerable lips to undermine him. He pulled out a cigarette to cover it. 'Don't blame me if I heave,' he said to Francis. 'Want one?' He shoved the cigarette pack forward.

Francis did not answer and his silence spoke more than any words. He took a few moments to look around the small room. The single bed was peppered with woodworm, three black and white photographs of men working on docks

27

adorned the bare pastel walls, while the plaster ceiling flaked and the heavy curtains released dust into a shaft of sunlight to the rhythm of a distant siren.

While Francis was a Bostonian with quarterback looks, a private income and an Ivy League education, Manny Rivera was a squat New Yorker from Spanish Harlem, with thick-set features and the kind of inferiority complex that fostered resentment and chain-smoking. Jeff Francis, on the other hand, had the mechanical distance of too much money, and Rivera thought his eyes seemed to expect things they could not have.

Rivera stood back and Francis crouched down and studied the two bodies, occasionally turning his head when the smell got too much for him. A car horn sounded in the street, and someone shouted from the stairs.

'He has bruising on his abdomen; and his neck's not right. And look at his head.' Francis looked over at the pastel wall again.

'Jesus, I think I'm gonna throw up,' Rivera said. 'So they were playin' naughty games with leather belts and white powder. I mean what kind of a name is Finger? Only the Krauts'd give a dumb name like Finger to anyone. Bet he was popular at school.'

Francis began to examine Violet Abery again, giving Rivera various descriptions. When he looked up, Rivera was looking at the floor. 'You are taking notes?' Francis asked.

'Sure. I don't wanna end up in some relocation camp in the Rockies, watchin' Japs play with themselves. I want a career. Maybe you'd be surprised what my name does for career prospects in this organisation.'

'You need some Irish in you,' Francis said. 'You know we used to be shit around here. Then they suddenly realised you can't do anything without shit. So we were in demand. And now we call others shit. It's called spreading it about.' He grinned the grin of the well-heeled when they are enjoying vulgarity then switched tack. His soft face, stitched together with small pocks and the pinpricks of approaching stubble, became firm. And the expectant eyes radiated ambition. 'I don't want to wait for forensic and pathology, Manny. So take the notes.'

Rivera took three more deep breaths. 'He's left-handed,' he said. 'There's tiny ink stains between the fingers. And calluses from holdin' a pen. He's left-handed.' Rivera pushed his handkerchief into his pocket and lifted Oskar Finger's digits.

'And the wound's on the right,' Francis said. 'Very good. You wonder how no one noticed her missing.'

'Own-key joint,' Rivera said. 'Cash up front. Know what I mean?' Then he looked at his notebook. 'And she goes south at the weekends. No one cared till the smell made them. Sick world, yeah?'

'I'll have to watch you, Manny,' Francis said. 'He could have shot himself with his right even if he is left-handed.'

'Yeah. But look where the gun is. And look at the way she was shot ... the blood ... the pillow.' Rivera lifted it. 'I've seen bodies like this before. Look where the depression is and the powder mark ... and the angle of entry. She was shot by a guy leaning over her like this.' He demonstrated. 'A right hand. It doesn't take a scientist to see that. Jesus, can we get outta here. My stomach's gonna pitch.' Rivera moved for the door.

When Francis closed the door behind him, Rivera was leaning against the far wall on the landing, holding his stomach. 'So, who else was in there?' he said between breaths.

News of Oskar Finger's death reached the headquarters of the Secret Intelligence Service in London that night at about the same hour Simon Penny failed to make radio contact with his British masters for the third time.

Five minutes later both pieces of information were in the hands of Colonel Claude Dansey, the Vice Chief, and despite his own angina trouble, the very heart of the Secret Intelligence Service, on the fourth floor of Broadway Buildings near Westminster.

People who saw Dansey in the spring of 1945 usually remarked on how age and illness had taken their toll of his bear-like physique and dagger stare, though none would ever think of saying it to his face. However, even Dansey's will could not overcome the almost constant breathlessness which accompanied his pallor during the final months of the European war.

'So tell me, have we lost Penny?' he said to the tall man sitting in front of him.

Deceptively modest in a way that often annoyed Dansey, Derek Boyd was the head of Huntergatherers, the deep-cover section at SIS. He helped himself to tea and biscuits before answering.

'It could still be a technical oversight,' he said.

A merchant banker before the war, Boyd had taken to espionage in the manner of one born to string-pulling but reluctant to release his own ruthlessness. Dansey had coached his career with a degree of interest he reserved for those whose potential only he recognised, before giving Boyd command of the Huntergatherers. Within six months they had taken over a second hotel in Earl's Court and Dansey felt his judgement had been justified.

'Do you think the Russians were on to him?' Dansey asked. 'What age is he?'

'Forty years of age ...' Boyd read that part of Simon Penny's life off a small sheet of pink paper, then paused to iron out a crease and go over a piece of faded type. 'Educated at Stoneyhurst,' he added.

'Catholic,' Dansey said. 'You do have a lot of Catholics in Huntergatherers, Derek. You don't think he's had a crisis and gone over to the Russians?'

Boyd was a convert Catholic, too. He had been in southern Mexico in the late thirties during the priest-hunting period, went to Mass most days and wore a miraculous medal. Sometimes, during a lunchbreak, when others would read the paper or chew a sandwich, Boyd might be seen in St James's Park walking up and down fingering beads.

'Cambridge men don't have crises,' he said.

'Is that a promise? He studied in Heidelberg?'

'Heidelberg and Vienna,' Boyd said. 'He was in Vienna in 1934, during the Dolfuss events. Came to us from the Royal Navy's volunteer reserve. I'd be surprised if Simon's ever had a crisis. It's not allowed in Huntergatherers. Your orders, Claude.'

Dansey nodded as if confirming something in his own mind. He had set up Huntergatherers a year earlier in an attempt to emulate the German Abwehr's Tod Programme, something which had raised eyebrows in the middle corridors of Broadway Buildings, and caused indigestion among certain senior civil servants. 'He's a good tennis player, if I recall,' Dansey said. 'Quite a formidable backhand.'

'And a proficient amateur actor,' Boyd said. Dansey raised an eyebrow. 'He worked in translation before the war,' Boyd continued. 'Lived in Paris and Berlin.'

'And you two were a team in Belgrade in forty-one,' Dansey said. 'What did you think of him?'

'It was not quite the success we had hoped for,' Boyd said. 'But that wasn't Simon's fault.'

'And then both of you travelled across Europe,' Dansey added. 'Quite some feat. Loud applause was heard in various clubs. Not Boodles, though. We're a quiet lot.'

'We were stuck,' Boyd said. 'Necessity is the mother and all that. Only way out was Spain. I played a priest.'

'And Penny?'

'Played deaf and dumb. Did it all very well. You're right, it was quite an adventure. Though I think I'm too old for that kind of thing now, Claude.'

'So what's happened to him in Washington?' Dansey asked. 'This actor of ours.'

Boyd had to pull out a small black book before he spoke. 'Well, if the Russians were on to him, then I think we can expect Simon to turn up in small pieces in some river.'

'But the FBI description is him,' Dansey said. 'Their suspect.'

'Why would he kill his source?' Boyd asked. 'Finger was the supplier of every morsel Penny was feeding Moscow about the Manhattan Project. All jumbled and useless. We made sure of that.'

'And you don't think he has gone over to them?' Dansey said. 'I mean, fed them more than we knew?'

Boyd made a few notes before answering. 'There is always that possibility, Claude. It's always a risk with Huntergatherers. Finger's trade was a godsend for us. Got Penny deep in position with the Reds for the post-war struggle.'

'And you believe there will be a struggle?' Dansey asked him. 'With our Soviet allies?'

'You do, too, Claude. Biggest prophet for it in the firm.'

'And now Finger's dead and Penny's vanished.' Dansey tapped the table. 'If there's any chance he's still in play, I don't want to risk him. Your Huntergatherers are very special to me, Derek. But if there's a chance something's going sour, I'd like to be on top of it.'

Boyd nodded. 'Should we let the FBI know?'

'Good God, no,' Dansey said. 'And have egg on our faces?'

He stood up and stretched and went to a book case. The slim volume fitted into his jacket pocket. Before Boyd left, Dansey turned off the light in his office, pulled back his blackout curtains and opened his window. He began reading just as Boyd shut the door.

It was snowing heavily when Simon Penny came out of the attic apartment near Greenwich Avenue in New York that evening. The street was brownstone, tree-lined, rather English in many ways. Steam rose from a grating on the sidewalk where birds landed to take advantage of the heat, and three men argued over a cab.

Penny crossed several more streets before he entered a small corner bar. He went straight over to the table in the corner. A blonde woman sat at the table, while two men, one wiry, wearing a long coat and a stiff-brimmed hat, the other solid but half-cocked, drinking a kind of pink infusion, sat at the bar, trying to read a newspaper and watch Penny at the same time.

'I need these documents all made out to these names.' Penny passed the two lists to the woman, and glanced over at the two men at the bar. 'Usual cocktail.'

'Your wish is my command,' the blonde woman said to Penny. She touched his hand and smiled. The smile reminded him of a teacher he had once had, with a smell of candle wax. He touched her hair and let his finger trace the line of her cheekbone. Her lips stuck to her teeth for a moment and he could see lipstick on them now. 'I imagined so many things.'

Penny pulled some money from his pocket. 'This is on account. And I want them by next week, Pam. So what does Moscow say?'

Pam Hanny nodded. 'I'm to watch out for you.' She shrugged then. 'There are accusations of carelessness, Simon. I told them . . .'

'. . . that I didn't kill him,' Penny said. 'He got nasty. I hit him, but I didn't kill him.'

She counted the money and put it in her pocket. 'So who did it?'

'That's what I'd like to know,' Penny said. He was feeling things he did not like and his unhandsome face contorted somewhat.

'I believe you,' Pam Hanny said.

Penny wanted to take her hand and kiss it and tell her how much he had missed her, but everything he was pulled the other way and he found himself virtually ignoring her. 'Who're the wiseguys?' he asked.

Pam Hanny called one of the men at the counter over. He smelled of fish. 'This is Angel,' she said to Penny. 'He's your contact when I'm out of circulation. He knows your trouble with the FBI.'

Angel Marcan nodded and rubbed newspaper ink from his fingers. 'Maybe we should just turn him into the Feds for the reward,' he said.

'Then you'd lose your life as well as the money I'm going to pay you. And any further business I might have.'

'He's a smart bastard, this guy,' Marcan said to Pam Hanny. 'I think we'll have to watch him.' He sniffed and looked at Penny, took the pieces of paper with the names and document requests, then stood up, put his hands on Pam Hanny's shoulder and rubbed it. He let his hand touch her hair. 'I take good care of her,' he said.

'I hope so,' Penny said.

When Marcan and his partner had left the bar, Pam Hanny flicked her hair and sniffed at her fingers. 'Don't mind him. He likes to think he's some kind of enforcer. He works at the fish market. I can't tell him he smells. Thinks he's the original bella figura.'

'Moscow should have sent someone by now,' Penny said. 'It's not like them to be this accepting. You look out for yourself, Pam.'

They strolled for an hour in the darkness and the remains of the snow, until the warmth of Washington had begun to arrive on the winds in New York. Penny kissed Pam Hanny near Central Park.

'I don't know what you see in me,' he said.

'You're a plain bastard,' she said, laughing. Then she started to cry, not for any real reason, but just to release the tensions which had been building in her. Penny's normal distance was shortened when she cried, because, like most men, he considered tears to be the source of great pain. In this, women will always have a secret advantage, no matter how much they try to explain it to men.

'Are you lonely, Simon?' she asked him.

'Loneliness is not permitted.'

They linked arms and walked through the remains of the night, until it came time to part. He kissed her lips and then disappeared slowly into the darkness.

When Pam Hanny reached her hotel on the upper west side, there was a cable waiting for her.

The following afternoon in Washington, the snowman across the road from Jeff Francis's apartment had begun to melt into the grass. Inside, the apartment was a shambles of disturbed furniture, files, plates, cups, bits of food, bottles and items of clothing.

'What if there is no other man?' Manny Rivera asked Francis. He had his feet hanging on the side of an armchair. 'What if all the circumstantial evidence is just what we want to think? There were no other prints. Maybe Finger did kill her, and then himself.'

'We have half a dozen witnesses who saw another man come out of that building!' Francis shouted. 'And we've accounted for everyone else.'

'So where is he? The woman ran a boardin' house, Jeff. Maybe Finger was a screwball. Who knows with these crazy scientists they have down in New Mexico.'

'You want me to go to Hoover and say that?' Francis said.

'I'm tryin' to help, Jeff.'

'They say you can tell when a man in the Bureau is going nowhere: he dresses too well and people open doors for him,' Francis said. 'No enemies, you see.' He walked back over to the window. 'Even a snowman leaves a trace,' he said.

5

The Ground Zero file was still lying across Thomas Heuzer's chest as he turned towards the slim rays of early daylight sneaking through his blackout curtains. He had given himself an hour's sleep, and the last thing he remembered was the sound of the rain on his window and the air raid sirens.

The rain was gone now but the bombers were back. Heuzer ignored the sirens again, ate some bread, drank some ersatz coffee, washed and shaved. He stayed in his office long enough to watch Walter Schellenberg leave for Heinrich Himmler's headquarters.

Karl Peiper was asleep in the anteroom. He snapped to attention when Heuzer woke him. 'You look worse than I do,' Heuzer said. 'That must be why I keep you around.'

Peiper began doing up his uniform. 'You need someone to look after you, Thomas,' Peiper said.

'I need you to lie for me,' Heuzer said.

Peiper consented without question.

Heuzer left the SD Ausland building an hour later and headed southeast. His rather beaten-up Citroen finally came to a halt at a checkpoint near a small country estate, and Heuzer had time to consider the body of a young soldier hanging from a tree across the road as it swayed in the breeze. The teenager had a placard hung round his neck. 'I was too cowardly to defend German women and children'. One of his eyes was still open.

The dying body eats itself, Heuzer thought, then censored what wanted to follow.

A military police corporal checked Heuzer's papers, then signalled to a man at the barrier. Heuzer looked into the eyes of the military police corporal again, but the corporal's eyes were devoid of thought and Heuzer could not compete. He dipped his own.

'We have another traitor over there,' the corporal said. 'We'll do him in an hour.' He gestured to an even younger soldier sitting under another tree.

Now Heuzer wanted to say something noble and brave, push his Knight's Cross into this subordinate's face, draw his service pistol and tell him to release the tearful young wretch, rocking back and forth beneath the poplar across the road. But that was another world. His world was silent and selfish and, frankly, disinterested, a detached observer of detail.

Heuzer drove on to a small chalet by the shores of a corrugated lake. When he entered the cabin, he placed his briefcase down on a table and his hands on his head.

'I'm glad you decided to come, Herr Hauptmann.'

Reinhard Gehlen preferred to stay in the shadows, hands in pockets, a thin film of dust veiling even the General's silhouette from Heuzer's eyes. A second man, who smelled of polish and acorn, frisked Heuzer and then backed off into the shadows, to be replaced by his boss.

'I was not aware I had a choice,' Heuzer said to Gehlen. 'Walter Schellenberg will have my head if he finds out about this.'

'I don't know about you but I had not planned on telling him,' Gehlen said. 'Anyway, you are following the direct orders of the Führer. And despite our current difficulties, he still outranks Schellenberg. Just consider Schellenberg a little local difficulty.'

'And Reichsführer Himmler?' Heuzer asked. 'I assume you

chose this place for effect. I would appreciate if you could intercede for the kid they're going to hang back there.'

'I wish I could,' Gehlen said. 'Anyway, I suspect we have too much work to do for ourselves, Heuzer.'

Chopin permeated every corner of the chalet while they talked, and there was a strong odour of cabbage and vinegar left over from the small meal they had eaten. Pieces of bread and cabbage lay across a large table between various papers and maps. Gehlen leaned against the table.

'If you had not been invalided out of Russia,' he said to Thomas Heuzer, 'you might have ended up working for me instead of Walter Schellenberg.'

'I think you have me where you want me,' Heuzer insisted.

'You were working for the state, Herr Hauptmann, when Admiral Canaris asked you to penetrate the Stauffenberg plot?' Gehlen said, as if to change the subject.

Heuzer nodded emphatically. And that was the first time Gehlen found himself drawn in by the captain, wanting to believe him. It was a brief diversion at the time but he would look back on it later when asking himself if he had made the right choice.

'Unfortunately,' Gehlen continued, 'it appears the little Admiral was playing both sides and stuck you in the middle.'

'I am a loyal German, sir,' Heuzer insisted, rather more than was necessary this time, and Gehlen saw another less palatable side to him.

'But there is something inside you that wishes to be free of that loyalty?' he said as if to test his theory.

'I was saved from the scrap-heap by the decision to re-arm,' Heuzer said. 'Unemployment makes a man very considerate of his position. I am tied to this state.'

'But if a different situation obtained?' Gehlen said. 'Tell me, how do you see your future?' Gehlen smiled for no reason. 'After the war.'

'Through darkness and thick mist,' Heuzer said. 'Night and fog. I think General Schellenberg is intent on sending me to the gallows.'

'Yes. Well, the Führer's *Nacht und Nebel* decree has provided the more poetic among us with many opportunities to regret their career choices. If you stick with me, though, you need not disappear into the night and the fog, Heuzer. If you obey Walter Schellenberg, you will be a guest of the Gestapo at Prinz Albrechtstrasse by the end of the month. Charged with treason. People are already realigning for the post-war era. I'll be looking for people after the war, you know. Reliable people.'

Heuzer looked around the chalet and his face began to take on a completely different expression from the man who had just admitted his most inner fears. 'So what's next?' he asked.

Gehlen smiled. 'I have a man,' he said. 'Someone I have taken great pains to have in the right place for the right event. Have you a large map of New Mexico?'

Heuzer hunted through his briefcase and pulled out a map. He spread it on the table and Gehlen leaned over it. 'I take it you have read up on Los Muertos,' he said. 'The kind of one-fly town dotted all over the mountains and mesas south of Albuquerque, here.' He touched the area to the east of the Rio Grande. 'The Spanish named this area to the south, *Jornada del Muerto*: The Journey of Death. The Americans use it for bombing practice and other things. But Los Muertos is far enough away from there and everywhere else not to be noticed. It has a jail, a bar, a barber, a store and a small railhead ...'

'And the plutonium for our bomb will be loaded on a train there,' Heuzer interrupted. 'I have read your file.'

'We know the day it will arrive. We know there will be no more than ten men with it, in two sedan cars escorted by two jeeps of military police. Very low key. All we have to do is intercept it.'

'And then what?' Heuzer asked.

'Leave that to me for the moment.' Gehlen took out a file

and passed it to Heuzer. 'This is something not in your file. His codename is Nativo. Read it all.'

Heuzer opened it. 'How do I keep such an operation from Walter Schellenberg?' he asked. 'And, consequently, from Reichsführer Himmler's anger?'

'You don't,' Gehlen said. 'You play Schellenberg's game. Tell him everything. Ask him questions. Now read, and I'll get back to you on the rest.'

'I'm going to need men. Our supplies of American English speakers capable of an operation like this are minimal. I should know. I led the last team over the lines.'

'Ask and you shall receive,' Gehlen said. 'I'll draw up a request I want you to sign. You can get Schellenberg to countersign it. Tell him it's for authenticity. It's to the head of the Waffen-SS, Reichsführer Himmler.'

Heuzer came to attention. When Gehlen was leaving, Heuzer asked: 'Why? Why do you wish it done? You don't believe the war is lost?'

'Wars are never lost, Thomas. Only battles. I do this to keep Germany intact.' And now the General smiled again. 'To keep myself in gainful employment. To give my family a future. Anyway, I do not fancy spending the rest of my life in Siberia. And considering your career in Russia, you should bear that in mind, Thomas.'

'I obeyed my orders,' Heuzer said.

'A noble defence,' Gehlen said. 'Now concentrate on Los Muertos, on Nativo.'

By the time Sheriff John Delmar had finished his morning rounds in Los Muertos, the sun had struggled over the subtle grey edges which dominated the three-thousand-foot mesa where the baked and jaundiced adobe constructions of the small town sat. The morning cold was giving way to a promising heat that would soon become threatening, and the wind was picking up from the north.

Delmar paused to watch, while somewhere between Los Muertos and the mountains, between the canyons and the flatlands, the desert rock and the sagebrush, the jagged bluffs and the small nipple peaks, the thin morning mist began to shred.

Behind it, the gathering sunlight caressed the snowlines, which seemed to bleed slowly on the barren rock and give the whole mesa a purple glow. And, in places, the distance seemed limitless.

Los Muertos was a single line scratched through a canyon in the mesa, a cave drawing where the wind scarred the walls and left people's faces coated with alkaline sand. The mesa was hard mesquite and sharp yucca, and the humans living there shared it with various insects, rattlesnakes, and spiders. A few people, like John Delmar, ranched. Most worked far away. And when they were home, the gypsum-fouled water played havoc with their bowels and left their hair stiff.

John Delmar was fifty-four, white-haired and mostly solid. Imposing in a thoughtful kind of way, he had brown eyes and brown skin with black hair, but a small neck on his strong shoulders impaired his physique.

'I got the purge again, John. Goddam water.'

The man holding his stomach was about the same height as Delmar, but more overweight, with thicker eyebrows and less hair on top. He wore oily dungarees and carried a chain watch and made a whistling noise through a gap in his teeth.

'Well, call a doctor. You're the mayor, Andy,' Delmar said.

'The purge don't respect office, do it?'

Andy Redrow winced and John Delmar touched his brow. 'How many times I gotta tell you to boil everythin' you drink?'

'Hey, we boil . . . we boil,' Redrow said. 'No sermons, please. A mayor shouldn't have to put up with that. Any news of Gus?'

'Just they're shippin' him home, that's all I heard. Nothin' official. Photograph arrived yesterday. I'll show it you next time we have you over.' Delmar opened his gate and helped Redrow up the path to the porch. 'Sit there, I'll get you somethin'.'

'You know, John, I'm kinda keen to see the war out as mayor.'

'Well, you have my support, Andy. Always have had.'

'And I appreciate it. Shame if I lost before the war was over. Don't suppose you wanna hunt anythin' this weekend?'

Delmar shook his head. 'Tell you what, though, why don't you and your Eadie come over for dinner, Sunday. We have a letter from Gus with the photograph.'

'You think that's a good idea?' Redrow said. 'I told Eadie she shoulda waited before comin'. Stayed where she was. God, she's all I got now but I don't wanna go through all that with her and Gus again.'

Delmar opened the screen door and then disappeared into the house without replying.

'You know Gus'll be wantin' a job when he gets out,' Andy Redrow said. 'I was wonderin' if you might take him on as a deputy. Till he finds his feet. Make a good deputy, your Gus.'

' 'Cept, I don't need one,' John Delmar said through the door. 'It's a part-time job for me. And I got help when I need it. Just a few drunks and wild Apache bucks from the reservation.' Delmar reappeared on the porch carrying a large bottle and a spoon. 'Be too expensive. Think about re-election, Andy. Here, drink this. Gus can take the GI bill. Go to college. I want him to go to college.'

They strolled while the morning sun performed a strange magical dance with the snow-capped mountains. The air was fresh and sharp and the sun reflected on the snow and broke the air in places.

'You out the reservation way yesterday?' Redrow said. He belched and sighed.

'I got a request to help bring in one o' them bucks caused a stir in Albuquerque couple o' weeks back.'

'Goin' in a bar he weren't welcome in,' Andy Redrow said, shaking his head. 'I don't know, John, I just don't know ...'

John Delmar watched his mayor sweat the intolerance of unwilling understanding, and wondered how such thin drops could come from such a fat man. And they strolled like friends.

Later, when John Delmar stepped inside his house again, he allowed himself to relax on a brief journey into his past, where the old men with hybrid names sat on broken porches in wasteland reservations and spoke of land and freedom.

Most of all, they talked of the freedom. And when they had finished, one or two would claim to have been at Little Bighorn the day the Son of the Morning Star was brought to earth, and a really drunk one might claim to have killed George Armstrong Custer, personally. The lies shamed John Delmar. The drunkenness angered him. Sometimes he would hear one of them say: 'It would have been better if they had killed all of us.'

Delmar's wife was a sharp-featured Methodist. Her mother's people had been Baptist once and Rosalyn Delmar spoke with something of a Baptist's urgency. She had a beauty which only allowed itself out once in a decade and that hard driven face only the Great Depression produced. Delmar bet himself he could tell Depression women thirty years later. He stepped out on to his porch and swung back and forth in a chair.

'What is it? That chant?' his wife asked.

'The sound of everythin' without a voice,' Delmar said.

'I'll never understand the way you let it eat you, John. Sometimes I wonder if you would not be better livin' on the reservation.'

'I feel my shame better here,' he said. 'Anyway, I would find no acceptance there, the same way I cannot accept here.'

'Sometimes I think you enjoy it,' she said.

'You wanna leave me?' he asked.

'With Gus comin' home and all? I'm happy, can't you tell?' She touched him. 'Are you all right, John?'

He turned to her for the first time in their conversation. 'No. No, I am not all right. Do you remember anythin' of the Faust story?'

'I wish you would not show off your learnin' around me. Gus's comin' home is all the brainstruggle I need.'

'Sure, Rosalyn, sure,' John Delmar said.

He stood up, and very slowly, without really wanting to, put his arms around her. She had a smell about her at that time of the day somewhere between sweat and dishwater, that no matter what she did to beautify herself, never completely went away. And her hands were sharp like the mesa rock.

An hour later, John Delmar saw his wife in the kitchen but did not speak to her. He climbed a wooden staircase to a small attic, locked the door and pulled a small suitcase from beneath the floorboards. It did not take him long to hook up the aerial. Then he opened another portion of the wooden floor and pulled out a series of typed sheets. As soon as he had placed his earphones on, he began transmitting.

Several thousand miles away, in a small room at German army headquarters in Zossen, outside Berlin, a non-commissioned officer who had lost one eye at the gates of Moscow in 1941, but who knew the touch, alerted his superior that Nativo was on the air.

6

Thomas Heuzer managed to get Walter Schellenberg's signature on every document he presented, and Heinrich Himmler's on five crucial orders. Schellenberg offered him the use of two secretaries, which he refused, saying he preferred to use Karl Peiper. Peiper had been a clerk before the war and took dictation moderately well. Schellenberg did not argue.

Heuzer and Peiper moved to a pretentious bourgeois mansion in the mountains about an hour and a half's drive from Berlin.

The house had as little proportion as taste, and Heuzer detested it, but for reasons other than the obvious. However, it was well hidden by hills and forests and listed as destroyed in official records.

'Bad fake or not, it's a perfect place to avoid Walter Schellenberg's eyes, Herr Hauptmann,' Karl Peiper commented.

That same Saturday, Reinhard Gehlen left a note to say he had gone to the Baltic coast. And with the note, a bottle of schnapps, some dry biscuits and Camembert cheese.

'Perhaps you are right, Herr Hauptmann,' Peiper remarked, 'perhaps we are condemned men. If he leaves us more special rations, I shall begin to be suspicious.'

'He's just trying to keep us working in this house,' Heuzer said, laughing.

Outside, as if nature agreed with Heuzer, the rain slapped against the window, throwing one or two hailstones at the glass, while inside, the floorboards creaked to the sway of the wind and some of the plaster fell from the ceiling.

'Well, I hope it's just as bad at the coast,' Peiper said.

The U-Boat pen Gehlen arrived at later that day was a heavy concrete construction between the Danish coast and Lübeck – or what remained of Lübeck – and concealed under camouflage netting which made it look like bomb damage. Seagulls flew over while the salted wind burned the pale skin of underwater faces and the sickly smell of sewage and bilge oil competed with soldered metal for the strongest sense of the men who stood to attention on the incoming submarine.

When Kapitanleutnant Dieter Vogl reached his commanding officer's office, he sat down prepared never to get up again. He had been on submarines since 1941, already well past the time when he should have been dead. Borrowed time had been mortgaged, and re-mortgaged. He had a girlfriend somewhere, and a child he had seen once, and a crew caught between suicide and mutiny.

'I tell you, sir, if we go out again, we won't come back,' he said to the balding man sorting through a sheaf of papers in front of him. The smell of ersatz coffee had replaced the harbour odours but it was the sight of an apple that turned Vogl's stomach.

The ruddy sea captain was having none of Vogl's protests and any sympathy in his voice was for himself. 'I'm sorry, Dieter. The order comes from the highest authority. General Gehlen is a persuasive man. So, for God's sake, don't say anything to him to get yourself into trouble.' He looked around and then as a pretend afterthought said: 'Or me.'

Vogl did not stand up when Reinhard Gehlen came in. Instead, he sat with his hands in his pockets and his feet stretched out. There were creeping food stains on his polo-neck and his jacket was torn. The Iron Cross, First Class, hung precariously from his jacket, and two of the buttons were missing where his Iron Cross, Second Class ribbon should have been. But what bothered his commanding officer the most before he was dismissed by Gehlen was that the General did not seem to mind Vogl's disrespect.

'You took part in the V2-A10 trials last autumn, Herr Kapitanleutnant?' Gehlen said to Vogl when the ruddy sea captain was gone. The General's slight frame and almost porcelain facade seemed to clash with his eyes, which Vogl could not help following.

'It was cancelled,' Vogl said. 'They needed us at sea.'

'Explain it to me,' Gehlen said, checking the windows. Vogl indicated that he did not think there was much point. But he volunteered the information anyway. 'The A10 is a two-stage version of the V2 rocket used against London. But the A10 has a much longer range than the normal V2. We attached the rocket and launcher to a submarine – a Japanese type I-400, a bloody monster we brought all the way round the world. The submarine was reinforced. The control box equipment for the rocket fitted into its conning-tower, and the rocket and launcher were built into the deck. Theoretically, assuming the two stages of flight worked, our range was over six thousand kilometres.'

Vogl paused and his face changed.

'We managed to hit an island off Norway,' he said then. 'Killed some fish. Then the arguments began. The Luftwaffe wanted to fire at New York, the Kriegsmarine wanted to attack British targets. It all ended when Admiral Donitz wanted to launch a fresh U-Boat offensive. Witness us. I've been trying to avoid death for three months now.'

'But you and your crew could still operate such a submarine?' Gehlen said. 'An I-400?'

'Sure. It's in Kiel, I think. Or Wilhelmshaven. You want to attack America?'

'No, I want you to take the submarine to America,' Gehlen replied.

Vogl swore and such was the strength of the insubordination in the remark that he stood up and came to attention while he was still speaking. More for the sake of his dispersed family than himself. And in doing so, he released all the pent up body odour of several months at sea. Gehlen was forced on the defensive, and he ignored Vogl's remark.

'How long would it take for you to reach the coast of Texas?' he asked the submariner.

'That depends,' Vogl replied. He sat down again, now resigned to his fate. 'On how we run. On how much risk we take. Up to two months if we're careful. Far less if we are not. I don't suppose you want me to be careful?'

'I want you there in three to four weeks.'

Vogl's swearing was down to a single word.

Gehlen pulled several files from his briefcase. 'Have you ever heard of nuclear fission?' he asked.

When the two men stopped for coffee some time later, Vogl was measuring the design specifications of a modified V2-A10 two-stage intercontinental rocket. On the plans since 1940, only five had ever been built. And there was one left.

'We don't even know if the rocket will fly,' Vogl said by way of a last-ditch protest, 'and even if it does, there's no guarantee it'll land where we want it to. Have you considered that? If this plutonium is as powerful as you say, we could ...' Vogl stepped back from the drawings and held his tongue between his teeth.

'You'll have a designated weapons officer on board the submarine,' Gehlen said. 'In command of all specifics surrounding the rocket and the detonation of the explosive plutonium. It will work. I appreciate your reservations but the risk is worth it. What other choice do we have?'

'We could just do nothing ... sir.' Vogl was shaking his head.

'I could have you shot for that remark,' Gehlen said.

'And who would skipper your boat?'

Gehlen smiled. 'Just get the boat into position, Dieter.'

'So I'm to be a bus driver to a lot of scientists,' Vogl said. 'If this explosive you propose to detonate over the Reds is as powerful as you say, then I am the devil's driver, perhaps.'

Gehlen pulled a map out. 'You'll begin your run to open sea from this island off the Fresian coast. Following a specific route mapped out for you. Please pay attention.'

'I've just come from there,' Vogl said, looking at the route.

'Then you should have no problems. Once out in the open sea ...'

'... I must run on the surface as much as possible. Wonderful. You know, I had hoped to be going home. I have a child ...'

For the first time, Gehlen adopted the full imposition of his rank. 'This is the last throw of the dice for Germany. You might just turn this whole war around for us.'

'Or blow a lot of what's left of our shattered country to hell,' Vogl said. 'I'm overwhelmed.'

'As you should be,' Gehlen said.

'And who have you persuaded to steal this plutonium for you?' Vogl asked. He was the one checking the windows now. And his iron cross had fallen off.

Gehlen returned to the mansion in the hills late at night. And it was raining again.

'You struck an officer,' he said to Thomas Heuzer as soon as he entered the library where the captain was working. 'In forty-one.'

'He threatened the safety of a Brandenburg operation,' Heuzer said after some thought. 'My men come first.'

'Do they indeed, Thomas? How honourable.'

Gehlen's ambiguity angered Heuzer. The captain felt the need to expand. 'We were behind Russian lines. The place was crawling with Reds. I had a hundred men, most of them Ukrainians and White Russians. My commanding officer did not appear to realise the seriousness of our situation. He was not cut out for Brandenburg work. Actually, they hung him last October for the Twentieth of July business against the Führer. He was friendly with Von Treskow and that lot at Army Group Centre. But when I hit him, he was a professional and I was not.'

'You carried out the mission, successfully.'

'I have six children,' Heuzer said by way of excuse. And he was able to draw sympathy from Gehlen in a way that made the General take a small drink.

'And the village?' Gehlen said, as much to re-establish his own authority as anything else.

'They knew our position,' Heuzer said. 'They had reported another unit to the Reds a week before. There was no choice.'

There was a detectable cadence of disbelief in Thomas Heuzer's voice. And his mouth had hardened to the point where the lips were no longer visible. That was the first time Gehlen really noticed that there might be the possibility of something truly monstrous in the captain. And it was attractive.

'Yes, well, I didn't come down here to lecture you on the morality of warfare,' Gehlen said. 'What have you come up with by way of men for this little foray?'

'Nothing,' Heuzer said. 'Operation Grief used up everything of worth, and anything it did not use up is useless. Grief killed everything we could use. Schellenberg knew that.'

'I refuse to give up,' Gehlen insisted. He pulled a sheet of paper from his pocket. 'From America. Things are going well there.'

7

The town of Los Muertos was founded almost by accident, by the Spanish conquistador, Iago Santavista, in the early sixteenth century.

Santavista, who had accompanied Cortez during the conquest of Mexico, was following the line of the Rio Grande in search of the legendary City of the Sun, where, it was said, the buildings were made of gold and the spires touched the heavens.

He disappeared.

In a letter which reached Madrid some years later, Santavista pledged himself to obedience, begged forgiveness for his blasphemy and warned all those who would search for the City of the Sun to abandon their quest and accept humility in their saviour.

At least five more expeditions attempted. One actually reached Montana in 1595. Then it vanished, too.

Los Muertos became a trading post and then settled into resigned obscurity until the United States Air Force chose the area to the south as a bombing range. And immediately to the north, Roosevelt's New Deal built a small dam and a railway line.

Simon Penny reached Los Muertos by car, after dark. He stopped in the plaza, strolled up and down the town, noticed the hispanic population took over the town after dark, then walked over to the only bar in town for a drink.

The bar was small and the ceiling low, which made it feel like the lower deck of a ship, and the smell was a combination of animal and engine. All the faces were frightened and many were bovine. The owner, a man named Pepper, looked something like a long-horn steer, only thinner.

John Delmar was waiting for Penny on his ranchhouse porch, reading. 'I see the stars better on a cold night,' he said. 'I can see my place then. And that keeps me even.'

'You're prepared?' Penny asked.

'I suppose I should be excited,' Delmar said. 'The culmination of two years' work. Suddenly things that were far away are very close. It all seems so unreal. My grandfather was killed at Wounded Knee, you know. For a dance. I sometimes do it myself, out there in the desert. And it seems more real than this. Perhaps you should either let your head or your heart rule you, but not both. He was ruled by his head.'

'Your grandfather was killed,' Simon Penny said.

'I was talkin' about this feller.' He showed Penny the book he was holding. 'Iago Santavista. Conquistador responsible for this place. He hated it, too. Do you know what it is like to feel loyalty to something you despise?' He held up the book. 'He says here he has been told the City of the Sun is over the mountains to the north, but his men are dying and near mutiny and he should turn back. But he cannot. And you can see, once he has written that, the tone of the rest of the letter is ... well, he starts regretting things ... should have trusted his heart, perhaps.'

'But there was no City of the Sun,' Penny said.

'Who says?' Delmar replied.

Penny laughed and rubbed his hand in the frost that had settled on the porch. A dog barked, then another, then three more. And somewhere among the dogs, a cock crowed.

The two men stared out at the mountain sky. There were too many stars to count, and the wind was rolling up clouds of dust to the north. You could hear the sound of the dust and the rushing water of the river nearby, and the water made you feel as if the whole world was beginning to melt, perhaps making way for a new one.

'You're Apache,' Penny said then.

Delmar broke off some tobacco and began to chew it. 'I'm part Ute and Sioux. Navajo and Cheyenne, too. This was a land of many tribes. And they moved with the seasons. Jeronimo raided this town.'

'And Billy the Kid shot a man down there where the railroad siding is now.'

'White man. Anyway, they all came through here at one time or another. Camino Real. The Royal Highway. I think you might be a gunfighter.'

'I'm nothing of the sort,' Penny said.

'Have you timed the drive?' Delmar asked.

'I need you to get me up there again. To Los Alamos.'

'Not back there,' Delmar said. 'Not there. I've done all you asked.'

Penny held the sheriff's arm. 'You're needed,' he said.

'I hate my people, you know,' John Delmar said by way of an excuse.

'Your motives are your own,' Penny replied.

'My wife's angry with me,' Delmar said then. 'I disappoint her. You married?'

Penny shook his head very deliberately. 'Not encouraged. I lived with a woman once. Didn't like her much, she was a spoilt child. From Ljubliana in Slovenia. Her name was Mita. They're all fascists there. Tito will probably make them pay. The Slovenians. I walked out on her one morning, Mita. Changed my life, moved countries.'

'I'm frightened, you know,' Delmar said. 'I've never done anythin' like that. Do you understand anythin' of the movement of the tides of history?'

'I like to think I am history,' Penny said without knowing why he had.

Delmar threw some stones into the darkness, and a small animal darted across their field of vision for a moment.

'I liked to think he was killed by his own men, Santavista. He gave them hope, then took it. He betrayed them and they hated him.'

'You are a sentimental man,' Penny said. 'That is dangerous. You display that naive sentimentality which Americans appear to have made their own. But then, very often, the most sentimental are the most ruthless.'

'Germany.'

'Germany is the soul of Europe, black or white, and without a soul, what is Europe?'

'You scare me, boy. And I'm not American.'

The lake where John Delmar fished the next morning was manmade for a reservoir, and it covered an ancient Indian cliff village. The rock around the lake was red run through with white, the water a very deep green, and the fishing better than in the river. The river was called the Vibora because it resembled a moving snake and changed colour during flooding. It fed the Rio Grande.

A few miles further east, the Vibora bordered Andy Redrow's small ranch. It was in full flood there, heavy with topsoil washed off the mountains, which meant it could only be crossed by the suspension bridge at the reservoir at that time of the year. Otherwise Eadie Shaffer would have crossed by the rocks and John Delmar would not have gone fishing.

Eadie was a series of delicate movements in the spring sunshine. To her left, the water rushed past angry, tearing at the banks, its course marked by small sunblasts and the hard crack of displaced rocks.

'Anythin' bitin', Sheriff?' she asked.

Eadie Shaffer had once stopped traffic in small towns. Five years on, she still made motorists with a gas ration pause before moving off. She lived away now, with a part-time husband no one had seen since he came to Los Muertos on a train, and left with her pregnant.

'This mornin',' Delmar said. 'I got quite a bite this mornin'. You look pretty, my dear.'

She blushed. 'You shouldn't say things like that, Sheriff. Makes a girl feel kinda queer.' She slid from the saddle of the chestnut horse, while the animal poked its nose into the green lake water. And Eadie straightened her denims.

'Someone said Gus was bein' shipped home,' she said. 'Why'd nobody tell me?'

'Thought you was goin' away again. Didn't seem no point in diggin' up the past. You leave Gus, Eadie. He left you.'

'Not before I left him,' she said without thinking. Her face showed she thought it was a victory; her eyes, a defeat.

Delmar cast again. 'It's been a while, Eadie, and things have changed. People's as won't accept that. Even here.'

Eadie thought for a while, looking at the scenery. 'I woulda married him.'

Delmar nodded, pulled his line in early and cast once more into the lake. 'We say things we want to mean so easily, my dear, and then we find we cannot take them back. How you gettin' on, anyways?'

'Oh, I make do. Ain't been easy since Mikey lost interest. But if it's a toss up between bein' with Mikey and bein' without Mikey, I'll take the second. I miss bein' married, though.'

'Maybe you should find yourself another man.'

She bowed her head and thought. 'I just wanna say hello, Sheriff. Nothin' more. Gus and me, like you say, that's history.' She picked up a stone. 'I sell these, you know. Shells, too. I pick them from a beach near me and I sell them. And I sew and other things.' She paused while he stared at her. The stare made her feel uncomfortable. 'There's some darkies moved in 'bout two miles that way,' she said then. 'Army engineers. I seen 'em. Big guys.'

'You'd do well to stay away from them while you're here,' Delmar said. 'Don't go gettin' ideas.'

'You're not my daddy, Sheriff. Anyways, I'm only here in passin'. I don't live here no more. Don't want to cause another scandal, do I? Your Gus is a queer critter, Sheriff. He didn't mind causin' scandal.'

'He's a boy who never recognised his own good fortune. Always lookin' elsewhere. All you young folk is.'

'I ain't so young any more, Sheriff. You see Gus, you tell him I was askin' for him.'

Delmar's mouth was dry now and he found himself shaking. As he watched her disappear into the distance, he considered the message he had received from Germany.

A brief shower laid a carpet of powder snow for the single Dodge truck that pulled up between the small railway station on the old spur line and the plaza in Los Muertos a few hours later.

The plaza had a handkerchief of mown grass, a bandstand, a replica cannon and a plaque. The plaque had two sides. On one side was an extract from the letter Iago Santavista sent to Madrid; on the other the names of the Confederate soldiers who died during the battle to capture the town in 1865.

The spur line connected the Atchison, Topeka and Santa Fe Railroad with a freight line to Dallas. Special cargoes could go all the way to Dallas undisturbed by regular schedules or the crush of wartime train travel. Otherwise, the spur line was often used to store old and redundant rolling stock.

The two US army officers who jumped from the cab of the Dodge that evening, one a major, the other, a lieutenant, drew long looks from the handful of people on the street at that time.

The major was of medium build, with short chestnut hair. He wore glasses, and looked more like a college lecturer than a soldier. The lieutenant, about six feet tall with brown eyes and black hair, wore two pistols, but no one who saw him much cared about such detail.

Andy Redrow strolled over from his feed and hardware store, arms folded, shaking his head.

The major put out his hand.

'Warren Brett,' he said, 'Army engineers. Up at the old Moore ranch. Just thought I'd drop in and pay our respects. Neighbours, like.'

'Yeah,' Redrow said. 'I heard you boys was up there. Come to help the airforce or some of those people from up Santa Fe way who don't ever stop and talk?'

'We're building a runway. And a road, maybe,' Brett said, as if he had just given away a state secret.

'Well,' Redrow's face beamed, 'any of you boys need anythin', my store's probably got it. Always willin' to help the military. No matter what the circumstances. Given the current emergency.'

'Good, good. This is Lieutenant Rand, my second in command.'

Redrow did not shake Philip Rand's hand. Rand acknowledged the insult, Warren Brett did not. 'We're just going to wet our lips in that bar over there. You care to join us?' he said. He pointed to the low building between Redrow's supply store and a three-storey foodstore, where two hitching posts stood guard before the road began bending under a low overhang from the mountains. 'Just the one, though.'

Redrow scratched his chin. 'Well, it'd be fine with me. But I'm not sure old Zach is quite as amenable to havin' darkies in his bar.' He glanced at Philip Rand. Rand felt the blood leave his face. Redrow smiled as if he had just pointed out a by-law. 'What say I go get you boys a soda and we hold on that drink, Major.'

He drew Brett away from Rand. 'You gotta learn to be sensitive to folks' sympathies, you know. I can tell from your accent that you're from back east, probably one o' them free thinkin' colleges . . .' He put his arm over Brett's shoulder.

Philip Rand was breathing very deeply and staring at the dust corkscrewing up the main street. 'I'm not very thirsty,' he said loud enough for the mayor to hear.

Redrow looked back at him then turned back to Brett. 'We should have a talk, Major,' Redrow said, ''bout bringin' your darkies into town. You know, we're not one o' them Mississippi towns where niggers get strung up if they give sass, no, but this is a small community and best not give any cause for trouble. As I say, I'm pretty free in these matters, have no problem with them bein' here, servin' the colours ... but that don't mean we gotta drink with them. Know what I mean?'

Brett nodded, then took Redrow's hand from his shoulder. 'I think I understand you, Mr Redrow. I have encountered this problem before, as you'll imagine.'

'Yeah. Well, then we understand one another. What say I get you that soda and it's on the house. By the way, if you want to come in with any more white officers, then please feel free. Ol' Zach does the best beer in these parts.'

'I'm sure he does.' Warren Brett looked at his watch. 'Look, forget the drinks. Perhaps some other time.' He saluted Redrow and signalled to Rand to get back in the truck. Rand stopped reading the plaque and rubbed his hands before getting into the cab.

They were out of Los Muertos, driving through a canyon called the Santavista Gap, when Rand spoke. 'You told them we're putting an airfield through their town, Warren?'

Brett shook his head and drew heavily on a cigarette. 'I couldn't find the words, Philip ... you know how it is.'

'I knew it was futile, Warren. We should be at the front. At least you know the enemy there.'

'Don't get on that again, Lieutenant.'

The truck had disappeared into the gathering snow and dust when John Delmar came very slowly from the direction of the sheriff's office on the other side of the plaza. A pickup backfired pulling out of the rusting gas station at the east end of town.

'Trouble?' John Delmar asked Andy Redrow.

'God, no. Just lettin' that feller know that there's protocol must be observed. I think he got the message. You think they'd have told him.'

'Know how many there are?'

'Fifty, I heard. My Eadie was out that way yesterday. They're just surveyin' at present. Might be a new base. Good for us. Good for business ...'

'Good for re-election,' Delmar said.

'God bless America,' Redrow said. 'You don't look pleased.'

'Rosalyn's ...' Delmar looked around him. 'Well, I have to arrest a young buck off the reservation again. Damn bastard cut someone up with a knife. I swear those people are children. I'll send him to Albuquerque for his own safety.'

'It's a hard life,' Andy Redrow replied.

8

Reinhard Gehlen arrived earlier than usual the next morning at Heuzer's mansion headquarters. It was misty, and some of the mist had settled on the General's cap and reflected the light in the room around his head, giving him a kind of halo. A guardian angel, Heuzer thought.

'I have the men you need,' Gehlen said.

'From where?'

'We were looking in the wrong place. They were listed as Spaniards.'

'Who?' Heuzer's impatience was getting the better of him and he was already reaching for the file Gehlen was pulling out. Heuzer handed a cup of coffee he was holding to Karl Peiper.

'Have you ever heard of the Stonewall Legion?' Gehlen asked him.

Heuzer shook his head. 'What are they, engineers?'

'No. Americans. Or rather, Confederate Americans. That is, men dedicated to the cause of the American Southern Confederacy.'

'But they were destroyed in 1865.'

'Tell them that.'

The Stonewall Legion of the Waffen-SS was probably the least publicised unit in the German armed forces during the Second World War.

Originally formed as a unit of the Spanish army during the Spanish-American War of 1898, the Stonewall Legion drew its first recruits from a nucleus of families who had left the defeated Confederacy to live in Cuba after the American Civil War.

Defeated in Cuba, its members fled the island before settling in Spain, this time as part of the Spanish monarch's bodyguard.

In 1918, much to the chagrin of the Spanish government, one hundred Stonewall Legionaries left to fight with the Imperial German Army in France. Much to the relief of that same Spanish government, they were all killed before they could meet United States troops in action. However, the Stonewall Legion remained in Spanish service and eighteen years later, to a man, joined Franco's Nationalist rebellion against the Spanish government.

Following Franco's victory, the Legion arrived in Berlin in early 1942 as part of the Blue Division, Spain's volunteer contribution to the invasion of Russia, intent on exploiting their position to get into action against the newly belligerent United States.

Three years later, Lieutenant Kyle Bedford Stuart III could dwell on all these things as he surveyed the remnants of the Stonewall Legion, by early morning light, in a slit trench near Kustrin on the Oder. The unit he commanded was down to twelve men, holding fifty metres of the line between two companies of various Scandinavians and a company of French and Belgian volunteers.

Stuart touched his Knight's Cross as he took a look over the parapet and straightened his camouflaged helmet. 'As soon as it's dark,' he said. 'Pickett's Charge. We seem to be forever facing that last charge at Gettysburg.'

The young soldier beside him, from an old Charleston family with property in Cuba and Argentina, nodded. 'Maybe we should unfurl the colours, Teniente. Maybe defeat is our destiny.'

'Nonsense, Crane, our destiny is how we shape it. But when

the Katyushas are raining down, you feel free to remind me of my foolishness.'

Kyle Stuart, then thirty-five years old, had been born near New Orleans to a family which never celebrated the Fourth of July and never partook in US elections. When his father was killed fighting with the Imperial German Army in 1918, young Kyle was sent to a small military college in Mississippi which trained men for service in foreign armies, while the family moved, first to Mexico, then Spain.

He was decorated by Franco during the Spanish Civil War. A rebel at last, he wrote his mother.

In 1942, he first saw action in Russia outside Leningrad. Wounded outside Stalingrad — Stuart was one of only fifteen officers and three hundred and twenty men to make it back to the main German lines before the pocket was completely surrounded — he was almost killed three months later during fighting to retake Kharkov. Then, in 1944, during the Russian Bagratian offensive, he was captured.

Sentenced to death by summary court-martial, Stuart escaped by killing two female guards. Friends noticed a change in him. As if he was struggling with himself. And losing. He refused leave and went straight back to the front. A month later he led a counter-attack near Warsaw, for which he was awarded his Knight's Cross, and in early 1945, he took command of what remained of the Stonewall Legion. But in all that time, despite many pleadings, neither he nor any of his men had yet met United States troops in action.

Stuart watched the dawn creep in on the Russian lines for the next few minutes, then signalled to the men beside him.

'I want a prisoner this time, *Brigada*,' Stuart said.

Larry Schwartz, a small Texan sergeant in his early forties, head shaven, missing two fingers of one hand, grinned and then slid over the top of the slit trench. Stuart followed him.

When Stuart and the Texan were fifty metres out, Crane and another private with a double-barrelled Franco-hispanic name everyone had condensed to Pierre, rolled over the top of the trench.

There were three men in the Red Army forward observation post, an old stone church, reinforced by several pieces of German halftrack and hung over with the remains of a circus tent. Two dead elephants in the middle of no-man's land had burst their sides the previous night and, now and again, hissing noises broke the silence between the lines.

Stuart watched Crane and Pierre work their way to the extreme flanks of the Russian position.

Crane fired. First one shot; then two more; then on full automatic until the magazine was empty. The Russian at the observation slit disappeared from view.

The other two Russians took positions either side of the hole and opened fire on Crane. Mortars and heavy machine guns opened up from the main Russian lines further back. Crane rolled into a hole and reloaded. Then Pierre opened fire.

Stuart drew a knife, Schwartz a P-38 with a heavy silencer attachment. The two remaining Russians in the observation post, a teenager with lice and an old man with a chest complaint were shouting at each other and at their own lines and trying to reload.

Stuart came in from the side and caught the younger one with his weapon still unloaded. Stuart drove his knife under the teenager's ribs and saw blood run from his mouth. The older man, watching no-man's land, swung to shoot Stuart, but Schwartz shot him in the shoulder and then in the leg. It took the teenager three minutes to die. Schwartz shot him in the end to make sure. Then the Russian mortars began to land.

Stuart shouted for cover. Crane and Pierre fired on full automatic and several trench mortars in the German lines backed them with a line of bombs. Stuart and Schwartz dragged the wounded old Russian under the fury of the exchange between both lines. Crane came forward to help. Pierre fell back to provide more cover, then threw himself across the German wire.

Stuart caught his prisoner by the neck, Schwartz grabbed him by the boot. They pulled him over Pierre, while Crane covered them. Then Crane fired a last burst, crawled across Pierre and pulled his comrade off the wire.

When they reached the German trenches, Schwartz was examining three bullet holes in the old Russian's back. 'Shit, he's dead,' he said to Stuart.

'I think I am, too.' Crane fell forward into Kyle Stuart's arms, a kind of glacial look in his baby eyes. Stuart dropped the cigarette from his mouth and the ash burned Crane's jacket.

A runner crept slowly along the trench, face covered by an angled coalscuttle helmet. He was spotted with mud and acne. When he reached Kyle Stuart, he made what might have been a salute. Or he may have been removing something from his eye. 'Sturmbannführer's compliments, but would you please report to him.'

Stuart looked at Crane's body and then at the rest of his men. 'We're doing no more patrols. If Himmler wants us out of the way so he can deal with the Yankees, then he can do it himself.'

The division command post was an extension to a farmhouse. The rest of the home was in ruins. A platoon of machine gunners and mortar men occupied the rubble. And there was a casualty clearing station under an improvised bivouac. Two dead bodies waited under greatcoats for collection. Kyle Stuart washed his face before going in to meet his commanding officer.

Sturmbannführer Leon Degrelle was the man Hitler once said he would have liked as his son. In his mid-thirties, he was the most decorated foreigner in the Waffen-SS and a supreme man of action. He wore a Knight's Cross at his throat and so many wound badges that his uniform had run out of space for them. On his shoulder he wore the legend: *Walloonie*. But his Belgian division was as much myth as reality now.

'You're being pulled out.' Degrelle looked more angry than Kyle Stuart. 'What do they think I should hold this line with?'

'Am I to know why?' Stuart asked.

'Perhaps you are right, Kyle, the Reichsführer does plan to hand you over to Eisenhower to gain credits. He certainly needs them. There's a military police escort.'

'I could refuse,' Stuart insisted. 'Technically we're Spanish troops attached to the Wehrmacht. Our SS affiliation is purely administrative.'

'That's a legal technicality that should go down well in a court martial.' Degrelle grinned. 'The order comes from SD Ausland. Walter Schellenberg's countersignature. Group S. Didn't you petition Himmler to join that thing Skorzeny organised in the Ardennes? Operation Grief.'

'We were refused permission,' Stuart said. 'The Führer did not want the vanguard of his offensive in the hands of foreigners. Quote, unquote.'

'Well, perhaps your dreams have come true, and they want you to launch an attack across the Rhine. Shoot Eisenhower, or something. Anyway, get your lads ready, and don't do anything stupid, Kyle. If they were going to hand you over, they'd have done it by now. Our esteemed Reichsführer would have handed all of us over to our respective governments to gain favour. Perhaps you will be decorated. We, here, on the other hand, will definitely be destroyed. I'm not sure I made the right choice with fascism. Perhaps I should have been a Communist.'

'I never had a choice,' Stuart said, as if he relished the notion.

9

Philip Rand ran ten miles a day when he was up to it, and five when he was not. A mile high on the Mesa de Los Muertos, he ran three and walked the rest. The road upon which he ran cut through the mountains at the west end of the Redrow ranch, where several tributaries drove deep finger canyons all the way from the Pecos to a junction immediately east of Los Muertos. There, they met up and became the Vibora, carving a sharp gorge at the Santavista Gap, and ploughed on to the Rio Grande.

Rand had reached the suspension bridge below the Santavista Gap when he heard the engine behind him.

'Bet I can beat you at a dash!' Eadie Shaffer slowed the pickup truck to Philip Rand's pace and shoved her head further out into the mountain breeze. 'You're with them black boys in the old Moore ranch, right?'

'You must be a spy to know so much secret information,' Rand said. He kept running, though he wished he could slow down.

'The Moores were forced out durin' the Depression,' she said. She stopped her pickup suddenly and jumped out. 'This is where Iago Santavista died, they say. Know that?'

'You are an obtuse lady,' Rand said.

'He's the conquistador who gave his name to this.' She made

a sweeping gesture with her hand. 'Conquistador's a Spanish word for ...'

'I know what it is,' Rand said. 'And I know about Santavista. I read the plaque in Los Muertos.'

'Well, this gap is for him. They say he and most of his men died over there.' She pointed to the other side of the river. 'They never found no bodies and the feller who brought back Santavista's letter refused to talk for the rest of his life.' She grinned. 'Bad medicine here, the Injuns say. He died in a monastery in Italy, the feller who brought back the letter, holdin' a copy of it to his breast. They say he died shieldin' his eyes as if from a great light.'

'That's a fine story,' Rand said. He sat down on a rock and examined the area.

'Isn't it? I been hearin' it all my life. Chirachauas on the mesa say Santavista's spirit still rides a white horse from one end of this gap to the other durin' a full moon, cursin' his blasphemy and beggin' God for a way out.' Eadie Shaffer shook her head.

The approaching police car took her thoughts and scattered them.

Sheriff John Delmar paused, holding the door, when he stepped out. Though he could not remember when he had fallen in love with Eadie Shaffer, if he even knew it at the time, or whether he showed it now, he feared it showed more than he feared most things. And fear was his constant shadow now.

'Sheriff's a student of Santavista. Ain't you, Sheriff?' Eadie Shaffer said with the embarrassment of one trying too hard to be amusing. 'Folks as say he's tryin' to find the City of the Sun hisself. Knows all them Injun legends, the sheriff does. That right?'

'It ain't legend. It's historical fact.' Delmar shut the door of his car, walked out on to the suspension bridge and looked back towards the Santavista Gap. Behind him, the mesa gave way to a purple serrated ridge. Delmar wiped the sweat from his brow and leaned over the bridge. The water below was red.

'Eadie, you get up and go on home. Your pa'd tan your hide if'n I told him you were talkin' here to this . . . gentleman. You best go home. And you . . . Lieutenant . . . you best learn what can and cannot be done here. For your own sake.'

Eadie Shaffer laughed and individual strands of her hair moved in the breeze. 'Sheriff, I ain't no schoolgal no more. I ain't your Gus's neither. And you got no right tellin' me who I may or mayn't talk to.'

There were two birds of prey floating on the morning thermals. Rand glanced at them. 'I have to be back at camp in thirty minutes,' he said. 'But Sheriff, I am an officer in the United States Army. I will be treated with the respect that is due my position and rank. If not for myself, then for the colours I serve.'

Delmar smiled. 'Well, you picked a place to do that, Lieutenant. Los Muertos, you see, is old Dixie territory. Over there is Texas. Not too much respect for the colours round here. Of any kind. Toleration when the military brings work, I suppose. Seems if the Devil himself brings work, then he gets the respect.' Delmar walked back to his car. 'Eadie! Get on home. Please.'

Eadie Shaffer blushed and hesitated before turning round and walking back to her pickup. Before she got in she waved at Rand. 'See you round,' she said.

John Delmar just stared straight ahead, while Philip Rand tried to maintain control of himself.

Later that day, watching John Delmar, Simon Penny worried that he had no fear anymore. He had not felt it for so long, he could not remember ever feeling it. And with fear had gone almost every other emotion, so much so that he had to force himself to laugh now.

He wiped away the thin coating of hoarforst that had settled on his saddle. After he had urinated against a fence-pole, he strolled back to the horse and pulled a small loaf of bread from a bag behind his saddle. The shadows were inching their way up the finger mesas to the northwest of Los Alamos and at least one vehicle was moving along the small dirt road to the north. A small animal stirred in the sagebrush.

John Delmar was watching it all through binoculars. 'It's all very ordinary from here, considerin' they're makin' a bomb that could be the end of the world.'

'You have a conscience?' Penny said. 'Or does it offend you that something so ordinary can be so powerful? Don't worry, what you see is unimportant. The power is in what you can't see.'

Delmar let his eyes survey the man-made intrusions of wood and concrete in the atomic complex, and then swung his binoculars to the mountains and mesas around it. They were overcoat brown scarred by scorched canyons and matted with pines and poplars and aspens. The mesas ran as high as ten thousand feet to the west and the colours there were different because of the rising sun.

'The City of the Sun,' Delmar said.

Afterwards, Penny and Delmar picked pieces of bread and drank coffee from a thermos flask, then wiped their hands and sat down on some long grass. A cow was grazing by a patch of sagebrush on the stretch of prairie to their right. A piece of sagebrush broke free and rolled towards a cabin among the trees in the distance.

'We better start moving,' Penny said. 'Security patrols will be around soon.'

From his vantage point, on the pointed rock of an Indian ceremonial site, Delmar could watch people moving around below him. They had the relentless automation of ants, he thought. A line of trucks was parked on one muddy drive and several military police threaded their way between the various buildings along the drive.

'My people have a legend about the end of time,' Delmar said. 'It will not stop, it will get faster and people will not be able to keep up. What these people are doing is pushing the accelerator.'

'So you do disapprove of such weapons?' Penny said.

'I have heard of men who are ghosts,' Delmar replied. 'The Germans use them. Tod agents, they call them. Many legends attach to them. I think only a Tod agent could come looking for the City of the Sun.'

'I think you should stick to the details of this operation and the weather, Sheriff,' Simon Penny said.

'Just so you know I am not as ignorant as you would like to believe. I know what I see.'

'Then you *are* dangerous.'

A truck appeared out of the trees. The truck swung round a mountain road. There were twelve military policemen in it and Penny shoved Delmar to the ground.

'And you are a ghost,' Delmar said.

All Manny Rivera's control died in the face of Jeff Francis' verbal onslaught, till the two men sank back in their chairs, one from exhaustion, the other from embarrassment.

'Look, I'm not blaming you, Manny.' Francis had to stand up to speak now. 'But it's my career on the line here. You know, I don't think Hoover likes me. How the hell am I supposed to find out what happened to Finger when I'm not even allowed to know details of what he was doing? They say it's a bomb, you know. So powerful it can kill a hundred thousand people.'

Rivera shook his head. 'You think our suspect might be hidin' down there in New Mexico makin' this thing?' he said. 'If it was just sex, then maybe they think this thing they're workin' on is bigger than the life of a twisted little ex-Kraut scientist. Maybe we're window dressin'.'

'Hoover keeps going on about sex. I think he wants it to be sex. He has this thing about sex. Says I should get a wife. Like I'm not trying.'

Rivera felt it easier to go along with his partner's self-pitying, but something was breaking between them, and it was not simply the complete lack of anything leading anywhere from the stiff body of Oskar Finger. Friendship had limits placed upon it by survival. Rivera had always known this; Francis came from a class which denied it; both men were content to leave it unsaid.

Francis kept looking at his watch, aware that he was in the process of losing something more than time. The power of the forces that would shape him caused him to pause, but he did not have the will to oppose them.

'You have a date,' Rivera said to him. 'Go on, we'll get back on this tomorrow.'

'Yeah,' Francis said. 'I want to go down to New Mexico. To Los Alamos. Find out more about him than we have on our files. You know, he knew a lot of stuff. He was lecturing generals.'

'You think it was political?' Rivera asked.

Francis shrugged. 'So what do I do? Tell Hoover everything about his secret bomb is in someone else's hands and scare this country to hell or tell him it was a sordid little sex game that turned nasty and wait for my reward? He wants the whole thing tied up yesterday. I have pressures, Manny.'

'Never make friends with your boss,' Rivera muttered when Francis had gone.

Derek Boyd might well have been thinking the same thing the way Claude Dansey had had him working that weekend. As if running a department dedicated to total deception was not a delicate enough task, now he was supposed to deconstruct the very deceits his men based their credibility upon. And the more he presented to Dansey, the more the old spymaster wanted. As if Dansey was conducting an interrogation of the whole of Huntergatherers through the only mouthpiece it had. Occasionally, Boyd found himself wondering who was the real subject of Dansey's suspicions.

The Monday night Boyd pored over Simon Penny's files and

records for the umpteenth time, noting down relevant details in a tiny pencil script that was barely legible, which, of course, it was meant to be, Dansey came back from a trip to the country with the air of a winter storm.

'He's just not there, is he?' Dansey said to Boyd as soon as the latter had sat down again. 'I mean, everything you need is there, but he isn't. But then that was what we wanted. I think you better see this. It's a photograph from Stoneyhurst. Taken when Simon Penny was seventeen.'

Boyd had to use a magnifying glass to look at it. His glasses were not good enough anymore, something he had hoped to hide. 'He might have changed,' he said after a while. 'It's a long time ago.'

'This boy died in Africa five years after this was taken. No relatives. I have the death certificate. Who vetted him?'

Boyd shook his head. 'I don't know. It was before my time.'

'Those plods over at Five. God knows how many stink-bombs were slipped past them. All ready to go off in our faces.' Dansey shoved his hands in his pockets and moved his pointed chin. 'I think we better travel, Derek.'

'Washington?' Boyd asked.

'No,' Dansey insisted. And for once his ill-health combined with his suspicions to stop him dead. 'Not directly. If I turn up there, Uncle Sam will want to know why. They may adore me but they don't like the idea of me prowling around in their back yard. No, you and I are going to Canada. Get Legends to prepare something and two covers, too. I don't want anyone to know I've left. Say I'm ill. It's true. I have contacts in upstate New York and we'll be able to slip in at Niagara without fuss. Have someone meet us at this address. This Penny business really is a wretched nuisance. Illness does that. You know Roosevelt and Winston got mauled by Stalin in Yalta. Roosevelt should never have been allowed go. Too sick.'

'I have heard,' Boyd said. 'What do you think it's about? This Penny thing.'

'It could be the Russians. But my old heart says there's more ... Didn't you use to chase them through the snow in Finland?'

'Yes, Claude. From bank manager to Bulldog Drummond, Sheila said. She doesn't approve. Thinks it's immoral. They're our allies now, aren't they? The Bolshevists. So perhaps she was right. God, it was cold, though.'

'Any news at all from Washington?' Dansey asked.

Boyd shook his head. 'Nothing of any quality. Except a thaw.'

'Real or imagined?'

IO

While listening to Thomas Heuzer deliver a briefing to Kyle Stuart's men, Reinhard Gehlen was reminded of an insurance salesman who knows the policy he is selling will never mature. But for all that, Heuzer held himself like a believer, spoke the words like a prophet and never took his eyes off Kyle Stuart.

When Heuzer finished, Stuart, who was sitting at an old harpsichord, began fingering the keys. 'As the old sayin' goes: beware of what you seek, you may get it some day,' he said.

Heuzer lifted his gaze to the rest of Stuart's men, perched precariously on various pieces of period furniture, helping themselves to five bottles of Tennessee bourbon recently liberated from an off-course American DC-3 transport aircraft. Mostly, they wore field grey uniforms with various pieces of Spanish and other personalised kit. A couple wore the arrow insignia of the Spanish Falange. And on all their cuffs, the letters: CSA. 'If we lose this war, then the Americans will probably shoot all of you as they shot our men during Operation Grief in the Ardennes,' Heuzer said. 'And our strategic situation is so precarious that getting back to Spain without help is well-nigh impossible for you.'

'We volunteered for Grief,' Stuart said. 'Himmler wouldn't let us go. Said he did not want Germany's fate in foreign hands. Now, it seems he's changed his mind. Why?'

'I suggest you ask the Reichsführer. I do not move in such

rarefied circles. I can point out to you that the Führer is far less sensitive about whom he executes these days.'

'You present a direct enough case without threat, Herr Hauptmann,' the Texan sergeant, Larry Schwartz, said. He and Pierre were sitting at a long window, smoking Spanish cigarettes. The Texan scratched a scab on his bald head and unclipped a gold wound badge on his uniform. 'May I remind you, we are Spanish soldiers. The Caudillo would not be pleased if we were taken out and lynched.'

'Yes, a very subtle diplomatic point, Brigada,' Heuzer replied. 'Do you wish to test it?' Heuzer smiled for the first time. 'You will be dropped off on the coast of Spain with the Führer's thanks if this succeeds.' Heuzer looked around the faces again. 'It's a chance to do what you have been asking for four years now. Fight the United States. And get back to Spain.'

Pierre, whose skin was so olive it reminded Heuzer of dead men he had seen in summer in Russia, lifted the red Spanish army beret he wore and fingered the edges. 'You're a fine speaker, sir.' He nodded as if confirming his position to himself. 'But you sound like a man tryin' to lay off a bet.'

Heuzer swung to Stuart but the lieutenant said nothing.

Then Schwartz began playing with the gold wound badge lying on a coffee table in front of him. He had other badges, on his uniform, including paratrooper wings and an infantry assault badge, but Heuzer could not help focussing on the wound badge.

'I bet you've sent many a man to his death with such fine words,' Schwartz said.

'I know most of you walked two hundred kilometres through the snow when Stalingrad was surrounded,' Heuzer replied.

'We left every second man in the Legion behind in the snow,' Stuart said. 'Standin' up. Always standin' up.'

'So what is your answer?' Heuzer asked.

None of Stuart's men spoke. A couple raised their eyebrows and one whistled slightly. He ran out of breath though. It seemed like an age before the next word was spoken.

'How can we refuse?' Stuart said. 'As you say, we've been askin' for this since we got here.'

There was a palpable release of tension, as if Stuart had just defused a bomb.

'Sure. Take the war to the Yankees.' Pierre clapped his hands. 'Hell, yes.' Behind him, someone gave what approximated to the rebel yell.

Reinhard Gehlen felt nothing but sadness. He was tempted to shake his head. 'I cannot promise it will do anything for you gentlemen or the cause for which you fight,' he said in a kind of apology. 'Frankly, I believe that it is a figment of your imaginations. You are fighting a war that has been over for eighty years.'

'You will allow us to be the judge of that, sir,' Kyle Stuart said.

'It is over, gentlemen,' Gehlen insisted, noticing that Heuzer was frowning disapproval. 'The American Civil War is over and you have lost. Before you were born.'

'If you're referrin' to the war of northern aggression, then you are right,' Stuart said. 'We did indeed lose. If you are, on the other hand, referrin' to the cause of the Confederate States of America, then you are wrong. That is alive and well and standin' in front of you.'

'All right, all right,' Gehlen said. He found he had to smile. He turned to Heuzer, but the captain had left the room.

The sirens started again when Thomas Heuzer reached Berlin that evening. He wiped his face with the towel and examined his own uniform. There was a button missing, and a tear between his Iron Cross and his infantry assault badge he had not noticed before. And his Winter War Ribbon was fading. When he had finished, he turned back to the mirror and looked at his face for the things he still recognised. It was a disappointment.

'You know, Thomas, I think you look younger.' Reinhard Gehlen did not come out of the shadows.

'But look at my uniform,' Heuzer replied. 'Have you ever read *The Picture of Dorian Gray* by Oscar Wilde, Herr General?'

Reinhard Gehlen laughed. 'Perhaps we are Germany's portrait,' he said. 'Or Germany ours.'

'I hope Walter Schellenberg didn't see you come in,' Heuzer said. 'It'll be reported anyway.'

'No, it won't.' Gehlen seemed unconcerned for himself. Then he thought again. 'Anyway, he's back up north with Himmler, terrified the Führer will ask to see him again. Unfortunately for Walter, Himmler is something of an irrelevancy now. His handling of Army Group Vistula has the high command and the Führer spinning. Sometimes Walter is a little shortsighted.'

Heuzer looked around the office, at the standard equipment, searching for signs of movement, disturbed dustjackets, too much symmetry. 'You see more than I do, Herr General,' he said.

'Tell me, do you still resent your demotion, Thomas?'

Heuzer thought for a moment and then his face took on that simplicity that made Gehlen nervous. 'I'm a captain. I might have been a colonel, but I doubt it. Even attrition cannot make up for breeding. I have no breeding. But, as I pointed out, unlike you, except for the present emergency, I would never have been a soldier. And definitely never an officer. I have done well out of the war. So you see how the thought of peace does not appeal to me. I know what it's like trying to feed a family without money.' Gehlen felt a sympathy for Heuzer which unnerved him.

'But you got very close to Von Stauffenberg and friends, he insisted.'

'That was my work,' Heuzer insisted. 'They were part of my army. A doctor must get very close to disease. But I was never disloyal.'

'You say that with a tone of regret,' Gehlen said.

'I have nothing but the Reich, Herr General.'

'And the Reich wanted to kill you.'

'Not the Reich.'

'But Schellenberg had to save you from a nasty predicament.'

'Others were not so lucky.'

'Does that prey on you?'

'I like life. I like the work I do. I do the job. I appreciate my fortune. Is there more?'

For a moment Gehlen thought Heuzer was trying to convince himself and the General felt the urge to back him up. 'And when was the last time you were in America?' he asked.

Heuzer grinned and for the first time since they had begun to talk adopted a completely separate expression from Gehlen. He leaned back in his chair, joined his hands and put his fingers to his lips. 'I used to be a salesman, Herr General,' he said. 'Something of a foot-in-the-door man. It has come in useful. Somewhat melodramatic, but useful. But it lacked honour. Fulfilment. Meaning. The army gives me meaning. I can focus. Meaning before anything.'

'But your father was American?' Gehlen said.

'Step-father. He was a good man who died for being too good. So I learned the value of cruelty. I used to work in a restaurant on 49th Street in New York. Cooking for rich people. Douglas Fairbanks came in once. And Chaplin. I shared a small apartment in Brooklyn with two Jews, a Hindu and much of the cockroach population of the region. Sometimes I begged on the street. Once or twice I did other things. And when I could not take it any more I took a train to California. Train guards beat one of the Jews to death outside Chicago. And I came back to Germany on a tramp steamer from Mexico. I'm resourceful. As we Yanks say, it ain't over till it's over.'

Gehlen took a small package from his pocket and handed it to Heuzer. 'Earl Grey tea. The only source left in the Reich. And you're not an American, by the way, Herr Hauptmann, you just think you are.'

'Something which afflicts all of us at one time or another,'

Heuzer said. He went over to the window. In the distance, a body hung from a lamppost. The rain had stopped and the clouds were clearing. 'My wife has left me,' he said. Then he buttoned his tunic, adjusted his Knight's Cross and put on his gun belt. 'Probably for the best. You know the law of Sippenhaft, Herr General? You are guilty and your family is guilty. That is always on my mind.'

'You have to give it to Schellenberg, he has you by the balls, Thomas,' Gehlen said.

'Do you hear me screaming? We just met some men today whose only reason for existence is a country that ceased to be eighty years ago.'

'Vogl's ready to leave,' Gehlen said.

'That's fine,' Heuzer said. 'I hope you've figured out a way to get us there. Because I haven't.'

'Meet me at Vogl's submarine tomorrow evening. I'll have a plane and two pilots.'

Because of the length of the days in northern Norway at that time of the year, Oliver Dasch did not know how long he had been held in the house. But, using a rule of thumb that involved hours of sleep and urinations, the Luftwaffe lieutenant figured it was probably about five days.

The house was wooden and red and there were fine carpets from Asia and plenty of meat and beer. But there were grates and shutters on the windows and five military policemen stood guard around it all day, and some of the beer was already flat.

Then Reinhard Gehlen was standing at the door, carrying champagne. 'Congratulations, gentlemen. Your escape from Britain has earned both of you a recommendation for the Iron Cross, First Class. If it wasn't for the fact that you allowed yourselves to be shot down in the first place, I'd say the Fatherland could do with more officers like you and recommend a Knight's Cross.'

'So why are we still here?'

Peter Heinck, the second Luftwaffe officer in the room, more tanned than Dasch, but sadder if you discounted the ruthlessness inherent in his expression, asked the question with the relief of a man whose dentist has stopped drilling for a moment. Then he took the glass of champagne offered to him, downed it in one and put his glass out for more.

'Because I want you to undertake a flight in that machine you escaped in, Herr Leutnant,' Gehlen said. 'That huge lumbering flying boat you two managed to steal from under the nose of our enemies. Quite a bird. Quite an escape.'

'And we need champagne?' Oliver Dasch asked. His slender physique bent back and he refused a second glass.

'Leutnant Dasch, you flew over the arctic before the war,' Gehlen said, glancing at the various protruding veins on Dasch's hands. 'Many times. Something of a navigational expert, they tell me.'

'If my record says so, then yes,' Dasch replied. 'Prison makes a man unsure of who he is. Boredom eats personality. Hunger wipes memory.' His voice began to shake as he spoke. 'I was a commercial pilot,' he said then. 'One was required to be flexible.'

'Imprisonment has not helped your manners either,' Gehlen said. He poured Dasch another glass of champagne and this time the lieutenant drank it. 'I appreciate that nearly five years in camps makes one a little brittle, if not resentful, but you are still a serving Luftwaffe officer.'

'Sir.' Dasch came to attention. 'What is it you wish exactly?' he said. The tone was funereal. The sense of dread and fatigue so obvious as to trip Gehlen for a moment.

'I need you to fly over the arctic for me,' Gehlen replied.

This time Heinck refused a refill. 'Where to?' he said. 'I've only been in prison two years, so my manners are better, sir. And I've never flown in the arctic.'

'New Mexico,' Gehlen said and poured both men another drink. 'And you're going along, Heinck, because you have flown a Coronado. Perhaps you should have escaped in a fighter.'

Dasch shook his head. 'Even a Coronado does not have the range to get back from New Mexico,' he insisted.

'You won't be coming back,' Gehlen said.

This time Dasch grabbed the bottle from Gehlen and filled the two glasses.

'At least not the way you think,' Gehlen continued. 'You will rendezvous with a submarine in the Caribbean. Your aircraft will be modified to carry enough fuel for that length of journey.'

'Which makes it a flying bomb,' Heinck said. He swore and grabbed the last of the champagne from Dasch. 'We should have stayed in that British prison.'

'Perhaps,' Gehlen said. 'But you're here now. You know your escape has drawn questions from the Reich Security Main Office in Berlin. The paranoia there at the moment is quite staggering. Norway is definitely a better place to be. I have had Reichsmarshal Göring sign the two of you over to my custody. You really have no choice. If this goes well, then you will be genuine heroes of the Fatherland. Think about it . . . in six years of war only one other German officer has managed to make an escape from an Allied prison camp. And that was from Canada into the then neutral United States. You can see the problem some elements of the Gestapo and SD might have with your remarkable escape.' Gehlen sat down. 'Me,' he continued, 'I'm only interested in the wonderful airplane you brought with you. And your skills. I need you. Why not prove your heroism? You have some catching up to do. What do you say?'

Both men put out their glasses this time. '*Sieg Heil!*'

II

Staring at a Japanese STo class I-400 submarine, displacing nearly 6000 tons through a length of 400 feet, you could be forgiven for thinking you were looking at a destroyer or even a light cruiser. Only a handful were ever built and they could carry and launch three reconnaissance bombers by catapult, or, if you had a mind and the technology, a massive two-stage 90-foot-long V2-A10 intercontinental rocket with a 10,000-pound warhead.

In 1944, after modifying her for just that purpose, the Germans had given the boat all the advantages of their latest underwater gadgetry. She now had an operating depth way beyond that of most normal submarines, could run for four days submerged on battery power, had a rubber skin which deflected radar and sonar, and theoretically, with the aid of a snorkel, never had to surface.

On the downside, while running on snorkel her diesels often borrowed oxygen from the crew, a process which caused what U-Boat men called slow hanging, and created a pressure differential that left people with excruciating pain in their ears. A cruising depth of 160 feet or more meant that sewage could not be pumped out of the boat, and the snorkel itself created a wake which could be seen quite clearly in daylight.

But when Dieter Vogl swung the command periscope round three hundred and sixty degrees and examined the massive two-stage rocket lying along the length of his deck, aware of all these deficiencies, he still could not be but amazed at the sheer size of the craft.

In order to increase her speed they had stripped the submarine of all but two torpedoes and half its crew, and souped up the engines. The bow was armour-plated to protect the submarine against the explosive power of the rocket during lift-off. It had advantages, but Vogl could not think of anything but the disadvantages.

He was feeling more strain than usual when he saw Reinhard Gehlen's slight frame coming along the dock. But his eyes soon left Gehlen for the slim woman beside the General. Vogl whistled, although she was not particularly beautiful, and a seagull squawked as if in agreement. The woman stayed on the quayside, while Gehlen climbed the conning tower. 'No women, it's bad luck,' Vogl said when Reinhard Gehlen reached the top. 'My men will rebel.'

Gehlen relaxed as much as he could. 'There is a line beyond which I will not tolerate your dissent, Dieter,' he said. 'Frau Doktor Hanke is your atomic explosives specialist, Herr Kapitanleutnant. And I am afraid, Vogl, that she is as important – perhaps even more so – to this operation as you. And when it comes to the firing of that,' he pointed at the V2-A10 stretched out along the deck, 'then she takes command.' The General then focussed on a group of Vogl's men watching the woman on the dock. 'And anyone who thinks differently will be on the Oder before the day is out, clearing minefields,' he shouted.

Doctor Irmgarde Hanke bore the fragility of too much time in laboratories, a broken marriage and a bad diet on her forty-five year old body. She climbed the conning tower with that degree of hesitation usually found in theoreticians, but when Vogl went to help her, she refused.

'I'm sorry, Frau Doktor,' Vogl said in an almost obsequious voice, 'but we submariners are superstitious. Perhaps when you are dressed in fatigues and oilskins ... so this is your baby?' He pointed to the rocket again, glad she was not handsome, but teased by whatever else it was about her that preyed upon him. Something he wished would go away, so he could tell her what he and his crew felt about women on their boat.

'If you can just get me to where I want to go,' Hanke replied, 'you can keep your irresistible charm to yourself, Herr Kapitanleutnant.'

'But of course,' Vogl said. 'I would not wish my appeal to hinder the course of an operation.' He put his hand out and Gehlen noticed that, whether through attraction or conflict or both, each held the other just a bit too long.

Vogl and Hanke were sitting on the dock, going through a check list when Thomas Heuzer and Kyle Stuart appeared. The camouflage netting overhead shuddered as the iron entrance gate to the dock was shut behind them and the tremor reached Reinhard Gehlen a moment later.

Gehlen thought Stuart had that swagger men on the wrong side of hope often employ, while Heuzer carried a responsible resentment the General had seen in men with command positions they needed more than they wanted. But, again, as he approached the General, Heuzer's appearance changed to suit the moment. He shook hands with Irmgarde Hanke but showed no interest until he saw Dieter Vogl staring at her for too long.

Kyle Stuart clicked his heels as if only interested in her reaction to him. Hanke felt the lieutenant was trying too hard, and chose Heuzer to focus on because he seemed the stronger of the two. It was a scientific rather than a social choice. Gehlen registered this.

In some way Heuzer drew all of them in, the General felt, and each of them felt the need to check themselves with him. It was not something Gehlen was completely happy with but there was little he could do about it. And it gave his project the focus he wanted, even if it did take it from his control. If Heuzer was aware of it, he was ignoring it.

Gehlen then clapped his hands and took Irmgarde Hanke back on to the submarine. As they walked the length of the deck, Dieter Vogl watched them. And then Thomas Heuzer watched Dieter Vogl come back to reality.

'So, Dieter, are you prepared?' Heuzer asked as Gehlen and Hanke were coming back down the gangplank. The whole sentence sounded prearranged and Vogl tried not to answer. But, as one of his superiors had once said in a report, Heuzer's questions could draw replies from the dead.

Gehlen found himself fascinated.

'Frankly, the thought of running the English Channel scares me to death,' Vogl said to Heuzer. 'But the thought of death does that too.'

'You just follow the directions given to you,' Reinhard Gehlen said. 'Don't deviate one metre from the course you have been given. You'll be fine.'

'I wish I shared your confidence. But then you know much more than me, Herr General. And now I am to be subordinate to a woman. The final humiliation.' He grinned at Irmgarde Hanke. She did not grin back. 'I expect I will end up as fish food at the bottom of the Atlantic,' Vogl went on. 'My Kriegsmarine career ending in the only fitting way. Such is the tragedy of duty.'

Heuzer looked over at Irmgarde Hanke and did a strange thing: he winked. 'Best thing for you, Herr Kapitanleutnant. Don't you think, Frau Doktor?'

She was so taken aback she did not answer. Instead she turned to Gehlen, as if she was trying to use him to break Heuzer's spell. But Gehlen refused to be drawn. A period of embarrassing silence was cut short by the arrival of Hanke's technicians, all of whom had the look of cattle going to the abattoir.

'It is illegal for you to fail, gentlemen,' Gehlen said then. 'Remember that.'

Kyle Stuart leaned his head back and watched a flight of airplanes pass overhead. 'Perhaps it's the right time to leave, Herr General,' he said. 'If we don't get to the States soon, I'm pretty sure they'll get here.'

'Well, I just hope we get some more snow,' Vogl said. 'Keeps the sub-hunters busy trying to stay warm.'

Three and a half thousand miles away, Simon Penny was wishing the snow would go away. Pam Hanny's somewhat overbearing little gofer, Angel Marcan, was leaning unconvincingly against the ageing black car he had driven to the gutted warehouse on the lower east side of Manhattan. And Penny had a headache. He had washed three times before the meeting but he still did not feel clean. He wanted to wash again.

The warehouse was used to store unsold foodstuffs and at that time of the evening, because the air was still, a distinctive tang of rubber, fuel and animal fat was everywhere, and even Angel Marcan's chewing on garlic cloves, a habit he had developed during his first stint in jail, had no effect on it.

The taste for limes Marcan had developed in his second term gave his face a florid and disappointed look. And this, combined with the smell of fish which seemed to dog him everywhere, made Simon Penny stand off while he examined various documents laid out on the dimpled car hood.

'You surpass all expectations, Angel. I shall recommend you for a bonus.' Penny held the different papers up to a single lightbulb and examined them closer. Then he reached into his pocket and pulled out an envelope. 'Here, enjoy yourself.'

'I'm afraid it's not quite as simple as that.' Angel placed his hand down on two of the documents, then pointed a Colt automatic at Penny. 'And my friend, Tommy over there with the thirty-eight, he'll kill you now if you blink.' He swung Penny around on the car.

As Marcan began to frisk Penny, the oily man who had been reading the paper at the bar two days earlier stepped from behind a broken-down truck in the corner of the warehouse. Marcan placed his pistol against the back of Penny's head. 'Kneel down, please.' He forced Penny's legs to fold. His various odours conspired with the warehouse to make Penny wince.

'Whose orders?' Penny asked.

'Does it matter?' Angel said.

'It might have saved your life.'

For the first time Marcan felt a shiver run up his spine. It was the last thing he felt. Penny brought a switchblade round and under Angel's ribcage in one action. The Colt pistol went off as he fell. Penny dived to the right.

Tommy Martin fired two shots at Penny, but Penny had rolled over the car. Tommy fired again, this time three shots, but Penny had vanished into the clutter of boxes, tyres and pieces of wreckage around the warehouse.

Tommy Martin rubbed his oily pale face as he backed off towards the door. 'I got one shot left,' he shouted. 'You come near me and I'll kill you. I walk and you live. I got one shot left.' He reached back for the door.

Penny's hand came down on his wrist and the Smith and Wesson went off again. 'No shots left,' he said.

Tommy Martin was kneeling on the floor, held tight by Penny's grip, switchblade to his throat. 'Who ordered the killing?'

'I don't know. I swear. Angel got a call, then said things had changed. Honest, I don't know. Honest.'

'I believe you,' Penny said. He patted Tommy's oily hair, pulled the knife from his neck and shoved the blade under the back of his skull.

Around the same time, in Bethesda, Washington DC, Jeff Francis rolled over to the side table by his bed and looked at his watch. 'I have to go.'

Pam Hanny sat up in bed and shook her head. 'When will I see you again?' She reached over and touched his chest.

Francis sat on the side of the bed and reached over for his trousers. Some keys fell out. 'This bastard can't have disappeared into thin air,' he said. More for his own consumption than hers. But she was meant to respond.

'I wish I could help,' she said. She rubbed his neck, which was just what he wanted her to do.

'We've talked to God knows how many people, and the guy just isn't there. It's just like he was never there. And the scientists, Jesus, they're difficult people. There's this place in New Mexico ...'

'You'll get him,' Hanny insisted. 'I'm sure of it.'

'Well, whatever I do today, I have to have it done by five this evening. I've got to be in Boston tomorrow.'

Pam Hanny fell back on the pillows. 'You're not married? Tell me you're not married, Jeff.'

'Worse,' he said. He was struggling with his shirt. 'My mother's birthday. I've got to cook dinner. It's kind of a family thing. She gets pretty damn upset if I don't. And I feel like a heel. Don't worry, you're invited. If you want to run the gauntlet.' He put his finger to his mouth and blew her a kiss.

Hanny sat up again, pulled the sheet over her and leaned her head on her knees. 'You don't think badly of me?' she said. 'I'd hate for you to think badly of me. I'm not cheap.'

Francis leaned his knee on the bed, and put his hand to her face. 'God, I know you're not. You know, I still can't get over this. Manny's the one usually gets the girls. I'm far too stiff and Ivy League. Puts women off.' He kissed her. 'Hey, I'm glad you're here.'

Pam Hanny shoved her head into his hand. 'My mother warned me against this kind of thing.' She grinned. 'You'll have to marry me, you know. And I'm engaged already.'

'Want to go get something to eat?' he said.

She shook her head. 'I think I'll rest some more. Anyway,

I don't think Manny likes me. Last night in the bar he just kept looking at me.'

Francis grinned. 'He's just jealous. Don't worry, I checked you out properly. I guess I should feel a heel playing around with a girl whose guy is overseas.' His face hardened and an arrogance re-appeared only to be checked by an innate modesty that bordered on timidity. The conflict was evident. 'I'll see you this evening then,' he said.

When he had gone, she went to the telephone.

That was February 14. Simon Penny arrived in New Orleans early on the morning of February 17, with his hair dyed dark and a growth of beard around his mouth and along his jawline. After walking around the city's French Quarter for a couple of hours to check for a tail, he reached the Plattner home after dawn.

Jesse and Jenny Plattner were married cousins who ran a brothel off St Charles Avenue. They were the sixth generation of an Acadian family, thrown out of Canada by the British, to run the institution, and Jenny had worked there before marrying Jesse and taking over the business from his father.

Jesse didn't work much at all. He smoked Cuban cigars, ran an illegal book and dealt in antiques near Bourbon Street in the French Quarter.

Jenny played music and did crochet. Both of them claimed lineage from Jean Laffite, the Louisiana pirate, and Jesse boasted that Jim Bowie, the slave-trader turned Texas independence fighter, who invented the eponymous knife, was a relative. Jenny kept a Bowie knife on display in the antebellum house they called Chez Nous, and Jesse often claimed it was given to him by a relative who had inherited it from Bowie's slave after the defeat at The Alamo.

Because of the peculiarities of their chosen trade, the Plattners had never been fond supporters of any forms of authority. Before and during the early part of the American Civil War, their great-grandfather had smuggled runaway slaves north, and when the Union occupied New Orleans, he had spied for Confederate guerrillas operating in the Bayou swamps.

Penny had inherited Jenny and Jesse from a Czech cavalry officer who had recruited them for the French secret service during the Depression. Then Penny became a customer and they became friends.

'Why Simon, you've lost weight.' Jenny Plattner kissed him when he was inside the white house, aware that a sign of affection in public would draw undue notice from those who wished them ill. 'All life is purely personal,' she always said. She took his bag, brought him into a small salon at the back of the house, called her husband and presented her guest with a meal of all the things that were hard to come by.

'I have to stay for a while,' Penny said. 'Can you look after me?'

'Anythin' for you, Simon. How are things at home?'

'Not good. I'm gonna need new papers.'

Jenny Plattner was carving some wood for a violin. She made them in her spare time, played them at concert evenings held in the house and sold them in her husband's antique shop as the work of more distinguished makers.

'There's a man I know in Dallas who deals in that kind of thing. Also moves items across the Canadian and Mexican borders without the interference of the authorities. I trust money is no object?'

'I didn't want you two involved,' Penny said. 'This isn't just aiding and abetting a fugitive, this is more serious, and it carries the death penalty.'

'Now, hush, you stop treatin' us like children,' Jesse Plattner said. 'I swear you're more superior the more we see you. Too much travellin' has done that to you. You'll pose for one of my pictures while you're here?'

Penny pulled out a wad of notes and placed it on the

table between his plate and a bowl of fruit. 'This'll pay for my keep.'

'Always rushin',' Jesse Plattner said. 'I suppose you'll want a girl now.'

'You read my mind, Jesse,' Simon Penny said.

12

If Gus Delmar was more like his mother than his father, then it was something deeper than physical characteristics or even personality. He had his mother's looks, which had always annoyed Rosalyn Delmar; a sense of justice which sometimes annoyed his father; and an approach to life neither Rosalyn nor John Delmar ever understood.

In the beginning they had taken his flirtation with the Japanese girl in Denver as just something that would pass, a bit like mumps or measles only more contagious. But when he announced the Japanese girl was pregnant and they were engaged, it grew from contagion to pathology. And then the war came.

On his first day in the army, Gus Delmar had deserted. 'One of your lost spirits,' he used to say in his letters. And the Japanese girl carrying his child hanged herself in an internment camp six months later. Gus found out in Africa, from a small postcard with the news in a single line at the bottom. The card was written in Spanish, and unsigned.

When he stepped off the bus in Albuquerque three days after his release from hospital, Gus Delmar was neither seeking understanding nor feeling very happy to be home.

'Andy Redrow fixin' to run me through town on a horse?' he asked his father. He handed the sheriff a small newspaper clipping reporting the medal he had won. 'Or will you do that?'

John Delmar placed his arms around his son, and his son

did the same, but there was no warmth in the embrace. 'Eadie's home,' John Delmar said.

'Yes,' his son said. 'Best pretend like nothin's happened. That's the Indian way, isn't it? Do a dance, maybe.' Gus grinned and shook his head. 'I could do with a beer.'

'Can you move proper yet, Gus?' John Delmar asked. 'I don't think you should if you shouldn't.'

'Your concern is noted, Pa. I still need a beer.' Gus tried to tell all the ways his father was different, but he could not.

'There's somethin' special cooked at home,' John Delmar said. 'Got extra cards for it. People gave.'

This time Gus put his arm around his father with some warmth. 'Slayer of Germans. Winner of medals. Savin' you all from them Nazi maniacs. And people gave. Good for people. But first I want a beer.'

After a long ride to Los Muertos in a car that might have been replaced but for the war, and several beers that might have been brewed before the war, the Delmars watched Andy Redrow approach Zach Pepper's bar with the gait of an unsure game animal in the presence of hunters. He shook his head from side to side as he walked and muttered to himself.

'Good to see you back, son,' he said to Gus Delmar. 'Heard you were due in. Decided to meet up.'

'I see the old town's had a few paint jobs since I was away,' Gus said. 'Some money around?'

'War's been good to us,' Redrow said. Then he thought for a while and put his political accent on. 'Well, some of us. Pete Swayge was reported missin' there last week and Billy Pepper was killed with the Marines. I guess you heard that. They're sendin' the body back. Zach puts on a brave face but he's cut up. You look fine, son.'

'I hear Eadie's around,' Gus said. 'Quite a homecomin'.'

'Yeah.' Redrow scratched his head. 'You don't gotta see her if you don't want to, Gus. Won't talk to me, she won't. Won't do nothin' I say. Drinks more than she should. Hangs around with . . . well, I guess there's no sense tryin' to undo what cannot be undone. You look fine, son, you look just fine.' He put his arm on Gus's shoulder. 'Another beer?'

'I think Rosalyn's got some food for us,' John Delmar said.

Redrow thought for a moment while a red vehicle with a faulty exhaust went by. 'I ever tell you I volunteered for the last one, Gus?' he said. 'All ready to ship out to France and I break my leg. Every one of my platoon was killed. By the time my leg healed, I was posted somewhere else, fillin' in forms. Now, I shoulda been concerned that all my buddies were killed and I was spared by my own foolishness, but then I thought, hey, no, I'm here for a reason. And I put effort into the rest of my life after that. Might could, you should too, young Gus. You'll see what I mean. Right, John?'

John Delmar almost found it impossible to move his head in the required way. But he forced himself. 'We gotta go, Andy,' he said.

Redrow nodded nervously. 'Sure, sure. Listen, we gotta talk about things, John. There's things . . . I think Eadie's stayin' only a few more days, Gus.' Redrow sounded like he was wishing something more than reporting it.

'We'll see you in the mornin', Andy,' John Delmar said. 'And thanks for the fence wire. I appreciate it. Maybe Gus'll help me fix it if that wound doesn't get in the way.'

'You thought about what I said about gettin' him work?' Andy Redrow said.

John Delmar did not reply and Gus walked on ahead of him, his face spontaneously changing expression.

Next day, Eadie Shaffer approached the Delmar ranchhouse with a degree of excitement and an anxious suspicion that she was looking at a dream. As she strolled up the driveway, the stone base of the adobe house broke up the light from the white caps of the surrounding mountains, and the stones seemed to draw in the cold mesa wind from the mountains and wrap it around the house.

Rosalyn Delmar watched from a window and then disappeared, and several gusts of wind swept the wooden porch where Gus Delmar sat in a swing chair, reading. The wind tipped a small pot on to the wooden boards of the porch and took the heads off several spring flowers sitting in pots on the wooden boards.

The flowers lay in the clay while the wind took some of their petals. And, far away, several animals moved across the horizon.

'You might say I looked well,' Eadie said to Gus. 'I think you look well. You look fit. For a man's been shot.'

Eadie picked some flowers from Rosalyn Delmar's small garden in front of the wooden porch and presented them to Gus. He took the offering without standing up, then stood up, wiped a seat of dust, and gestured to Eadie to sit down.

'I think I seen Iago Santavista last night,' Gus said. It was an old joke and Eadie did not laugh.

When she sat down, Gus picked up the pieces of broken pot from the wooden boards of the porch and placed them on a wooden table. Eadie tried to read the book he had put down but Gus laid her flowers on top of the pages. Then he picked up the flowers from the broken pot, and the clay they lay on. He did this in small handfuls, until he could not scoop up any more. 'So, how are you, Eadie?' he asked. He kicked the remaining clay off the wooden porch.

'I expected you to call,' Eadie said. 'And I'll have some tea, Gus.'

Gus nodded and looked at her. 'You do look well, Eadie,' he said when he was going to get the tea. She put her flowers to one side and picked up his book.

She was still reading Iago Santavista's letter when he came back.

The mesa wind had all but died and the colours from the purple mountains had remixed with the sunlight. She pointed to the Santavista Gap. 'He says here that a man who never changes, dies.'

'I bet you meant to write,' Gus said.

'No,' she said. 'I never meant to write. I'm sorry about what happened. I'm sorry your girl died. I have a heap of sorrow. I'm not sorry I had my daughter.'

'The cruelty of it is, I wished you were,' Gus said.

'And now?'

He reached over and took the book back when she was sipping her tea. He put it out of her reach. 'How long you stayin'?' he asked.

'Nothin' here for me now but lazy looks and embarrassment,' she said. 'Don't know why I came back.'

They sat for a time, and once or twice each of them looked like they were going to say something. The wind picked up again and a motor vehicle passed on the road from Los Muertos. A joint creaked and one of the wooden boards became loose.

When she was going, Eadie Shaffer looked back at Gus Delmar.

'Give my best to your husband and child,' he said.

She tried not to cry and held back her tears until she reached Los Muertos. The only other sound there was fine gravel on the bars of the jailhouse where John Delmar stood in the doorway. He had just received a message from Simon Penny, the first in ten days, and what he had allowed to slip into the recesses of his mind had been dragged back to the forefront of his concerns, along with his son and Eadie Shaffer.

Simon Penny put the telephone to his ear again and drew back the curtains. The hotel was buried in a thick clump of poplars, just off a main road in west Texas. The curtains were cheap and the same colour as the leaves on the poplars. Across the plains a golden glow lit up the mountains while a fresh frost had settled outside. The morning moon was smiling on the frost, giving the landscape a translucence similar to his eyes, which it did not deserve, Penny thought.

'Pammy ...' He said her name with a degree of reverence that in different circumstances might have suggested a medium talking to a spirit. Penny could not get over the respect and anticipation in his voice, so he drew breath, wiped his lips and held his tongue.

After allowing the unspoken words to sink in, Pam Hanny replied, then paused. Her unspoken words questioned his, and for a while their conversation remained completely silent.

Hanny was at an address they had pre-arranged for emergencies. One of several bought or rented by either one of them. There was a time, usually once a week, when contact was possible at each venue, and this was the first time she had gone to this address since Penny had broken off contact.

'I called your apartment,' Penny said.

'Someone turned my apartment over,' she said. 'Angel and Tommy are missing.' She paused for a long time, made longer by the fact that it was a long-distance telephone call. 'I thought it might have been you, Simon.'

'No.' Penny had a way of denying things which did not need clarification and he could feel her relax at the other end of the line. He relaxed when she did and that made him think. 'Moscow,' he said. 'It must have been.'

'Where are you?' she asked.

Ten minutes later, Pam Hanny stood before Claude Dansey in the next room. 'He won't say,' she said. 'I told you he wouldn't say where he was.'

'Let's go where we can be safe,' Dansey said. He kept rubbing his chest.

Dansey had set up office in a small apartment in the Foggy Bottom area of Washington, DC. The apartment was owned by a company director friend of Dansey, who had once been a member of a country club the spy had run in his younger days. Boyd had a British nurse installed in the apartment next door and several more SIS staff were staying at a small hotel on the Virginia side of the Potomac.

'I'm not happy with all this,' Pam Hanny insisted. 'I'm not happy, Colonel.'

Sometimes she had that tiring self-righteous manner middle-class girls who, but for the war, would have been office workers and housewives, carried around in their handbags. Dansey's ailment did not make him very tolerant of it then, if he ever had been. And her end-of-sleeve patriotism irritated him as much as his breathing difficulties.

'I don't really care, my dear,' he said. 'One of my Huntergatherers is up to something annoying and I want to know what. What did Finger do that made our Simon kill him?'

'He says he didn't, sir.' She had been at this game so long that giving the right time of day had become a strain, and now she was caught between two stools, ever widening, and the floor below was covered in every conceivable sharp instrument and jagged edge. Pam Hanny often wished she had stayed deciphering.

'And you believe him?' Dansey said.

'He said Finger was an addict. Things had become difficult. Why would he kill the source of his best trade?'

'Precisely,' Dansey said.

'Where might he go?' Derek Boyd asked her then. He had the air of a father who's lost his favourite son, and his concern for Penny made Hanny more comfortable.

Until her mind regained control and she remembered Dansey's reputation. 'If you care about him, you'll think hard, my dear,' Dansey said. He could detect weakness at three hundred miles, they said in London, and a lie at any distance.

'I don't know him that well,' she said.

'That is unfortunately the problem with trying to tie down a Huntergatherer,' Dansey said. 'None of us know him that well.

There is, by nature, nothing to tie down with these chaps. You see the problem? The only thing we have by way of trace is the effect they have on others. And that, in this case, is you, my dear.'

'He'll kill me,' she said, 'if he suspects. And if he has gone to the Russians, they'll kill me. It would be foolish to move before he does.'

'I'm supposed to be getting married soon, you know,' Dansey said. 'You probably think it's foolish at my age, with my health. But I love the woman I am marrying. Just so you understand me.'

They were both about to say something when one of Derek Boyd's men came in. He looked at Boyd before speaking.

'The FBI have found two bodies in New York.'

Manny Rivera sniffed the formaldehyde, pushed the steel trolley containing the mortal remains of Angel Marcan back into the wall and pulled out a cigarette. His thickset features fixed on the police lieutenant to his right.

'Old Angel never looked more beautiful,' the policeman said.

'Beautiful,' Jeff Francis agreed. 'And all he was carrying was forged green?' He pulled out a twenty dollar bill and examined it.

'That and some personal items,' the police lieutenant said. He was chesty and the formaldehyde was irritating him. 'We don't smoke in here,' he said to Rivera as the FBI agent began to consider lighting up.

The two agents then pulled the second trolley out and looked at Tommy Martin.

'Where were they found?' Rivera asked. He still had the cigarette in his hand and the vulnerability of his lips was exacerbated by the prohibition placed upon him by the police lieutenant.

The police lieutenant fiddled with his spectacles and cleaned the lenses. 'Downtown,' he said. 'One of the warehouses. We figured it was a family or a union thing. Angel ran a couple of locals and did a little enforcin' on the side. Always strayin' out of his territory down the fish market, Angel. I liked him, personally. Kinda idealistic. Stood up for the workin' man. Well, he talked like he was.'

Outside, Manhattan island was bathed in the vagaries of a March sun and two cars had crashed across the street. A policeman on horseback was arguing with one of the drivers, who appeared to be a relative. Francis and Rivera hailed a cab and headed for their train. Francis pulled out the forged twenty again.

'It's in the spiral decoration,' he said to Rivera. 'See? You'd never notice it if you weren't looking for it.'

'So what have Angel Marcan and Oskar Finger got in common that they both carry the same issue green?' Rivera asked.

13

Thomas Heuzer reached his Berlin office late on the night of 28 February. He took two tranquillisers and slept before eating bread and drinking some real coffee Reinhard Gehlen had given him. Then he went through his mail.

His wife had written her third letter in as many days. He put the letter with the others, unopened, and took out a map of New Mexico. Then the air raid sirens sounded.

Heuzer was already on the way to a shelter when he received a request to come to Walter Schellenberg's office. He paused to collect some papers before complying.

Schellenberg's face had more horror than anger in it. His feet were on the desk in front of him and he was leaning back in his chair with his hands behind his head. He looked like he had been drinking.

'What the hell are you up to?' he demanded. The gap in his teeth produced a strange sound in his words, and his eyes moved around in a panicked terror.

Heuzer feigned ignorance, but his tiredness and irritation with Schellenberg, and his curiosity for what was going on in the skies over the German capital, made him relax and betray the residual insubordination that Schellenberg had often sensed in him but had ignored up to now. Something Heuzer was angry with himself for. His anger was a seventh sense. 'My friend and protector', as he once described it.

'I am obeying your orders,' he said. 'On Ground Zero.'

'I ordered you to kill Ground Zero. Kill it, Thomas. With a thousand reasons why it was impossible! And what do I find? You're seen at Foreign Armies East headquarters in Zossen, having lunch with Reinhard Gehlen five times in the last two weeks. He's been seen here. And now there's a bloody Japanese submarine with a V2-A10 on board out in the Atlantic, while you have a dozen American dreamers training up in Norway for a commando strike.'

Schellenberg pulled his feet from the desk and his cheek began to twitch. 'Now you had better have an explanation for this, Thomas, or I'll have the more salacious details of your Abwehr record on Gestapo files so fast you'll be swinging from piano wire before you next draw breath. Which will be your last!'

Even Schellenberg was frightened by what he had just said. But Heuzer remained calm and that frightened Schellenberg more than the thought of piano wire or the bombs beginning to fall outside.

'My job was to infiltrate the Stauffenberg circle,' Heuzer insisted. 'I carried it out. I informed Admiral Canaris of everything. You know that.'

'If that's still the basis of your defence, then you had better take something strong and lethal,' Schellenberg countered. 'Remember, Admiral Canaris is now almost on the scaffold. One more push. And anything he touched is likewise tainted. I saved you, Thomas, and look how you repay me.'

'It is a Führer order,' Heuzer said. And Schellenberg found himself drawn by the captain's words. He broke free suddenly.

'You work for me!' he shouted. 'And I ordered you to bury this atomic thing. I want to stop this bloody war while we have something left to deal with. And I want the Americans to think well of us before the whole population of central Asia descends on us. Have you seen the newsreels from the east?'

'But it will work,' Heuzer said.

'I don't want it to work. Reichsführer Himmler doesn't want it to work. We want to make friends with the Americans. Do you understand, Thomas? What the hell does Gehlen have over you?'

'Nothing.' Heuzer leaned over Schellenberg's desk. 'But he sees what I see.'

Heuzer's courage in the face of Schellenberg's anger upset the senior officer.

'Does he now?' Schellenberg said. 'You stupid bastard, Thomas. Can you not see he's using you to get at me? And when we're both swinging, he'll be sitting at the side of the road, bags packed, ready for a nice job with whoever offers the best salary in Washington or London.'

Heuzer was not listening. He leaned closer and appeared to think before he spoke. 'General Gehlen has a recording,' he said, 'of a conversation involving you and Reichsführer Himmler, at the Reichsführer's Army Group Vistula headquarters ... sir.' Heuzer pulled back from Schellenberg for the next part. 'And you appear to be urging the Reichsführer to have the Führer killed ... sir.'

Heuzer's sense of his place got the better of his insubordination now. He almost came to attention. 'Very indiscreet, sir,' he said. 'You should have realised that now Himmler is in charge of Army Group Vistula he has moved out of the protective mantle of the SS and comes under the watchful eye of Foreign Armies East. All army commanders on the eastern front are routinely wired in case of staff leaks. Perhaps you should not drink so much, sir. I have heard the tape. And I have a copy of the transcript. Care to read it?'

Schellenberg's face went pale. Heuzer's eyes looked straight into his superior's and the two men did not speak any more.

South of Berlin, some hours later, Thomas Heuzer and Reinhard Gehlen watched the searchlights take position in a moonlit sky and small bursts of flak break the silence which had descended after the first raid. Then the sirens began again.

The ritual of defeat moved to the rhythm of the sirens now, Heuzer thought, like some ancient funeral dance. And with it, the sense of his own importance increased.

'So you have burned your bridges,' Gehlen said.

'Perhaps a sea voyage would have been better,' Heuzer said. 'Got us out of the way. Left Schellenberg with a fait accompli.'

'I considered sending you with Vogl but the concentration of resources was too risky,' Gehlen said. 'Anyway, the distances overland are too great. Penny has arranged a suitable landing area with Nativo.'

'You have shown me no file on Penny,' Heuzer said.

'There is none,' Gehlen said.

'A Tod man?' Heuzer inquired. 'How did you manage to get a Tod man?'

'Before your time, Canaris gave me a handful,' Gehlen replied. 'You may have met Penny once. He was in Berlin in 1943 when Canaris proposed we kill Stalin, Roosevelt and Churchill in Teheran.'

'Let me guess, the Führer called it off, saying it tempted providence,' Heuzer said.

'No,' Gehlen said. 'The Reichsführer didn't like the idea. He said it tempted providence. I suspect he was contemplating treason already. Canaris, who was up to his neck in treason, was all for it. He had recently met his American and British opposite numbers in Spain. I think they were the ones who put him up to it. Perhaps the British and American intelligence organisations wanted to put the frighteners on Stalin. He was still open to a separate peace then.'

'I don't remember Penny,' Heuzer said. 'Abwehr II Tod did not encourage memories. Perhaps, given what happened to me there, that is a good thing.'

'You volunteered as an agent for the Tod Programme, I understand,' Gehlen said then.

'I was turned down,' Heuzer replied. 'I had too much of a life behind me. Or lives. Only suitable for behind the scenes work. And spying on my comrades.' For once, all masks Thomas Heuzer had were off, and Gehlen knew the captain would go on to the bitter end. But the anger in Heuzer's expression made Gehlen move away from him.

'Berlin is the most dangerous terrain of all,' Gehlen remarked. 'What about Schellenberg? What do you think he will do?'

'What it takes to survive. Isn't that what drives us all? Survival. Even Stuart and his men. The thing we all need to know, however, is how far we are willing to go to ensure it.'

'Sometimes I think you need too much, Thomas. I say that as a friend.'

'I have no friends,' Heuzer said. The revelation took something from him and he dipped his head.

'Well, Germany is so crazy now,' Gehlen said, 'I can't see Walter interfering at all now that he's compromised. Walter will keep his head down and his various passports ready. And he'll stick to Himmler as long as he needs the old chicken farmer. The Führer ate the face off him the other night, you know. Himmler. Army Group Vistula is a shambles. He's back in bed. That little offensive that wore out last week was our last throw of the dice with what we have. We need this bomb, Thomas.'

Heuzer was happy to snap to attention. 'And you shall have it,' he said. It did not matter whether he truly believed what he was saying, just that he said it. They waited for an hour, watching the skies, but the bombers did not come again.

Heuzer cleared most of his Berkaerstrasse office the following day and moved to Norway pending a transfer to Foreign Armies East. Stuart's men were billeted in the remains of a small whaling station destroyed during the German invasion of 1940. Two or three of the wooden buildings had been rebuilt and the remainder were transformed into a mockup of Los Muertos, about as incongruous a sight as Kyle Stuart's men taking position among its facades on a lonely peninsula just inside the arctic circle.

Sitting in an American jeep, hands in his pockets, woollen cap under his American helmet, blowing clouds from his cherried lips, Thomas Heuzer kept looking over his shoulder as if he expected someone unwelcome to approach at any moment.

Behind him, the wind threatened to flatten the mockup of Los Muertos for the seventeenth time, and the sound of creaking wood reminded Heuzer of agony. Only Peiper recognised his superior's concern. 'Don't worry, Herr Hauptmann, I have a sense of these things.' He touched the back of his neck. 'I can feel policemen right here at great distances. Himmler won't move on us. The way Germany is now, my guess is he and his lot will be just too damn interested in saving their own skins.'

Heuzer patted his sergeant on the shoulder. They had never been very close until the past few weeks. And now their closeness was that of survivors, each trusting their survival to the other. Heuzer looked on his sergeant as a kind of talisman. When Stuart's men had rehearsed the raid for the twentieth time, Heuzer called a halt.

'We can do it blindfold, Thomas,' Kyle Stuart said later.

They were drinking beside a small stove in a long hut. Snow in the roof of the hut combined with the wind to produce a landslide sensation for those inside, and Heuzer found himself looking up once too often.

'I like my men to have their eyes open, Kyle,' he replied.

'You can tell you were never in the line much, Herr Hauptmann,' a corporal said.

Heuzer looked at Stuart and then at the corporal, Billy Watkins. It wasn't the man's familiarity, it was the lisp that caused the captain's hesitation. Watkins had been hit in the mouth by a piece of tank.

'Sitting in dugouts,' he said. 'Gets you used to imminent burial.' His family owned parts of Brazil and he had never been to the United States in his life.

'I have seen my men executed for wearing American uniform,' Heuzer said. And his eyes held Watkins with an intensity that forced the corporal to swallow.

'We are aware of the penalties,' Kyle Stuart said, as much to draw Heuzer's attention as anything else. 'I think Billy was tryin' to reassure you, Herr Hauptmann.'

'I'm grateful,' Heuzer said to Watkins. The switch in mood made Watkins' mouth dry, but he could not help himself smiling.

'They'll shoot you too, Herr Hauptmann,' a very olive-skinned man with a slow Louisiana drawl shouted from the back. 'Just the same as us.'

This time Heuzer only feigned anger, then smiled. 'Menton,' he said. 'Don't you know? I intend to hand you over to save my skin.'

David Menton laughed well after everyone else.

They drank whatever was available well into the morning, singing songs and exchanging stories of the Russian front, each one more harrowing than the next. Reinhard Gehlen appeared at dawn, in a black Mercedes, and the party broke up. Only Kyle Stuart remained at the stove. It was a moment of extreme concentration for him, when all of his life presented itself in a single instance of struggling hope and doubt. The period passed, but when it had gone, it had taken some of Stuart's faith with it. And he went looking for Heuzer.

Five minutes after Dieter Vogl's next message was deciphered, Thomas Heuzer went walking alone to the edges of the cliffs. Peter Heinck and Oliver Dasch were coming up a small path from their aircraft hangar, tucked in at the foot of the cliffs.

There was something very comforting about a raging sea, Heuzer thought, as he watched the foaming water below him attempt to take more of the land away than it could. His wife needed money and that might have had something to do with it. But there was more to it than that.

The white seawater surged up the fjord and bit off a large chunk of Norway before retreating. Smooth dark rocks from the cliffs toppled away slowly into the foaming sea like petrified tears. It brought a curious emotion to Thomas Heuzer, something he was not used to.

'We'll have to get that aircraft into shelter or she'll be pulverised down there,' he said to the two pilots. 'Dry land or no.'

Peter Heinck wiped his nose and nodded. Nothing seemed very dry, even on dry land. The flying boat he had helped to fly from Britain sat on the end of a slipway, facing down the fjord. Like a contemplative albatross, he thought. 'You just hope there's good weather when we try to lift off, Thomas,' he said. He turned to Oliver Dasch. 'Remind me why we volunteered for this.'

'The money,' Dasch said. His eyes had dulled to the colour of the water. The regret on his face was so obvious, Heinck felt sorry for his partner.

Behind them, strolling up the stone path, Reinhard Gehlen and Kyle Stuart were talking. Gehlen wore a long greatcoat with the collar turned up, Stuart was in full American Ranger combat dress. Yet despite their different sizes and states of dress, Gehlen looked as incongruous as Stuart, and definitely more threatening. Except that Stuart carried himself with the determination of a crusader and had the eyes of a man who really did believe in things, which came as close as anything to really frightening Peter Heinck.

Thomas Heuzer concentrated on Karl Peiper, who walked behind the two officers. And Peiper smiled on cue. Heuzer had come to rely on the sergeant's instinctive feeling for a situation, and very often one glance at Peiper would make up the captain's mind.

'It seems there is a small problem with some of the accents, Thomas,' Gehlen said. 'You were right. Exposure to Spanish and German has diluted them. I've had an expert in Berlin listen to all your accents.'

'Perhaps you should have signed him on,' Heuzer said. 'To watch over us.'

'Too old,' Gehlen said. 'Anyway, the problem will be solved.'

'We're taking a crash course,' Stuart said. Then he looked at each of the officers in turn. 'We'll be ready,' he added.

'I expect it,' Heuzer said.

'Even a native might not pick up the intonations, but someone curious just might get suspicious,' Gehlen said as if to excuse Stuart's men and himself. 'It should not be difficult to iron out.'

'You and I are perfect, Herr Hauptmann,' Karl Peiper said, 'since we've been playing Americans for some time now. I speak better English than the Teniente. But then I lived in Chicago, so I am a Yankee.'

Everyone laughed.

'Other problems?' Gehlen asked. He glanced down at the mockup of Los Muertos. One of the facades had blown down in the wind and three of Stuart's men were trying to re-erect it.

'The cold,' Stuart said then. 'That place you have us billeted at, it leaks warmth.' He looked down at the flying boat and then out to sea. 'Quite a beast,' he said to Dasch.

'The sea or the aircraft?' Heinck asked.

'What do you think, Oliver?' Reinhard Gehlen asked.

Dasch squinted and shook his head. 'I don't think any more, Herr General. I wonder why I made the stupid move of leaving a prison camp for this.'

'Because you are a German officer. Because it was your duty,' Gehlen said. 'And because that is the man you are, Oliver.'

There was something in the statement that caught all of them off guard.

Then Stuart clapped his hands. 'Look at all the glum faces. Thank God we're not stuck in a submarine several hundred metres below the Atlantic now. I am decidedly claustrophobic. I wonder how Vogl's getting on out there.'

'Oh, they're fine, I'm sure,' Gehlen said. 'Easiest part of the operation, believe me.'

It was often said that U-Boat service was good for the intellect, because if you did not lose your sanity the only pastimes were reading and writing. When Dieter Vogl sat down to write a letter to his mother, ignoring the incessant spray which came in to the control room through the hatch from the bridge, he acknowledged the second watch officer, a young ensign straight from school, who smiled before he climbed the ladder to the conning tower. Stubble and acne competed with anxiety on the young teenager's face. Vogl said something encouraging he did not mean and went back to his letter.

Sitting across from him, wiping her face of the spray which she found irritating in a way Vogl did not, Irmgarde Hanke was making calculations and sketches on either side of a notebook.

'Where are your family, Herr Kapitanleutnant?' she whispered.

'I'm not sure,' Vogl said. 'The bombing. My mother is in Munich, so my girl may well be with her. I'm sending this there. My sister was in Berlin. But her husband died. And you may call me Kaleu, all the men do. Or Dieter if you wish. Do you have a family?'

'A son,' Hanke said. 'My men are sick, can you do something about it? The smell back there is unbearable. How do you stick it?'

'I could tell you the joke about joining the navy to see the world. Truth is, we get paid more and I'm greedy. It helps if you learn to anticipate the boat's movements. For seasickness. Otherwise there is nothing to be done. You seem fine.'

'So long as I can smell fresh air,' Irmgarde Hanke said. 'But those diesels ...' She offered him a piece of bread.

'They are our life, Frau Doktor. Our way home.' Vogl took the bread. 'Though I sometimes feel this is home.' He called one of his men over, whispered in his ear and then gave another man a piece of paper. 'I'm surprised we've got this far running on the surface. We should by rights have run into Royal Navy trouble. Incredible. Quite a degree of luck. Almost makes one hopeful. Perhaps we will change the course of the war. Though that presents a whole new set of arguments.'

'I take it you are not a Nazi?' Irmgarde Hanke asked. She offered Vogl more bread. Vogl refused and went back to his letter.

'And you're not with the Gestapo?' he said.

He glanced at her a couple of times. She noticed. She was about to comment when the watch officer came sliding down the ladder from the top of the conning tower.

'Alarm!'

Vogl had just enough time to see the ship coming at them before they dived.

14

The next depth charge felt like it was inside Irmgarde Hanke's head. She shone a torch beam down the line of men crouched along the floor of the submarine, a nauseous feeling in her stomach feeding on the diesel and sewage fumes, trying to equalise the pressure in her ears while the noise of the explosions all round beat a rhythm inside her brain. In a corner, one man vomited. But all eyes were turned upwards.

A little bearded submariner from Dortmund, dressed in oilskins, chewing on a piece of sausage, crept towards Hanke. 'Kaleu's compliments, Frau Doktor, but would you join him please in the *Zentrale*. And if you could ask your men to limit their breathing, please.' Helmut Otto was Dieter Vogl's first officer, though he looked old enough to be his father. The permanent look of exasperation he carried did nothing to ease Irmgarde Hanke's fears.

Dieter Vogl was scribbling under torchlight in the control room. 'There's at least two of them,' he said. 'That way and that way, we think. In figure eight patterns. Now, with our rubber skin they normally shouldn't be able to pick us up on their instruments. But we have your rocket and its launcher. Reinforced steel has its disadvantages.'

Two more depth charges went off either side of the boat.

'I'm bringing us down to maximum depth,' Vogl continued. 'I don't know what that'll do to your rocket, but, if we don't, then we're in trouble.' He passed his sketch to Hanke and shone his torchlight on it. 'They'll maintain this pattern, then, if we're really unlucky, two more will come in, then two more. And so forth. If we don't break free before they gather, then the Führer will be very angry. I knew it was going too well for us.'

'Can't we attack?' Hanke asked.

'With two torpedoes and God knows how many of them gathering? No, silent running for the moment. The weather coming in from the west is bad. So we can hope it turns ugly up there and we lose them. Hope for a thermal down here to block out their instruments. Hope ...'

'What about playing dead?' Hanke asked.

'You think those boys would fall for some old clothes and a few litres of oil?' He grinned and drew his hand across his neck. 'Anyway, our oxygen supply is limited. And the batteries were not fully recharged when we dived. So, I can either turn on the diesels and suck our air and draw more fire or run on batteries till they die and then turn on diesels and suck our air out or ... I'm open to suggestions. You're the scientist.'

'How deep can you go?' Hanke held her stomach and prevented herself from vomiting, then sat back against the hull.

'How long is a piece of string? Our operating limit is about three hundred metres. After that, it's in the lap of the gods. If we stay here, just silent running, they'll get us, sooner or later.' Vogl looked at his calculations again. 'Unless, of course, we can get to a trench.' He touched the chart of the western flanks of the mid-Atlantic ridge. 'Some of them are very deep and we might just run into something and sink anyway.'

'Charming,' Hanke said. 'You have a depressing way of putting things.'

Vogl pulled a chart from the seat behind. A depth charge exploded nearer the boat and knocked one of the crew from his seat. Vogl pulled him back and then laid the chart out. 'Here,' he pointed with his torch, 'is a possible hiding place. Now it's about four to five hundred metres deep. Quite beyond our depth.'

'But the surrounding peaks and rocks might just be enough to confuse those boys above,' Irmgarde Hanke said.

Vogl grinned and rubbed his tongue along the line of his teeth. 'Or kill us,' he said. 'If we drop in there and then crawl our way through by sound, we might break free ... or we might not.'

'Well, let's do it,' Hanke said. 'That rocket we're carrying might not work either. And the plutonium Heuzer intends to steal might blow up in our faces. I might even refuse your advances.'

'Our hull probably won't take it,' Vogl said, shaking his head. 'And then you'll never know.' He pulled out a coin. 'You call.' He flipped the coin.

Irmgarde Hanke called.

'You win. We'll be running blind, relying on sound alone to get us through the trench.'

'A blind date,' she said.

Two hours later, Dieter Vogl sat in his sound room, looking at his charts, listening to his hydrophones. Ahead of him, at the door to the control room, a man indicated the depth they had reached with his fingers.

'The deep red zone,' Vogl whispered to Helmut Otto. He winced at the figure. 'We should touch something soon. Jesus, we have to.' He looked over at Irmgarde Hanke and pointed to his charts. 'You see this fracture here, this is where we are going to attempt to slip through whatever net they're preparing. I'm banking on the bad weather up there getting worse. So, if you believe in a god, pray for bad weather and a cloudy night.'

With the toxicity levels in the submarine rising, Vogl ordered the engines switched off. Now all they could hear was the echo sounding and the cushioned thud of various explosions above them. And the eerie strain on the skin of the submarine and its colossal payload.

Men sat looking up, tapping fingers, discomfort registering on their faces with each atmosphere they sank beneath, small beads of sweat pouring out of pores with the same regularity the piping began to spring leaks. And the boat creaked and groaned under the weight of the ocean, and men continued to look up, as if they were looking for something, some indication that they would be saved, or some true sign of their doom.

About fifteen minutes later, when Irmgarde Hanke looked at the young submariner sitting next to her, he was white. And the boat had hit a shelf.

The hours ticked by to the drip of one leaking pipe and then another. Once or twice rivets shot loose and tore holes in lockers and instrument panels. One or two of Hanke's technicians lost their nerve and had to be restrained. Some of Vogl's old hands took bets on when the final moment would occur, most stayed alone with their thoughts. Occasionally, Irmgarde Hanke thought she could hear the thoughts of men, and wondered if they could hear hers.

She made her way back to Dieter Vogl vaguely puzzled by her own lack of fear and her sense of fascination at their predicament. She examined what she could of the boat by torchlight, every centimetre of its agony, and only ever wondered in a loosely objective fashion what the moment of destruction would be like. She wondered if she was deceiving herself or whether her determination was something she had never noticed before.

Dieter Vogl sipped on the small cup of water and put the earphone to his head again. 'There's one still there ... damn ... bastard!' He passed it to Irmgarde Hanke, who nodded. A valve burst and water began to trickle in. A freckled submariner dealt with it.

Vogl looked around him at the men struggling with the pressure of the depth. The oxygen ratio was starting the long dip out of their favour.

Vogl took a torch, climbed through the decks, and walked the length of the submarine, viewing the crew who were all suffering from pressure pain, oxygen deficiency and atmosphere toxicity.

For a while, all he could hear was the strain of the submarine's skin under the multiplicity of atmospheres. When he reached the control room again he had come to a decision.

'We have to move, Kaleu,' Helmut Otto said as if to comfort his friend. 'We're being crushed here.' He rubbed the kingfisher on the side of his *schiff* and put his hand on Vogl's shoulder.

'And what if there are more out there, waiting for us?' Vogl asked. His nerve almost failed him but the sight of all the eyes looking to him for salvation drove him on.

Vogl leaned over and whispered into one sailor's ear. The electric motors began and the submarine pulled from the bottom and started to crawl its way up from the fracture.

The ascent was a hundred times more nerve-wracking than the dive, Hanke thought. Hope had been restored and with it all the expectations that rely on it, and all the possibilities that may damn it. Then, suddenly, they were out of the danger of depth and back in action. Men who had remained frozen for hours suddenly thawed out and went to work and the hope now inspired will and the will seemed unstoppable.

The submarine reached periscope depth after dark, no more than one hundred metres away from the faintest silhouette of a small British destroyer.

'They must have been from a convoy,' Vogl said to Hanke. 'Left this one behind. He hasn't picked us up. The weather, perhaps.'

Hanke saw another Vogl now: the hunted had become the hunter.

Vogl hung on to the periscope and pushed his cap peak to the back of his head. Behind him Helmut Otto waited with a stopwatch for the orders.

When he thought he could not miss, Vogl gave the order to fire.

The two torpedoes hit the small destroyer amidships.

'And now we are defenceless,' Dieter Vogl said.

15

While Philip Rand rushed to dress, Eadie Shaffer stretched on the mattress and rolled over on to her stomach. She folded her arms and leaned on them. 'You really are beautiful,' she said. 'I don't want you to think I don't appreciate your beauty.'

'You make me sound like a piece of furniture,' Rand said.

'Made of ebony,' she said.

Rand swung round. 'Don't you ever say that again. Ever! You hear?' His fists were clenched and his body taut in the strong light.

Eadie Shaffer put her hand to her mouth. 'I'm sorry. I was just kiddin' you. You didn't have to see me again,' she said. She went over to put her arms around Rand, but he moved.

'Hey, no sense in getting ourselves worked up,' he said.

'No,' she said. 'No sense. Men always say that in the mornin'. Every sense in gettin' themselves worked up when it's dark and they want you so much they'd kill, but when it's light and it's done, there ain't no sense.' She opened the door and went out on to the small porch and stared across the mesa. 'I'd like a swim,' she said. 'You want a swim?'

'I have to get back to camp. I'm late and I have work.'

Eadie began to whittle a small piece of wood with a foldaway knife. 'I woulda liked to hear you say you cared some. It's a nice feelin' havin' someone who cares. My daughter cared.'

'You should go back to her then.'

'She's dead.' Eadie began to cry.

Two small desert creatures were fighting by the side of the river, and they sounded as if they were crying, too.

'Look, I'm sorry,' Rand said.

'Do you know how many times I've said I'm sorry?' she said. 'I know the value of sorry.' She was wiping her tears away. 'Don't tell no one about my daughter.'

Rand kissed her and touched the piece of wood she was working. 'What's that?'

'Totem,' she said. 'Brings you luck.' She handed him a small round piece of wood with a serpent carved into it. 'It was Iago Santavista's sign. Came here lookin' for the City of the Sun, found snakes. And I reckon folks been comin' here and doin' the same ever since.'

'I'm from back east, remember? Anyway, we're going to put an airfield right through your town, you know. That's why we're here. Right through your precious little shithole town. You're supposed to look surprised.'

'I'm relieved,' she said. 'Some things it's best to be rid of. This town was always a blasphemy, they say. Born of a proud man's blasphemy. That feller, Santavista. And I know about blasphemy. I had the misfortune to be born pretty. Know what I mean? Born pretty, with men and boys and even some women tellin' you you're pretty and askin' you places and buyin' you things and payin' attention to what you say and all the things that go to a girl's head and make her think she's more than she is. When you're that pretty you expect things.'

'I wish I had time,' Rand said, wishing she would leave him now.

'I'm scared now. Scared of when my looks go. I seen women that was beautiful when their looks go. I seen the ones men used to swarm round like skeeters on a warm dusk, and I see 'em now, when they try to pretend. I won't pretend. There's a price for beauty. Tell me I'm beautiful.'

✻   ✻   ✻

There were two bottles lying in the sand when Andy Redrow reached the Delmar porch. And Gus Delmar was already well into the third. Redrow stood leaning on the rails of the steps leading to the house. Several legs of lightning were dancing silently across the rims of the jagged mountains in the distance. And the colours had changed.

'I been lookin' for Eadie all night,' he said. 'Don't suppose she came here?'

Gus Delmar shook his head. 'I ain't seen her, Mayor. I don't much wanna see her. She don't much wanna see me. We embarrass each other.'

'Gonna give me a drink?' Redrow asked. 'Or are you gonna sit there pissin' into history. I bet it was all they say it is. The war, I mean. I bet you're twistin' inside. I bet if I wasn't older than you, you might like to swing at me. I bet. I wish it was better for you, Gus.'

'You like ice?' Gus asked him.

'Only when it's cold.' Andy Redrow climbed the five steps to the porch with difficulty. 'I'm not what I used to be, Gus. Pieces o' me are fallin' apart. And I only got Eadie. Makes me scared, I'll tell you.'

'And you'd hate me for helpin' you,' Gus Delmar said.

Andy Redrow paused for breath at the wooden porch, then slumped into the nearest easy chair. Gus Delmar passed him a drink and he lay back in the easy chair and drank it in one. 'How're your wounds?' Redrow asked then.

'You got any gas in that automobile?' Gus asked him.

Rosalyn Delmar came out, tying her dressing gown. 'He hurts all the time,' she said to Andy Redrow. 'Don't you, sweetheart? You'll stay for lunch, Andy?'

'Might take a trip to Mexico,' Gus said. 'Eadie and I were gonna go to Mexico.'

'Thanks for the offer, Rosalyn,' Andy Redrow said. 'But I was lookin' for Eadie. I'll have this and go. John around?'

'She's with that nigger lieutenant, Andy.' John Delmar

appeared on the porch without anyone seeing where he had come from. 'And we don't want you to go to Mexico, son. So don't.'

John Delmar checked his revolver, spun the chamber and returned the revolver to its holster.

'I'm tryin' to avoid Eadie,' Gus said. 'Seems she even prefers a darkie to me.'

'Gus, put that bottle away,' Rosalyn Delmar said. 'And let's all have lunch. Andy, stay ...'

'Where'll I find her, John?' Andy Redrow asked the sheriff.

'River ways maybe. I saw 'em this mornin'. You want I should do somethin' there?'

Andy Redrow shook his head. 'I'll take care of it.'

John Delmar slapped his son's shoulder. 'Maybe Gus should take care of it.'

'No,' Rosalyn Delmar insisted. 'No one take care of anythin' that doesn't need takin' care of. Too many people want to take care o' things round here. That's the problem. John, you should take care o' what's your business and leave other people's business to them.'

Gus Delmar rubbed his face and held his emotions. 'All right, all right ...' He raised his hands. 'They used to have nigger hunts when I was in England. Know that?'

'Pour me another drink before I cry,' Andy Redrow said. 'We gotta do somethin'. Or folks won't ...'

'Re-elect you, Andy,' Rosalyn Delmar said.

'Well, I got other work to do,' John Delmar said. He stopped and turned to his wife. 'Eadie foolin' round with them nigger soldiers ain't gonna do no one no good.' He looked at Andy Redrow. 'You're right, Andy, you better sort it out before she causes more trouble again. By God.'

None of them said a word.

Simon Penny arrived in Los Muertos that night and found John Delmar sitting on his porch, alone.

'I've fallen in love,' Delmar said. It sounded even more pathetic than it should have.

Delmar looked around at the house. 'What happened to you anyway?' he asked. 'I thought you was gone. I thought this whole thing was gone. You know, what we're doin' here . . .' He shook his head. 'I don't know. I just don't know. Jesus, I thought the Feds had you, you know.'

Before Simon Penny could answer Gus Delmar appeared out of the moonlight, hands in pockets, shoulders hunched, collar high, undirected stride taking him towards the house in an uneconomic fashion. Gus stopped at the porch and greeted Penny. 'You boys takin' a trip?' he asked.

John Delmar introduced his son.

'I saw you in the bar earlier,' Penny said.

'I'm drunk,' Gus said. 'Zach Pepper likes me to tell him what a hero I was in Europe. Makes him feel good about his son bein' dead.' Gus put his hand out and Penny shook it. 'You two goin' fishin'?' he said then.

'No time,' Penny said. 'Next time.'

'Never is,' Gus said. And he went inside.

'Finger had a cocaine habit. Angel Marcan sometimes sidelined in stuff like that,' Manny Rivera said. 'So maybe they had a fallin' out.'

Jeff Francis pulled up a wooden chair while Rivera just sat back with his feet up on a table, shoes off, moving his toes, a pack of playing cards in his hand. He reached over for a notebook.

'So how come they both end up stiff?' Francis asked. 'Even supposing Angel was Finger's supplier, that's a coincidence. And that police lieutenant said a strange thing. He said Angel Marcan was idealistic.' Francis looked to Marcan for confirmation.

'He was a union organiser. That kinda thing. But that don't make him idealistic in New York, Jeff.'

'But what if he was?' Francis said it like it was the last thing he wanted to think. 'Idealistic, I mean.'

'Finger, too? All we have for evidence is a possibly left-wing hood and some forged green, Jeff. Not much to go to Hoover with.'

'So let's dig into Angel's life, see what he was up to. If he was a Communist ...'

Pam Hanny came in from the kitchen and Manny Rivera let his imagination do a quick circuit of her before allowing his reason to interrupt and ask if she was as beautiful as she looked. He laughed to himself and took the coffee she offered but refused the cake. Jeff Francis stopped taking notes.

Pam Hanny paused and looked at the two men. 'You want me to go in the bedroom?' she said to Francis. Her eyes pleaded justification and she put her hands together so that the long fingers began to make shapes. 'Sometimes I get lonely, Manny,' she said. 'Washington is a lonely town.'

Manny Rivera gave her the benefit of whatever doubt jealousy had placed in his mind and raised his hand. 'Sure. Listen, if you two want to do somethin', I can go off and get this thing movin', Jeff.'

'All right,' Francis said.

'I won't finish my coffee,' Rivera said. But he did finish it and ate some of the cake he had refused.

'You think anyone in Los Alamos knew about Marcan?' Francis asked then. 'Scared to talk now. Look at them. They get out of that place once a year. Maybe there's a well-worn trail to Angel. Maybe he used his white powder for other things.'

'If any of them do know, they're not gonna say,' Rivera replied. 'People like that don't talk to people like us if they can help it. And if they were messin' with powder ... Hoover has them all lookin' over their shoulders, scared.'

'We have to find that guy with Finger and Mrs Abery,' Francis said. 'Whoever he was.'

They both went a little pale.

'Tomorrow,' Rivera said. 'Tomorrow we go over everything we have.'

When Rivera had gone, Pam Hanny sat on Jeff Francis's knee. 'I should have told you I'd be here,' she said. 'I was lonely. And I missed you.' She found it quite easy to bring sentiments to her lips. They were there in abundance and she had no one to use them on now that Simon Penny was gone.

'That's okay,' Francis said. He asked her if she wanted coffee again. She said no and this diverted things on to rationing for a few minutes. They went to bed after that.

Derek Boyd arrived at Claude Dansey's apartment to find the Vice Chief of the British Secret Intelligence Service gone. When Pam Hanny met Boyd on a lonely country road in Virginia he thought she looked like a woman he had once sent into France, knowing she might be caught. Hoping she would.

'You were recruited in the Far East,' Boyd said to her by way of chit-chat. 'I worked in India and Singapore for a couple of years.' His blue eyes froze while he spoke.

'We were tea planters. Then rubber. My mother's in a Japanese camp.' Pam Hanny's eyes fought off tears.

'You were hired in Australia?'

'And they sent me to London. Then here because I had spent two years in Virginia. I think I have a conflict of interest, Derek.'

'You have no interests save those of His Majesty's Government,' he said. 'How long will you be gone?'

'I don't know. Jeff Francis doesn't tell me details. He's not very intimate.' Suddenly, she looked vulnerable and Boyd wanted to reach out and embrace her. 'I want a desk job, back in London,' she said. 'I'm not happy here.'

'You're our only link, Pam. I know your cousin, you know. She thinks the earth of you. And I hear you played a mean game of hockey when you were at school. Simon was a tennis player. But I suppose you know that.'

'No.' She shook her head in disappointment. 'I can shoot the eyebrows off a fly at a hundred paces,' she said. 'And I feel I'm losing myself. Am I a prostitute?'

Boyd was thrown completely off balance. He just reached out and took her arms. They spent about ten minutes, with her leaning on his shoulder. 'I'm addicted, I suppose,' she said finally. 'Like Finger and his cocaine.'

'Keep in touch,' Boyd said.

When she was saying goodbye, Boyd leaned out of his car. 'We want to find Simon, you know. Alive. If there's a problem then I want to sort it out.'

'You have a wonderful believability about you, Derek,' Pam Hanny said. 'If he's Moscow's man, why is he running? Why kill Angel and Tommy?'

'I don't know. If he's running from them, why doesn't he contact us?'

Dansey was waiting for Boyd when he got home. 'Do you think she's still onside?' he asked.

16

The following day, Thomas Heuzer began the clean-out of his Berlin office with a collection of American jazz records and a book of quotations. He played one of the records and opened the book to a quotation he had marked. From the Book of Proverbs, it was the only quotation he ever read. The book had been given to him by his father, and when Heuzer read the quotation he mouthed the words and nodded to himself: 'Death and life are in the power of the tongue: and they that love it shall eat the fruit thereof.'

The remainder of his office was taken up with ancient rusting cabinets and files he had no interest in any more.

His personal effects, apart from the the book and the jazz records, were five pencils, a spare shirt, some coffee and a spare Russian pistol. The pistol was wrapped in cloth and secreted in one of the rusting cabinets. Heuzer unwrapped the cloth, placed the pistol on his desk and pulled a full magazine from his pocket. He laid the magazine beside the pistol, placed his watch beside the magazine and stripped the pistol. Then he began to reassemble it.

'Not planning to deprive us of the pleasure of your comradeship, Thomas?' Walter Schellenberg's top buttons were undone and he was holding a bottle. His eyes had a mosaic look and his skin was loose around the neck.

'I like to time myself,' Heuzer said, snapping the magazine into the pistol and cocking it. He placed it back on his desk.

'I have been officially informed of your transfer to Foreign Armies East, Herr Hauptmann. I thought I'd pop along and salute you. Stand up!'

'Sir!' Heuzer stood up.

Schellenberg began to shake his head. 'I would have saved you, you know. You stupid, stupid man.'

Heuzer came to attention and Schellenberg collapsed, muttering to himself.

'You cannot even save yourself,' Heuzer whispered, placing Schellenberg in a leather armchair. When he left his office, he put out the light.

Heuzer caught an airplane back to Norway that night, touching down in time to have breakfast with Reinhard Gehlen. There was a subdued mood at the Stonewall Legion camp, men preferring to check their equipment than talk. Occasionally, Kyle Stuart went among them, asking questions. Heuzer saw something between them that he had rarely experienced in military formations before, something based not on command or even respect, but friendship. Reinhard Gehlen's insistence that *he* was the captain's friend only irritated Heuzer, but he never said so.

An hour after breakfast, a coded message came through for Gehlen. The General looked up very slowly at Heuzer, a vague disbelief in his eyes.

'Vogl's made it!' he said. 'He's bloody well made it.'

'The clock is wound,' Heuzer replied. And they shook hands.

Dieter Vogl was fixed on his stopwatch. They were off the northwest tip of Cuba, at a depth which ran off the dial. And their air was beginning to taste of salt.

'If we make it, I'll buy you dinner,' Irmgarde Hanke said to him.

'If we make it, I'll buy everyone dinner,' Vogl said. 'You know, we definitely ought to go on a date.'

'I thought you had a girlfriend.'

'I'm allowed one act of infidelity per month. We have an arrangement. Just to show I'm not a robot. As you've noticed, these boats are instruments of torture.'

'Heuzer's men will have to suffer, too. The cold of the arctic,' Hanke said.

'Are you trying to tell me it could be worse?' Vogl asked. 'The Caribbean is an American lake. Getting in is the easy part. Getting out might not be so much fun.'

'So, when do we surface?' Hanke asked him.

'You're too eager for me, you know.'

Simon Penny received Vogl's transmission late in the afternoon, in the attic of John Delmar's ranchhouse. Delmar was standing behind him, spinning the chamber of his revolver, obviously disinterested in what was coming in from the submarine.

'She was with that nigger again,' he said.

Penny swung round. 'What are you taking about, John?'

Delmar shook his head. 'Kids used to paint me red, you know.'

Penny packed away the radio set and pulled away a section of the wall next to Delmar. He placed the radio set in a small nook and the coding papers on top of it, before securing the piece of wall and shoving an old piano up against it.

'We've got to prepare the landing site,' he said to Delmar. The sheriff barely acknowledged him.

Jeff Francis was delivering a report on his own failure when the humiliated tone of Manny Rivera's request interrupted him in a Washington FBI office that evening. Francis thought he was about to score a point off one of his superiors. His first reaction was to dismiss Rivera in a manner he usually reserved for times when his friendly face was away being cleaned, something he was not particularly proud of. But Rivera got the upper hand in the facial expressions and Francis excused himself from the meeting and left.

Outside, in an ornate corridor, Rivera shoved five twenty dollar bills in Jeff Francis's face. 'Found in New Orleans.'

'When?'

'Two days ago,' Rivera said. 'Military asked the local cops to crack down on the whores. The local PD staked out a few well-known pick-up joints to please the military. And this came in to us because we were interested. It's thin but it's a chance.'

'Get down there yourself,' Francis said. 'Take Albie Rice, he's a good sniffer. You have full authority. But do nothing without telling me.' Francis looked back at the office he had recently been defending himself in. 'And tell no one else what you're doing,' he added. 'Okay?'

'How's the meeting goin'?' Rivera asked.

Jeff Francis knew the inquiry was not about his meeting. 'I haven't seen Pammy for three days, Manny. When I call she's not there. I guess I've lost her to the job, as they say.'

'Maybe she's just scared. Best you keep her away from all this.' Rivera backed off.

'I really cared,' Francis said. And he headed back towards his meeting. 'Oh, Manny,' he added. 'You take care. We're dealing with a killer.'

It did a little to restore what had been broken between them.

As Pam Hanny opened the door, Simon Penny swung his arm down on her wrist, punched her on the side of the face and threw her across the room. A pool of Arkansas sunshine flooded the bed for a moment and then evaporated.

'Now, you have five seconds to give me a good reason why I shouldn't pull this trigger.'

'Because I'm here,' she said. The suddenness of her composure made her words touch Penny, and the release of emotion stunned him. He placed the gun he held in the belt of his trousers.

'What's going on, Simon?' She wanted to tell him everything, expected she would tell him everything, but when it came to it she stuck to procedure. She just could not break free of it.

'You might tell me,' he said.

'You killed Angel and Tommy.'

She had seen people become involved before, usually by circumstance, often without care, whatever they had being simply a dumping ground for their excess emotions, sometimes their shared experiences ensuring they could not turn anywhere else. Like people with a rare disease, she thought. And if they were lucky, and they survived, they might try and make something out of it until the time and the distance from the events which brought them together would gradually limit its effects and they would drift apart. Cured.

Penny sat on the side of the bed later, examining his watch. He had a fascination for mechanical things. He stared at Hanny. She put her hand to his hair and rubbed it the way he liked, and continued her movements in the mechanical fashion he found reassuring. 'I haven't told anyone where you are, Simon.'

Penny walked over to the window before answering yes. There were tall trees in the garden and leaves of different greens and the beginnings of fruits, and to his left, blossoms. And the blossoms were like snow on the wind.

'They were ordered to kill me, Pam,' he said. 'Angel and his sidekick.' There was something beginning to shift inside Penny and he was bending under the strain.

Pam Hanny lifted herself from the bed, wiped her lips and touched the bruise next to her eye. 'Well it wasn't my order.'

He shoved the watch into his pocket. 'I need time,' he said then. 'A week. Maybe a little more. You're supposed to be looking out for me, Pam. Moscow must have ordered them.' He turned to her and what he saw made his conclusions bend. 'This is Moscow's doing,' he insisted. 'They didn't buy the Finger story. They had Angel try to kill me. And they probably intend to kill you.' He did not believe that but he could not act against her. He felt like he was standing on the edge of a cliff and she was the only thing holding him from falling – or jumping – over. 'What the hell did you tell them?'

'What do you think I told them?' she shouted. 'But I'm not going back to them, Simon, not after Tommy and Angel.'

Penny thought some more. 'I need time, Pammy. You've got to get me time. You go back to Washington. Find out what they think. Buy me time.'

'And if they kill me?' she asked.

'Buy me the time.'

She came over to him and put her arms around him. Then she leaned into his chest. 'Why don't you just get out. Leave it all. Go south. I'll come. You trust me? I want you to trust me, Simon.'

'A week, Pam, then it won't matter.' He touched her face.

She slapped him so suddenly and with such force, he stepped back paralysed. 'You ever pull a gun on me again,' she said, 'you better damn use it.'

Up close the Consolidated Vultee Model 29 PB2Y Coronado looked like a small hotel with wings. The massive American flying boat ordinarily had a range of 4000 miles, and could carry 16,000 lbs of material. Carrying extra fuel, she could still hold Heuzer's team and three jeeps and make it to New Mexico in one hop. But, as he stared at the various star constellations that night, Oliver Dasch could only see dice rolling ahead of him.

The Germans had painted Dasch's Coronado in the colours of an air ambulance, and Reinhard Gehlen touched the red cross while three jeeps were loaded on board a specially adapted hatch. Then Heuzer's men did final checks on weapons and ammunition, and Peiper and Schwartz checked the radios.

'No doubts now we're here?' Gehlen asked Oliver Dasch.

Dasch nodded like he did not mean it. 'So many I cannot

count them. Anyway, it's not the taking off with these babies that matters, it's the landings. And I have to do two. But compared with the prospect of facing a grilling from the Gestapo, I think I have the better deal.'

'It should be what you flyboys call a milk run,' Gehlen said.

'I hope your man is in position to guide us in or we're going to look like a broken milk bottle.'

Gehlen did not take this in. His mind was elsewhere. 'Take off as soon as word is in,' he said to Dasch then. 'Don't wait.'

Out to the west, the weather was a solid wall of black and only the anger of the sea was there to tell them what lay ahead.

'Frankly, I'm glad to get out of here.' Peter Heinck, whose nose was running, had small cold rashes on his neck, which he was scratching. One had become slightly infected. 'I can't stand this place any longer.'

'Perhaps I should come, too,' Gehlen said.

'I don't think Hauptmann Heuzer would appreciate it,' Oliver Dasch said then. 'This is his show. What on earth are we involved in, Herr General?'

Kyle Stuart's men lined up on the jetty. Heuzer and Peiper appeared out of the dark. Heuzer and Stuart then proceeded to inspect the men. Gehlen stood back.

'I hope we will not meet again for some time, Herr General,' Stuart said to Gehlen.

'Have some coffee ready for me in Madrid. And keep out of trouble.' Gehlen put out his hand and shook Stuart's. 'Good luck, Teniente.'

Stuart saluted and his men came to attention. Gehlen saluted them and stepped back. One by one they climbed into the huge seaplane.

'I could wish you luck,' Gehlen said to Heuzer. 'But I think you already have it, Thomas. Pull this off and you can show the Führer a detonator from last July's bomb plot: he won't care.'

'I shall take your word, Herr General. My life has been in

your hands for some time now.' He saluted and Gehlen shook his hand.

About ten minutes later Oliver Dasch started the engines. And fifteen minutes after that, the huge seaplane lifted off. Gehlen watched it crawl its way up into the darkness. By the time it reached cruising height it had vanished.

Peter Heinck wiped the sweat from his face as the airplane settled into its struggle. And blood came back to the faces of the men sitting in its belly.

Below them, Reinhard Gehlen arched his neck. 'I'm not sure I believe in God,' he said to himself. 'But I think God believes in me.'

Claude Dansey read a report he had written during time he spent in Africa forty years earlier, while his nurse took his blood pressure that Friday afternoon.

'I used to hit sentries over the head with sand,' he said to Derek Boyd. 'Very effective.'

The telephone rang before Boyd could reply. Dansey pushed his nurse to one side and answered it.

He put the receiver down two minutes later and turned to Boyd. 'The money found on Finger and Marcan is part of the same sequence as a batch found on a German agent named Peter Pohl picked up in Canada last year,' Dansey said. 'Pohl was a saboteur. The Canadians handed him over to us last month.'

'Simon's been passing the Germans Manhattan?' Boyd said. His thin face elongated. 'It doesn't make sense. They're this close to defeat. They haven't the capability to make such a bomb any more. We saw to that.'

'Get everyone in here,' Dansey said. 'All the information we have on Penny. Get on to London, have them do the same. And find out what the hell's going on down at that New Mexican bomb factory. Break limbs if you have to, I want to know what Finger knew by Monday, Derek.' Boyd was already pulling his coat from behind the door.

17

The single-storey adobe farmhouse serving as his officers' quarters always made Warren Brett sigh. As he made his way through the maze of small rooms and empty beds, surrounded by military clothing and oiled equipment, the unhealthy alliance of claustrophobia and stale odour and the deep fissures bleeding ferrous moisture on every wall, forced him to struggle physically before he could concentrate on the master sergeant standing before him.

'Jesus, Helm, get some bodies in here and do something about this place. I've been in chicken sheds smelled better than this.'

Master Sergeant Bobby Helm saluted. He was taller than Brett and he used his height to blunt the edge of the major's order. 'I was visitin' the lieutenant, sir. Officers' quarters is not my area of expertise.'

'Well, I know that. But you're here and this place is ...' Brett often had trouble with his own authority. He changed the subject. 'How is the lieutenant?' He gestured to the figure sitting on a single occupied bed in a tiny room at the far end of the house.

'He was lucky. They cut him up good, sir. I seen it before. He was lucky.'

Through the windows, clouds drifting along in phalanxes outside meant the sun burst through the windows intermittently, changing colours inside, and the grey metal beds and the various pieces of kit and equipment lying around occasionally seemed to catch fire.

A solitary table, to one side of the door, with a heap of yellowing paper, gave an official flavour to what might have been an ad hoc refuge. Philip Rand was cleaning a rifle. There was a bruise down the side of his face, a bandage on the side of his head, some stitching on his wrist, and a series of deep scratches on his neck, with small pieces of stone still embedded in the skin and coagulated blood. There was iodine on this wound.

'What happened, Philip?'

Brett knew the answer but he felt he should ask the question anyway.

'Several men – I'm not sure how many – ran into me with their automobile.' He continued cleaning the weapon.

'Now you're not going to do anything stupid, are you, Philip?' Brett asked.

Rand looked at the rifle and shook his head. 'I am not going to let them get to me, Warren. I am an officer and a gentleman. Not a common brawler.'

'Doctor says it's mostly bruising,' Brett said.

'Does he? Next time I hear a car behind me, I'm heading for the hills, though.'

'It might have been an accident. It was dark?'

'Drivers in accidents don't get out and kick you on the ground. Don't worry, I feel kind of blooded actually.'

'Then you'll be glad to see this.' Brett shoved an official notice into Rand's hand and stood at ease on the balls of his feet. 'We've been given combat notice, Lieutenant. I think your endless missives to the various powers have succeeded in getting us all killed.'

Rand could not conceal his joy, but he managed to temper it. 'Oh, come on, Warren, it won't be for months, and they don't even say where – Japan or Germany. My God, but we are being posted. Hell, Warren, that's what we're here for.'

Warren Brett kept rubbing his face, as if he was trying to wipe something off. 'Well, I hope you're happy, Lieutenant. I hope you're proud of yourself. Damn, I thought I'd get through this one without that.'

'Don't be like that, Warren.'

'Major, Lieutenant. Major. And you're an engineer and we need engineers to build roads and runways here. Not makeshift rubbish while people are trying to kill us. You know any damn fool can fire a rifle, but you've got to go to college to be an engineer. Just bear in mind that some time in the next few months we'll be trying to do what we're doing now with a million krauts trying to kill us. Not just a bunch of cowboy rednecks out for some fun with ...'

'... a nigger,' Rand said.

Brett blew out. He went to the window. 'I'm not like you, Philip. You're a fighter. You're a doer, I'm a ... well, the opposite of all that. I got sick when they drafted me, you know. I was never so happy as when they put me building runways and roads around here.'

'It'll probably never happen, Major,' Rand said. 'Not with my luck. They'll post us the day this war ends.'

Brett held himself on his toes for a while, then looked out the window at the rain. A rainbow had formed from one side of the camp where a wall of timber rose twenty feet to a series of bulldozers. Two soldiers in capes smoked a cigarette under the shelter of the bulldozers.

'You want to make an official complaint about that?' he said to Rand. 'I did tell you to stay away from that Shaffer girl.'

'You too, Warren,' Rand said.

'You know I'm not like that, Philip. You know that.'

'Yeah, well, forget the complaint, Warren. Like you said, I'm a fighter.'

'You're a fool, Philip,' Brett said with the conviction of a man who is not easy with decisions. 'And what does that make me?'

The horse told Eadie Shaffer someone was there. She had been lying on a rock, looking into the river. The river was brown, and the rock was red. A tornado in east Texas threw veils across the eastern horizon and there were small pieces of construction timber in the river. When she rolled over on to her back, Gus Delmar was standing there with his hands in his pockets.

'Bet you thought I was your nigger,' he said.

'You think I'd make that mistake?' she said. It was not serious, more mocking, and Eadie put on a mocking face that could not be mistaken for anything else.

'I don't want to talk about him,' Gus said, more to get away from her face than anything else.

Eadie rolled over again and put her hand in the water. It was cold and she kept her hand there until the pain of the cold forced it out. 'You not gone?' she said.

He sat down beside her. 'I got nowhere to go.'

'Big war hero,' she said. 'Sure, you do.'

He placed his hand on her back and began to rub it. 'I'm not such a hero. I missed you.' He did not mean it.

She pushed his hand away. 'You got no call for doin' that, Gus. No call.' She did not mean it either.

'I got trouble, Eadie,' he said. He felt ashamed. 'Things I done.'

'We all got trouble, Gus. Now, go on, get outta here before I get upset. You and I is back there where the water's calm and the sun always shines and there's possibilities. Thousands of possibilities.'

'What's my pa been like since I was away?' Gus asked.

'How would I know? Same as my pa, only worse, I guess.'

He put his hand on her again. This time she pushed him off and rolled away. She stood up. 'Just go, Gus, just go.'

'I wanted comfort,' he said. 'I just wanted comfort.'

'I ain't got none for you,' she said. She threw some stones at him and Gus Delmar backed off. Then Eadie Shaffer mounted her horse and rode off. He threw a stone after her. In the distance, John Delmar put away his binoculars and got into his car.

So many eyes stared at Philip Rand as he walked into Zach Pepper's bar in Los Muertos, he felt they would kill him simply by looking at him. He walked into the bar without looking anyone in the eye, and the wide eyes of the dozen or so men in the bar bored holes in the shadows while Philip Rand leaned on the dry counter and signalled to Zach Pepper with his eyes.

Pepper was short and bow-legged from rickets. He held one shoulder down. He had a cloth and a glass and he put them on the counter and came over to Rand like he was approaching something organically unpleasant.

'A glass of lemonade,' Rand said.

Pepper smiled, but there was no affection in the expression. 'You might wanna reconsider your position, Lieutenant,' he said to Rand. 'I don't want no trouble ... so why don't you turn around and let them well-trained legs take you outta here.' The smile dissolved into a stare which went way past a threat. And others did the same. Rand recognised at least two of the men who had attacked him the night before. Small things gave them away, nothing you could prove, just a tone and the look in their eyes and the pace of their breathing.

'A glass of lemonade,' Philip Rand repeated.

'Get out, boy!' Zach Pepper said then.

Two or three of the men moved forward and then hesitated. Rand turned to them and his demeanor changed their hesitation into retreat.

Then Gus Delmar hobbled out of a group of men sitting around a table. He was pale and his left arm shook when he walked. He took the trouble to introduce himself but there was an implied supremacy in the motion, something Gus himself did not like.

'There's a cantina 'bout ten miles that way caters to hispanics and others,' he said. He put his hand on Rand's arm. 'Now my advice to you is about face, Lieutenant, and strategically withdraw. To use a military term.' He looked at the other customers and grinned. 'We're peaceful folk here.'

The men now standing around Rand all grinned but none of them laughed. They were the middle-aged and they had taken the place of the elderly, who were all sitting again. What the middle-aged held in their hearts and minds they let out in small packets. But venom laced most of their sentences and their Adam's apples seemed to move in harmony with the small beads of sweat on their moonscape faces.

Philip Rand looked around at them. 'I want a glass of lemonade,' he said. He removed his hand from under Gus Delmar's.

'Yessir,' Gus Delmar said. And he saluted. 'You heard the officer, Zach. A lemonade. If you please.'

'You're drunk,' Philip Rand said to Gus Delmar. He paused before tacking on the end, 'Corporal.'

Delmar might have hit him if he had been fit. At least that was what he told himself and that was what the spectators said.

Zach Pepper poured the lemonade in front of Gus Delmar. 'He knows my name,' Gus said. 'Did you hear that? The officer knows my name. Well, guess what, sir? I know things, too.' Gus picked the glass of lemonade up and drank it in one. 'You look pretty beat up, Lieutenant. Been in combat?' He touched Rand's stitching and bruises.

'I was hit from behind,' Rand said. 'By a coward. Or cowards.'

'Oh, a coward,' Gus Delmar said. 'Well, maybe you should watch where you run ... sir. Dangerous out here. I was in the European Theatre myself. What theatres have you served in ... sir?'

'I want a glass of lemonade,' Rand said.

'No can do ... sir,' Gus said. 'Didn't Zach tell you, this bar's only for combat veterans. Everyone here's a veteran. And I bet you thought it was because you're a gentleman o' colour.'

'You're gonna cause trouble,' Zach Pepper said to Rand.

'Now we can do this easy or I can get Sheriff Delmar and he'll get mean. My boy died in the Pacific, son ...'

'That makes Zach a kind of veteran, too,' Gus said. 'What stories did you tell Eadie, I wonder.' Everything on Gus Delmar's face said he did not want to know.

The other customers dipped their eyes and talked to one another. 'Get out, nigger,' someone said.

Philip Rand slipped a hand in his pocket and pulled out a hand grenade. He showed it to Zach Pepper's moist eyes. Pepper's moist eyes froze so much you could almost see the icicles.

'A glass of lemonade, please ...'

There was a moment when Philip Rand thought he was going to pull the pin on the hand grenade. Andy Redrow came over to him and put a hand on his arm. 'Why don't you put that away? You're in trouble as it is.'

'Just defending myself, Mayor,' Rand said. 'Like I'm entitled to.' He drank the lemonade Zach Pepper had poured. Then he ordered another and drank that. No one else in the bar drank until Rand had replaced the pin in the grenade. He replaced the grenade in his pocket, put some money down on the counter and backed off.

'Your commandin' officer will hear of this,' Andy Redrow said to him.

'I fully expect him to,' Rand said.

'You're causin' trouble, son,' Redrow said then. 'For my Eadie. For me. For this town. For the military.'

'You don't have to worry about that, Mr Redrow. Not any more. Your Eadie's gotten as sick of me as you are. She's just like her father. Be proud, you should be.'

He saluted.

'Evening, gentlemen.'

Andy Redrow went over to the bar counter and slapped Gus Delmar on the back. 'What the hell was he thinkin'?' he asked. 'I'll get your pa on that boy.'

Gus Delmar shook his head. 'It scares me, Andy,' he said. 'It scares me to think what he's thinkin'.'

Rosalyn Delmar had a frame that suggested an unsustainable plan battling with an unshakable will. But when you studied it in conjunction with her face all you saw was frustration secreted behind irritation.

She had waited in vain for her husband to come home on many nights but this was different, she felt. Simon Penny sat across the room from her in silence.

Rosalyn Delmar only dropped a stitch when Gus finally came in. 'Have you met Mr Penny, Gus, your pa's friend?' she said as Gus stood looking at Simon Penny.

She led Penny across the Mayan rug on the living room floor, and he shook hands with Gus.

'You're lookin' better than when I last saw you, Gus,' Penny said. 'You were a bit out of place then.'

'What did you say your name was?' Gus said then.

'Penny. Simon Penny. I was on the porch with your father. Some few nights ago.'

Gus did not remember him. 'And what's your connection with Pa?' he asked. The suspicion was born of a paranoia Gus was now finding hard to control, but it weighed on Simon Penny.

'They're fishin' friends,' Rosalyn Delmar said.

'He invited me to come down for the weekend, to cast a few lines,' Penny said. 'I'm from Virginia, and your pa sometimes came up that way to visit some years ago. Your ma, too.'

'Ma never liked fishin',' Gus said.

'Simon's a good friend of your father's,' Rosalyn Delmar said. 'You wanna keep him company? I'll do some bakin'.'

'Yeah, well, you can see it's an inappropriate time since I'm drunk,' Gus said. 'And I'm damn rude when I'm drunk, sir. I been out all day and all night and you can see my mind ain't quite caught up with the rest o' me. I assume you're stayin' here?'

'I think I might ...'

'No, I would not have it any other way,' Rosalyn Delmar said. 'You'll stay, Simon.'

Gus Delmar was about to put an argument up but his attention was distracted by Andy Redrow's appearance at the screen door. Redrow was white and his head had drooped and the way he moved suggested he had no strength left. Behind him a thin wisp of dust shaped itself against the horizon.

'Somethin' terrible ... 'bout three miles outta Santavista Gap...' Andy Redrow started to cry.

18

Philip Rand woke with a hangover. His head moved before his eyes opened and the only thing he saw was John Delmar holding a rifle to his head.

'Just give me an excuse, boy.'

Rand's face betrayed a resignation that was just about overwhelmed by his confusion.

'We found Eadie Shaffer out by the Santavista Gap, you bastard,' John Delmar said. He followed Philip Rand out of the bed and kicked him across the room. Two more men with badges and rifles, whom Delmar referred to in monosyllabic terms, stood either side of the door. They were shaking, obviously unused to this kind of thing.

Rand was still dressing when Warren Brett forced his way through the door and Delmar's two deputies. John Delmar shoved a badge in Brett's face before he could speak.

'Country sheriff's business, Major. And since you ain't got no military police on camp, we're takin' this man in on suspicion o' murder. Local girl found in a gorge this mornin'.' John Delmar paused like he was preparing to retell something so awful it might not get out. 'Without clothes ... son of a bitch!' He swung his rifle and hit Philip Rand across the back of the head.

Rand picked himself up and tried to come to attention. There was a shocked expression on his face. And it spoke more in two gestures than any words he could think of.

'I swear ...' Rand raised his hands to his chest and his eyes almost begged Warren Brett.

'Lieutenant Rand is a serving officer in the United States military and will be accorded all protection,' Warren Brett said. His own face was betraying all the nervousness he could feel in his guts.

'We found this,' John Delmar said. He tossed a unit identification patch at Brett. 'His, I'd say. Everyone knows they played together.'

Brett walked across to Rand's clothes locker and went through his uniforms.

'I gave it to her. A gift.' Rand was recomposing himself.

'Hangin' round her like a dog around a bitch,' John Delmar said. 'You think we didn't see it. Jesus, you vicious bastard.' He went to hit Rand again but was pulled back by his deputies and Warren Brett.

'You couldn't leave well enough alone, could you, boy? I mean, Jesus, man, what kinda animal are you?'

'Philip, is this true?' Brett demanded.

'What should I say, Warren? That I got what I deserved?' Rand was desperately trying to preserve whatever dignity he thought the situation required. Several small birds landed on a window sill and then flew away.

'Get your things,' John Delmar said. 'We're gonna do this by the book. I want you to know that. When they do you, boy.'

'I'd like someone to accompany him,' Warren Brett said. 'He deserves that. I don't want him disappearing into the mountains or being shot while trying to escape.'

'Might be a better result than waiting for the citizenry to come one night,' Philip Rand said. 'Right, Mr Delmar?'

John Delmar began reading him his rights. And they sounded like a list of charges.

Rand slowly put his uniform on, having difficulty with the buttons. No one helped. Then he stood to attention. 'Warren

. . . do something, Warren. For God's sake. I'm dead if they take me there, Warren. I'm dead.'

One of the deputies, who now seemed very uncomfortable with the whole event, cuffed him and led him to the waiting police car. 'You'll inform my family when I'm found face down in the dirt,' Rand said to Brett as he was being led out the door.

Warren Brett looked away.

In the fading light of Saturday evening Simon Penny stopped his car about two miles east of the Santavista Gap. The two headlights coming towards him dipped below the horizon for a time and then reappeared as a shooting star crossed the sky. Penny waited for the other car to stop, pausing to take in the smell of the broken leather upholstery and gum boots that floated on the warm air.

The temperature was dropping and a mist forming along the river. He tried to time the mist but he could not see its extremities.

'Another night here, Mr Penny. You must like night fishin',' Gus Delmar said, closing the door of the old car he drove.

'I enjoy the solitude,' Penny said. 'I was expectin' your father. I left word.'

'Yeah, well there's still a heap o' business needs takin' care of. You ever been in love?'

'No,' Penny said. 'I like fishin' too much. I am sorry about the girl. Your father said you were close.'

'I'm his son, Mr Penny. I have to fake things sometimes. Love, hope, and such. That is what sons do. My father never spoke of you, you know.'

'He always speaks of you, Gus.'

Gus Delmar walked to the river bank and looked at the gathering. 'I think he truly believes he will find it,' he said.

'What?' Penny asked.

'You know what I'm talkin' about.'

'I'm sorry, I don't.'

'I'm talkin' about Iago Santavista,' Gus Delmar said. 'That's what you boys is lookin' for here. I know.' He touched his nose. 'He believes in the City of the Sun, my father. And I know it's just Injun talk.'

'I'm familiar with the story,' Penny said.

'My father is obsessed with it. He is a man of obsession. 'Specially the things he can't have. He does not want what he has because he cannot deal with it. He must seek what he cannot have.'

Gus Delmar strode back to his car and drove off.

Simon Penny blew out. The mist had engulfed him. Half an hour later, he was in the mountains, listening to a final transmission from Norway.

Dieter Vogl's radioman slipped on a piece of sausage skin as he made his way to the submarine's control room. He swore. Vogl was reading an old pre-war novel and sipping the last of a store of coffee he had looted from a British merchantman two years earlier. His hands were streaked with oil and his face had several days' growth of beard. The radioman shoved the message into Vogl's hand.

'Did they repeat it three times?' Vogl asked.

The radioman, who was experiencing salt rash in his groin and fatigue brought on by the bad air, nodded a halfhearted acknowledgement.

Vogl called Helmut Otto over. The first officer's eyes were watering. He took out a pair of steel spectacles to read the message. Vogl grabbed his own map off a bench.

'Set a course for the rendezvous, Helmut.'

'I believe some of Hernan Cortez's men landed near there in 1519,' Otto said. 'They were never seen again. Cortez said they had achieved their destiny.'

'Let's hope it isn't catching,' Vogl said.

Otto gave the relevant orders and five minutes later the

submarine began to rise. Further down the submarine, Irmgarde Hanke nodded to a respectful sailor, slipped from her bunk and quietly moved to the control room.

'Ah, Frau Doktor,' Vogl said. 'Couldn't resist me? It seems we're in business. You and your men should prepare for action. All that fancy explosive. Tell me, does it concern you, the devastation we may cause?'

Without a word she made her way back to the bunks where her team of scientists and technicians lay in a degree of claustrophobic misery which had occasionally led to arguments and physical sickness. One by one, the men rolled from their bunks and began to leave their thoughts behind and enter the safety of their work.

Dieter Vogl watched the periscope rise in front of him and put his book to one side. When he took the periscope handles in his hands, he wrapped his arms around them and looked out at the ocean. 'Good. Nothing.'

If Walter Schellenberg was happy at finding nothing behind him, his body language just wasn't translating it. He had sent a messenger to Sweden, to a contact in the SIS station in Malmo, with a note detailing Ground Zero. For two hours he walked around the charcoaled centre of Berlin, periodically pausing to turn round and study the faces still on the street. Then the evening brought the cold and the cold brought the mist and the mist broke up the light, and all that was left was sound. And every sound was his name.

He drank himself to sleep finally and did not wake up when the bombers came again.

Over the middle of arctic Canada, Peter Heinck took out a flask of coffee and passed it to Oliver Dasch. 'I'll go back and check on the passengers,' he said.

'If you do, I might just fly us to Mexico.'

Dasch was holding the steering column very tightly, and Heinck noticed how tight his face was and the way the nose broke the freezing air in the cabin. Dasch did not turn his eyes to his co-pilot, merely took the flask, drank from it and then handed it back.

'We'll get out of this, Oliver,' Heinck said. He put his hand on Dasch's shoulder.

He realised that their talk had so often been diversionary, that he knew so little about Dasch beyond the country childhood, the dead father, the girl he did not marry, the career cut short by being shot down. He took the flask, screwed the cap back on and made his way back down the aircraft.

'We're east of the Rockies,' he said to Heuzer.

'How can we fail?' Heuzer said. He looked around at his men. Most of them smiled.

Kyle Stuart was helping a former tanner from Georgia, named Stephen Harris, to cope with air sickness. The smell of leather was still faint on Harris's hands and his left eye was damaged from a ricochet in Russia. He threw up in his helmet right as Peter Heinck offered Stuart some coffee.

'And the Canadians?' Karl Peiper asked Heinck then.

'We came in low enough. Now we rely on deceit. Should be no problem.' Heinck laughed. 'Aside from trying to negotiate this monster on to a lake in the dark. What can stop us now but rough waters, bad visibility and no beacons? Lie back and relax, Sergeant, we have long passed the point of no return.'

Philip Rand lay back and watched the slivers of light enter his cell, and, as the door opened, he let the shadow of John Delmar gradually blot out much of the light before he sat up. 'I'd like some water,' Rand said.

'You'll get water when you need it. Not when you want it.'

'I didn't do anything, I'm telling you. I assure you, I am the wrong man. I would like to see my commanding officer ... the military authorities.'

'Where'd you get them scratches and bruises?' Delmar asked.

'You wouldn't believe me if I told you. I didn't kill her, I swear.'

'Don't tell me you loved her or I will get angry.'

'No, I didn't love her. There was no love between us.'

Delmar leaned against the stone wall. It was cold and small trickles of water were running down the yellow stone in one corner. There were mouse droppings in another corner, and one of the bars on the door was exposed where the wood had worn away and the bar was rusting. But the gap was too small to do anything. Insect remains on the door, caked there from the previous summer, began to crumble and fall away.

'You're not doin' yourself any good, boy,' Delmar said then.

'I am telling the truth.'

'If you raped her, we'll know. I'll have someone do an examination. They can tell, dead or not.'

'Sir, I did not kill her. Where is my commanding officer? Where are the military authorities?'

John Delmar closed his eyes. 'You know you're beginnin' to try my patience. Now I got people out there would probably tear you into small pieces if I took a mind to lettin' 'em. She was a dear friend of mine. Do I make myself clear? A dear friend of mine. My Gus and her ...'

Philip Rand shook his head. 'Shit, you haven't even contacted the military authorities, have you?' he said. 'What the hell are you holding me on, Sheriff? I want to see my commanding officer. I demand a lawyer.'

John Delmar raised his finger. 'You demand nothin'. You will get nothin'. But I swear I'll get justice from you.' He walked to the door. 'There's a storm comin', you know,' he said.

'You've got the wrong man,' Philip Rand yelled. He lay back on his bed and watched what remained of the light vanish as John Delmar closed the door to the cell block.

AT THE GATES

19

An hour after the last rainstorm on Sunday, II March, 1945, a single jeep with four men in it and a thirty-calibre machine gun mounted on the back broke through the haze of dust and moisture at the Santavista Gap end of Los Muertos, rolled down the main street through several puddles, and came to a considered halt on one side of the plaza. As Kyle Stuart stepped out of the passenger side of the jeep, covered by his Texan sergeant, Larry Schwartz, the smallest drops fell from the bandstand to their right, each one catching the furthest limits of the sunlight.

Their driver, a Virginian named Albert Murphy, stayed in the shadow, his engine running, while Steve Harris swung the thirty-calibre machine gun to face the street. Harris's damaged eye caused an hispanic woman across the street to stop and pause.

Then the sun broke through the remaining clouds and reclaimed the mountains. Long, sharp rays scorched the arid peaks, then filtered through the tall thin trees on the brown slopes around the town, spreading a sharp golden hue on the landscape behind the sudden bursts of reflective light.

Two or three ranchers from distances of ten to thirty miles, dressed in denims and carrying tools, chickenwire and animal feeds, stood around a beaten-up truck, and joined the hispanic woman, watching Stuart and his men check their weapons. Then the hispanic woman called her children and led them across the street. They moved like they were tied together.

Kyle Stuart had time to notice an inflexibility on the faces around him as he placed his helmet on the seat of the jeep and pulled on his side cap, making sure his rank badge was in the right place. The noise of his helmet on the back of his seat interrupted the Sunday afternoon sounds, except, perhaps, for the sound of the heavier rain drops falling from the rim of the bandstand.

Stuart reached the bandstand right as the onlookers had lost interest. The beaten-up truck rolled down the main street towards the dust and moisture mix. Another woman, white this time, stood at the other side of the plaza, scratching her head. She had heard the noise of the helmet.

Andy Redrow came out on to the porch in front of his supply store, stopped and looked at the Rangers drawn up at the plaza. And for a moment he hesitated. Then he strode across the road, buttoning up his flies and pulling his suspenders over his shoulders. His face was ruddy and creviced, and he had broken into a sweat.

'Gonna be a fine day now, looks like,' Kyle Stuart said as if he was a neighbour. 'Kyle Stuart, United States Rangers. You must be ... Mr Redrow.' He offered his hand to the mayor.

Redrow glanced at Stuart's jeep before taking the lieutenant's hand. 'Yeah, what's up?'

'Just some routine business at the station,' Stuart said. 'We'll be gone by dark. You don't mind us makin' ourselves conspicuous?'

Redrow wiped his face of unwanted mucus and sleepy tears with the back of his hand. He sniffed.

A second Ranger jeep drove into Los Muertos just as he did, its field radio buzzing with static from the remains of the storm, Pierre at the wheel, wearing a woollen cap and leather gloves. Behind him, on the thirty-calibre, was a New Yorker named Vernon Kell, who had only joined the Stonewall Legion from a POW camp in late 1944. The jeep pulled in beside the first, and Pierre nodded at the mayor.

'Southerner?' Andy Redrow asked Kyle Stuart.

'Several of us are Southerners,' Kyle Stuart said. 'I'm from Louisiana myself.'

'Hell, I'm from Louisiana originally,' Redrow said. 'Right near the state line with Mississippi. You?'

'Family used to own land around Baton Rouge,' Stuart said. 'But we moved around. I spent time in Europe.'

'Your accent's kinda light, all right. I wasn't sure.'

The two men stood staring at each other. The mayor glanced at the other Rangers again. Larry Schwartz had a map out and was pointing positions out to his men.

'Our business won't take long,' Stuart said then. 'Sheriff Delmar didn't speak with you?'

Redrow shook his head. 'No,' he said then as if to confirm himself. He thought for a moment, tried to regain the sense of official composure his daughter's death had robbed him of, then looked back up the west end of the town. 'We've had a tragedy,' he said, nodding to himself.

'Sheriff Delmar mentioned it,' Stuart said.

'Got the boy who did it,' Redrow said. 'Army'll deal with him.' He did not elaborate.

That was when Larry Schwartz told Vernon Kell to check the small railway station they had passed on the way in, then whispered something to the man beside him. Charlie Race, who had metal plates in his head, lifted a Browning Automatic Rifle and some spare ten-round magazines from the floor of the jeep, and followed Vernon Kell to the station.

When he saw Vernon Kell appear on the roof of the train station, Andy Redrow's face suddenly registered like a one-armed bandit with three fruits. 'Sure ... sure ...' He kept nodding. 'Yeah.' He wiped his face again. 'I was with our boys in the last one,' he explained to Stuart. 'I didn't get to do any fightin' but I sure wanted to. Never mind tellin' me what you boys are doin' here. I know.' He touched his head with a callused finger. 'I know.'

Just then, Karl Peiper drove the third jeep past him and on past the plaza and the jailhouse and several low houses, and moved it into a position where it covered the east end of the town. The swiftness of the takeover obviously caught Redrow offguard, because he spent the next ten minutes bombarding a reluctant Kyle Stuart with questions. Once, he mentioned Eadie again, but only in passing. His official self would not allow his private self to impinge on office hours.

Finally, Stuart raised a hand. 'You'll have to excuse me, Mayor, but I have to take care of business.'

Redrow took Stuart's hand again. 'Yeah, sure. Listen, anythin' you boys want, I'm over there.'

'And I'm sorry about your loss,' Stuart said when the mayor was halfway back to his store. Stuart wandered up towards the train station and Pierre then backed his jeep across the plaza and down to Zach Pepper's bar. A Tennessean named Jimmy Mitchell, who remained in the back, manned the machine gun on Pierre's jeep and now covered Kell and Race at the train station.

A couple of dogs made their way up the main street sniffing at some garbage. One of them cocked its leg at Pierre's jeep. Pierre kicked out at the dog, and it barked and ran off towards the train station.

At the east end of Los Muertos, near a dump for old farm machinery, Corporal Billy Watkins, whose lisp seemed more pronounced at altitude, led a wiry legionary named Harry Pellicer and David Menton across the street, where they took up positions on someone's porch.

Rust from the farm machinery ran into the soil and down a furrow in the street.

Menton walked with the same pace as his accent let him speak and drew a remark from a small boy standing in the shadow of an arch. When Menton turned, the boy saw the scar behind his ear, which curved and ran down his neck, and from there on all the way to his groin. A Russian Cossack had almost cut him in two. Menton winked at the boy but the child ran off.

'We should have someone up on the hills,' Kyle Stuart said to Larry Schwartz. They were standing at the bandstand, examining a map. Stuart saw a curtain move across the street, made a note of it and put it to one side.

Schwartz scanned the slopes around the town. He pointed to a sharp rise with tree cover. 'They call it the Sun's Peak,' he said to Stuart. 'Murphy, get yourself up there. Take field glasses, a walkie talkie and some water. And keep in the shade.'

The blond Virginian sighed, grabbed a hand radio and checked his own water bottle. When he had fished about for some field glasses in the back of their jeep, he strolled towards the summit by way of a small track leading past the jailhouse over the railway line and across a footbridge over the Vibora river.

The bridge shook as he walked across because of his weight and because the river level had swollen even more overnight. There were cacti and a dead animal in the river. The dead animal was swollen, too, and it had changed colour. The cacti were the same.

As he climbed, Murphy saw a dull-coloured car put another crack in the peaceful Sunday monotony on the main street in Los Muertos. John Delmar and Thomas Heuzer stepped out of the car and, together with Stuart and Schwartz, went into Delmar's jailhouse.

Fifty miles to the north, Simon Penny was shivering. Dug into a sharp mountain, wrapped in a blanket, carrying a pair of field glasses and eating an onion sandwich, he was soaked through with rain.

About a mile in front of him, in the middle of a refracted vision of dust and spray, two jeeps and two Ford sedan cars approached from Albuquerque at a steady thirty-five. The plutonium was on the move.

When he had clocked the vehicles over two separate distances he went back to his own car and took out a field radio.

The sun's fingers now stretched along the main street in Los Muertos, interlocking with the lengthening shadows of the afternoon. Thomas Heuzer stood in front of the jailhouse in one of the shadows. Kyle Stuart approached from the sunlight.

'Position two,' he said to Heuzer.

'Get ready to cut the telephone lines,' Heuzer said. He was experiencing a feeling of strength he only ever experienced in the field, tinged only with the slightest of fears. Not for what might happen to him, but of what he might do. Still, everyone looked to him, and he had the sense that if he had asked anything of his men at that moment, they would have obeyed. 'And remember,' he said to Stuart, 'we're letting them in, Kyle. So tell everyone to be polite. And make sure Race and Kell keep their heads down. We don't want to spook them. Where's that train?'

John Delmar was rubbing his head. He gave a short almost defensive shrug. 'It'll come,' he said.

'Murphy'll see it,' Larry Schwartz said. He was standing beside his jeep watching Andy Redrow approach again from the other side of the street. A small group of people were on the street now, watching the Rangers, asking questions of them, getting nothing in reply. Stuart told Schwartz to go round the men and tell them to prepare.

'Sheriff, be about your business,' Heuzer said to Delmar. 'You have been of enormous help.' He smiled at the sheriff who tried not to smile back. He failed. John Delmar then went back into his office and Heuzer started to walk towards the train station, examining the town.

Andy Redrow caught up with Heuzer before he reached the

station. Stuart introduced them, but Heuzer did not give Redrow anything but monosyllabic answers. The captain kept looking at his watch and when he turned to face Redrow directly, his face was hard like it was preparing for a fight. Andy Redrow backed off immediately. 'Man's got a job to do,' he said to anyone who would listen.

Redrow found John Delmar drinking in his office.

'Goddamn Captain thinks he's God Almighty hisself!' he said.

'I got work to do, Andy.'

'What you gonna do with *him?*' Redrow asked, gesturing to the door that led down to the cells.

'Due process,' Delmar said.

'Well, you better think about due processes by tomorrow, 'cus them boys from Albuquerque is gonna be askin' questions if'n we don't present them with a suspect for Eadie.'

'I know my duty, Andy,' Delmar said. He downed his glass and put it on his desk. 'I said I'd deliver a suspect, I'll deliver a suspect. But we gotta hear what the military want first, and they're awful slow.'

'Yeah, sure, John,' Redrow replied. 'I know you felt for her, too. I know that.'

Delmar came over and put his arm on Redrow's shoulder. 'I need to be alone, Andy.'

That was when Gus Delmar looked out an upstairs window of Andy Redrow's store. Sitting on sacks of seed, hung over and barely dressed, his eyes were drawn to the two Rangers in the jeep below him. He tried to read their insignia. Jimmy Mitchell glanced up and saw him. He waved and Gus Delmar nodded back. Then he closed the curtains and poured a glass from the same bottle of spirits he had almost emptied the night before.

He had not slept properly since the day before he enlisted, and had barely slept at all since he came back from Europe. Once or twice after waking up that morning he had considered killing himself, but he had not been able to do it when Eadie Shaffer was found dead, so what chance had he now? He pulled the curtains apart again and watched the Rangers. Then Andy Redrow came into the storeroom.

'You can't sit here and drink all day, Gus,' he said. He began stacking boxes. 'Workin' eases the pain. You might consider that. Your drinkin' irritates me, Gus. And, to be honest, you irritate me, Gus.'

'Who're the Rangers?' Gus said after a long silence.

'Not allowed to say. Your pa's handlin' it. You best sober up, son, before your pa sees you. And I won't have you seein' off Eadie like that.'

Gus Delmar pushed past the mayor, trying to straighten his clothes while he leaned on his stick. He almost fell over.

'You listenin' to me, Gus?' Redrow said.

'Don't worry, Andy, Eadie probably won't do your re-election prospects no harm,' Gus said.

Redrow went to grab him but his size went against him and he stumbled on to some bean sacks. Gus went to apologise and then decided against it. 'There's things I done I ain't so proud of, Andy,' he said.

'She was my daughter,' Redrow shouted at Gus. He repeated it a few times.

Below him, Gus Delmar stood by a low arch, watching Thomas Heuzer leave town. He was sobering fast and no longer listening to the Mayor.

When Thomas Heuzer reached John Delmar's ranch, Simon Penny was standing on the porch, reading. 'Iago Santavista's confession,' Penny remarked. 'Hard to resist it here.' He handed it to Heuzer and explained the story.

Heuzer read the book for a minute or more and then stared at Penny. The captain looked like he had been woken from a sleep. 'The convoy?' he said suddenly.

'About thirty minutes that way, making steady progress.

Plutonium in each sedan. Guards in the jeeps. Just as said.'

'And Heinck and Dasch?' Heuzer asked.

'Ready to go. If it clicks we'll make Mexico before the gringos know what hit them. And then the darkness will make everything else irrelevant. Except landing on the sea, of course.'

'You're coming with us?' Heuzer asked.

'I would be a liability otherwise.'

'We should be about our business then,' Heuzer said. Then he re-opened the book. 'You are a Tod man?' he asked Penny.

Penny took the book off him. 'How's the sheriff?' he said.

'Will he come, too?'

'I took his wife to Albuquerque.'

'I got the impression she had no feelings for him,' Heuzer said. 'That things around her were bare. A hard woman.'

'I don't know her that well, Herr Hauptmann,' Penny said. 'You obviously have a facility for discerning people. I wish I had your insights.'

'There is a saying in this country, Mr Penny. Don't kid a kidder.'

'Fishing does that to me,' Penny said. 'I think the sheriff would rather not have sent that black boy to Albuquerque yesterday.'

'We'll have to watch him, then,' Heuzer said.

'I have things to see to. I'll follow you, Captain.'

'I appreciate your work, Mr Penny,' Heuzer said. 'Germany does.'

'*Deutschland Uber Alles.*'

'So long as she is not under all, I will be happy,' Heuzer replied.

Heuzer was feeling confident when he reached Los Muertos ten minutes ahead of the plutonium convoy. For the first time in months he felt he had completely regained control of himself and his sense of confidence radiated to his men. Penny arrived about five minutes later and neither he nor Heuzer saw Gus Delmar hobble out of a small shed across the street from his father's jailhouse and stop by the bandstand. If they had he might have noticed the blanched expression on Gus's face, the hurried almost pained strides he made to make it to the jailhouse, the dry breathlessness, the sweat pouring from his face. Gus stopped at the jailhouse porch and squinted while Kyle Stuart and Heuzer studied a map and then broke up. Only Jimmy Mitchell noticed Gus but he was too busy to think anything of it.

Gus stared up at Albert Murphy and then at the other Rangers and then at the jailhouse. His mouth went so dry then he had to reach into a pool of water on the ground for moisture.

The insect Gus Delmar saw wriggling across the stone floor as he limped into his father's office was, in fact, several, but Gus stamped on them all the same. Nervous energy rather than anything else.

The sheriff was sitting at his desk with his head in one hand and a pen in the other. There was a plate of half eaten food on the table and two revolvers hanging in their holsters on the wall behind. John Delmar lifted his head slowly.

'We gotta talk ...' Gus said.

John Delmar put his pen down and looked out the window.

'Sure, Gus, but I can't let you near Rand.' The sheriff nodded to his cell block. 'There's a transfer team comin' from Albuquerque tomorrow, then it'll be outta my hands. I'm doin' this by the law, Gus.'

Gus looked behind him, through the window. Two Rangers crossed the road to the plaza and measured out a position. Gus followed them and studied their movements, as if he was trying to clarify something he was already sure of but had not the final courage of his convictions to act upon. 'I ain't here for that.' Gus looked around him and then rubbed his face. 'What are them Rangers here for?' he said then.

John Delmar rubbed his palms together, fingers entwined.

'Government business, Gus. I can't say more. There's a train due here any minute now, for a very special cargo. Those boys are here to make sure it gets to the right place.'

'How special?' Gus asked.

'I don't know,' his father said. He went back to his writing, more because he could not bear to watch his son's hangover than because there was work to do. 'I don't get told everythin'.'

'Well, they sure as hell know,' Gus Delmar said after some thought. 'They're Germans.'

John Delmar's face lost and regained its colour twice. He scratched the stubble on his face.

20

John Delmar composed himself and pulled his mouth from the telephone and replaced it with his hand. 'They're who they say they are,' he said to his son. 'Colonel on the end of this line is askin' me to give your name, rank and number, Gus. You took him from a golf game. I'll say you're gone.'

'I shot myself, Pa,' Gus said to his father again. 'I watched that captain out there slit Ira Stern's throat and I did nothin'. Then I watched him and his men blow six tanks to hell and I did nothin'. And then I shot myself. You think I'd make that up. They're Krauts. Gimme the telephone.'

But John Delmar put the telephone down. 'Look, son,' he said, 'you've been under a terrible strain. You may think you've seen that captain before, you may even believe it. But it's the hurt you suffered ... And now Eadie ...'

Both men could feel the vibrations of a railway engine entering Los Muertos when Andy Redrow came into the jailhouse.

Redrow came into the office with a gust of wind and the accompanying dust, panting. 'My goddam telephone is dead, John. I been tryin' to get a line to Albuquerque for ten minutes ... can't get a thing. Same with Zach Pepper. And them Rangers has the town blocked off. No one's allowed out. Now I know somethin's goin' on down the station, but what the hell are they doin'?'

Gus Delmar took in what the mayor had said almost in slow

motion, as if he were an observer, calculations flowing through his head like streams dribbling together to make a river and the river building to full flood. He instinctively picked up the telephone receiver across the desk, listened, then replaced it and sat back in the small chair. He swung round to see his father pointing a .38 revolver at him. 'I wouldn't move if I were you either, Andy.'

At the same time, the small plutonium convoy of two jeeps and two Ford sedans that had left Los Alamos earlier that morning approached the Santavista Gap, breaking slowly because of the winding nature of the road and the drop to the river below. And as the road began to climb towards Los Muertos, the vehicles' speed decreased even more, something the drivers were used to.

To their left and right were small cactus fields buffering the red and brown cliffs and the drop to the river was planted with strong skeletal trees and cacti and was darker than the cliffs.

The lead jeep in the convoy, with four military policemen in it, had to drop another gear to climb the curve to the edge of Los Muertos and the pencil lane to the railway station.

Then Kyle Stuart stepped out of cover.

The driver of the lead jeep in the convoy braked, skidding on the sand and dirty gravel, leaving the marks of his tyres in the road, and one of the military policemen in the back of the jeep almost fell out. His companions had to put their weapons down to prevent him, and the sedan behind them almost hit his head before it stopped in a slow skid.

Only the second sedan hesitated before stopping. It hit the car in front of it, and the last jeep had to swerve to the left and on to a bank. Its wheels stuck in a mud rut.

Immediately afterwards, Thomas Heuzer moved a jeep in behind the convoy, cutting off its retreat. Larry Schwartz cocked the machine gun on the back.

Kyle Stuart leaned into the passenger side of the lead jeep

in the plutonium convoy. 'United States Rangers. I'm afraid there's been an incident.'

The fat military police captain on the passenger side of the lead jeep in the stalled plutonium convoy, a man of about fifty with shocks of grey in his hair and a smell of aftershave and body odour, leaned out towards Kyle Stuart.

'Incident?' he asked.

If a man approaches you, dressed as you are, speaking your tongue, and tells you the sky is falling, you look up. The fat military police captain looked over at the diesel engine parked at the railway station and then back at Kyle Stuart's sub-machine gun. Then he looked back past the two sedans and the rear jeep and saw Thomas Heuzer and Larry Schwartz, and to the right Charlie Race and Vernon Kell pointing carbines at the sedans. And Pierre was kneeling with a bazooka on his shoulder on the other side of the road.

Andy Redrow's smile was his automatic reaction to a crisis. Then he became officious. 'Sheriff, what the hell's goin' on?'

John Delmar hit him with the handle of his revolver and the mayor fell back across the concrete floor and hit his head on the brick wall. 'I've been wantin' to do that for years,' John Delmar whispered. 'Ignorant bastard. Now you get down to the cell block, Gus. Just do as I say and you'll be fine.'

'You!' Gus Delmar finally came out with what was the closest thing to the feelings he had. He wanted to move, might have attempted to move if he had not been so crippled, but could not move because of the implications of what he had just witnessed.

'I can't explain it, Gus. Not now,' his father said.

They moved down into the cold of the small cell block below the back of the jailhouse, Gus Delmar dragging the semi-conscious and bleeding mayor along the floor and down the steps, the mayor asking inane questions of John Delmar, losing his dignity in the bottomless well of the truth he had discovered, and then trying to pick himself up and maintain his official front. John Delmar fumbled to find the right keys while keeping his weapon pointed at his son. In the end, he gave the keys to his son and told him to open the cell.

Philip Rand was standing at his cell door, demanding to know what was going on. John Delmar drove the barrel of his revolver through the small bars in the wooden door and told Rand to lie on his bed, face down.

'I suppose you're gonna kill me,' Gus challenged his father.

'No, Gus, no,' his father said. He still held the gun up but his mind was not in control of it any longer. 'No, son ...'

'What's happening?' Philip Rand shouted.

'You shut your mouth,' John Delmar said.

'My father's a ...' Gus Delmar could not get the word out. 'There's Rangers in town,' he said. 'They're Germans. Come to steal somethin'.' He stared at his father. 'Somethin' very special.'

'It's for a bomb,' Andy Redrow said. 'And they say it can wipe out cities.' Now he looked at John Delmar. 'I heard talk up in Santa Fe.'

'Now you have to kill all three of us, Pa,' Gus said.

John Delmar struck his son across the head and knocked him over Andy Redrow right as Redrow was managing to lift his large body from the floor again. 'You ignorant bastard,' John Delmar said to his son. 'War hero! I'm the goddam war hero here. I'm the goddam ...' He could not complete his sentence.

Thomas Heuzer gave a command and his men shot out every tyre in all four vehicles they were covering.

The fat military police captain with the shock of grey and the aftershave and body odour smell touched his leather sidearm holster. But it was closed. Kyle Stuart did him the favour of glancing at the Thompson sub-machine gun beside his seat. The fat captain put his hands on his head. The two military policemen in the back of the lead jeep lowered their weapons.

'If you co-operate, no one will be hurt,' Stuart said. 'You understand, Captain? But any other moves and you get it first, sir.'

Then the back door of the rear sedan opened and a reserved, bespectacled and freckled slab of a man stepped out. 'My name is Dr Ashton, Silas Ashton. What we carry, and you seek, is my responsibility, Lieutenant.'

Simon Penny slipped round behind Ashton, put a gun to his head, and pulled a small box from the rear seat of the sedan. 'Then you won't mind us relieving you of your responsibility,' he said.

Heuzer did the same with the back-seat occupant of the other car.

In the distance, he could see the outline of a huge rainstorm descending on the plain of west Texas.

John Delmar had Philip Rand kneeling against the far wall of his cell with his hands on his head. His son backed into the cell in shuffled steps.

'You never did understand, Gus. Always one step behind. Your precious Eadie . . . she was damn worthless.' John Delmar almost apologised to Andy Redrow. 'Always goin' with the wrong ones, always makin' a fool of the right ones. Well, maybe she got what was comin' to her, got it surely as if God hisself had ordained it. I'm sorry but I had to say that, Andy.'

'You killed her,' Philip Rand said very softly.

'You say another word, Lieutenant, it'll be your last.' John Delmar shook his head. 'Kneel down beside him, Gus.' The sheriff turned back to Andy Redrow. 'I didn't kill her, Andy.'

'For God's sake, John, you're an American,' Andy Redrow said. 'What the hell are you doin'?'

Delmar made the mayor come into the cell on his knees. 'Am I an American?' he asked the mayor. 'I always did resent bein' named for an Italian adventurer. Apache. Chiracaua. Cheyenne. Now they are good names. Noble names. Names founded in tradition. Not somethin' drawn up by a public relations firm. And his name was Amerigo, not America. Vespucci. You couldn't even get that right. See my skin, son? See any red in it? No, I bet you don't. I bet if you looked for a lifetime you would not see any red. And I used to be so proud of that, so proud of no red and so proud of the whiteness ... proud to the point of shame. America! The misspelt name of an Italian liar. He never went half the places he said. Vespucci. An invention of convenience. This whole damn country's a convenience store.'

'You don't have to do this, Sheriff,' Andy Redrow said.

'I saw men die in the cold when I was young. They had no food and their souls had fled.'

'Well, I'm not gonna let you kill me down here like a dog on the street, John,' Andy Redrow said. 'I'm gettin' up.' He pulled himself up.

'Get down!' Delmar said. He went to strike Andy Redrow across the back of the head but Redrow moved faster than he should have. He brought his leg across the back of Delmar's knee and the sheriff stumbled back against the wall. Redrow threw himself on John Delmar, with a fury he did not know he possessed, and knocked the sheriff across the small metal bed. Gus dived on his father right as Andy Redrow hit his head on the bed and ran out of steam.

The struggle moved across the floor, Gus Delmar and his father fighting for the revolver which seemed to slide with each of their movements, Andy Redrow now devoid of any momentum he had built up. Philip Rand took his place.

Rand grabbed John Delmar from behind and should have been able to hold him, but Rand mistimed his hold and the big sheriff was able to throw the soldier. The following kick winded Rand. Gus then rolled away to the left and tried to reach the gun, but John Delmar got to him just as he was picking the gun up.

Delmar punched his son in the back of the neck. The gun fell from his hand. The sheriff picked it up. And in that moment, Gus knew he was dead. Philip Rand tried to stop it. John Delmar tried not to shoot his son. But before he could control himself, he had stepped back and pulled the trigger. He shot his son through the chest.

It did not feel like he had been shot and Gus managed to pick himself up and say something about Eadie Shaffer before he slumped to the floor in a heap.

The sheriff swung the gun at Rand.

But Andy Redrow had recovered himself. He shoved the metal bed at John Delmar and Philip Rand pitched himself forward at waist height and hit the sheriff right in the centre of his body, forcing him off balance. Delmar fell back against the open door and out into the corridor. Redrow collapsed and Rand followed the sheriff and hit him again.

Delmar levelled his gun at the same time.

The first shot from the jailhouse caused most of what was happening at the railway station to slow. Kyle Stuart lifted his hand from the fat military police captain he was frisking, and other men turned their heads, but Simon Penny and Thomas Heuzer kept staring into the two small boxes they had taken from the sedans, each containing a metal hemisphere, warm and coated in nickel and gold, and the draw of these was enough to distract a man from a gunshot.

It took the second shot from the jailhouse to distract them.

Heuzer looked around for a few seconds, trying to determine where the shots had come from, then at Silas Ashton, whose previous calm had begun to desert him now. Simon Penny was already moving back up towards the plaza, shouting at Harry Pellicer and Dave Menton at the eastern end of Los Muertos to cover him. Menton, who was sitting near a pump at the small gas station, smoking, dropped the cigarette, then came back to stamp it out before running towards the jailhouse.

Kyle Stuart barked an order and Larry Schwartz took Jimmy Mitchell with him up the other side of the street.

When Simon Penny got to the jailhouse, Andy Redrow was lying over John Delmar, whispering into his ear. John Delmar's lips were moving and he was trying to touch his dead son across the floor. Penny pulled Redrow off the sheriff.

'For heaven's sake, the man killed his son,' Redrow said. 'He killed his son.'

Penny leaned down to John Delmar's lips and listened.

'What's he sayin'?' Kyle Stuart asked.

'A prayer,' Penny said. 'He's saying a prayer.'

21

'When did this come in?' Jeff Francis put his coffee cup at the corner of the table and looked at the telex.

'I don't know. Director wants you now, though.' The young agent in front of Francis was salivating from the side of his mouth and pushing his hand through his curly hair in a nervous action. 'There's a plane at your disposal,' he said. 'Santa Fe's been alerted. But it'll take them some time. And whatever lines there are in that area are down.'

Francis looked at his watch and then the telex, then slammed his hand down on the table and knocked his coffee cup off. 'Jesus!' He paced up and down the room and slowly nodded his head. Then he leaned back from the table and held his hands together. He noticed how the veins protruded and how much his hands shook. By accident, he let his fingers touch the pulse point on his wrist. It was remarkably slow. 'Jesus Christ!' he said very softly.

While a gathering of grey clouds threw threatening hail at the dry walls, teasing the fragile fissures in the flaking aridity of the clay, and a dead dog lay in the middle of the main street swelling by degrees, the shadows began to increase their length, and the thick stumps now pointing from the Santavista Gap began to stretch out towards the singular pool of fading light in the centre of Los Muertos.

Thomas Heuzer's men had rounded up the thirty-five civilians left in the town that afternoon and sat them down on the verdant mat surrounding the bandstand in the plaza. The town's cultural budget, Andy Redrow once called it.

To their left, the fat captain and his military policemen lay face down in the middle of the street, their hands spread.

Silas Ashton, who had been granted the privilege of sitting with his legs crossed, had managed to regain some of the calm he had lost when the shooting started at the jailhouse. He cleaned his glasses with rainwater. 'I take it that you are familiar with the substance in those boxes,' he said to Heuzer, gesturing at the two plutonium containers placed behind the jeep to his right.

'As I need be,' Heuzer replied. 'Doctor ...' Heuzer had to look at his notebook to remember the scientist's name. '... Ashton.' Heuzer grinned, as much to relieve his own growing tension as anything to do with the small talk he was making. 'I want none of us in a grave.'

Ashton shifted his legs and pulled his hands from his head, looking at Heuzer to see if he had permission. When Heuzer did not object, Ashton pulled out a pipe and began cleaning it with small blades from the scarce grass. His pipe dropped to the grass.

Thomas Heuzer leaned down and handed the pipe to him. 'I have no desire to harm innocents.' He sounded more genuine than Ashton was comfortable with, and the German's expression only made the scientist want to co-operate, something that shocked him. But the difficulty in maintaining distance was immense.

For Heuzer, the difficulty began and ended with the dead body of Gus Delmar and the feeling that, for the first time in his life, there might be forces at work over which he could exert no control.

'But you propose to use it,' Ashton said, 'the plutonium?'

'And you did not?' Heuzer replied. 'I too have family and friends, Doctor. I would quote Shylock's speech on the nature of being a Jew in *The Merchant of Venice* if I could remember it. Don't worry, I appreciate the irony of a German using a Jew as a metaphor. Perhaps you might recall the speech for me. And if you would keep your hands behind your head, I will not have to shoot you. I am a soldier, not a murderer.'

Andy Redrow's coming out of the jailhouse prevented the conversation going any further. He was holding his arm and his eyes stared past the horizon. He made an attempt to swing at Billy Watkins. Watkins' carbine caught him under the ribs and sent him down on to the street. Redrow almost looked disappointed when Watkins did not shoot.

Kyle Stuart shoved his pistol into Redrow's mouth, while Watkins and Menton held him down on the grass. 'You have just used up all nine of your lives, Mayor,' Stuart informed Redrow. 'Now, I am a patient man, but I have my limits. You would do everyone a favour by co-operatin'.'

Redrow's anger once again gave way to his politics, and he relaxed. A small trickle of blood ran from his mouth. Stuart patted him on the head, something Heuzer noted.

Then Heuzer called out the names and one by one individuals and families took the positions assigned to them. Once in a while a white man or woman objected to being placed beside hispanics. When Heuzer or one of his men forced the issue with a gun, the complaints were usually dropped.

'You will kill yourself and your men,' Ashton said to Heuzer then. 'And many others around you.'

'Just what is that stuff they have, Andy?' Zach Pepper asked his mayor. Pepper was wheezing from fear and his shoulder had drooped so far it looked like he might fall over. But like most of the people there, his main emotion was confusion. When he looked at Silas Ashton for an explanation, others joined in, as much to keep their nerves as from curiosity. Ashton refused to tell them. Redrow wanted to speak but felt he would be betraying something if he did.

'It is an explosive,' Heuzer said slowly, moving his hands as if to emphasise his own power, something he suspected might do the exact opposite for him, 'and a quantity the size of an orange can destroy a city. Powerful medicine, as the Indians say.' He glanced over at the body of Gus Delmar, lying across the street with his father's, in two canvas tarpaulins. Some of their blood was trickling into the sand on the street. 'And we're borrowing it,' he said. 'Our need is greater. But it is for your benefit, too, I assure you.'

Andy Redrow dipped his head and Thomas Heuzer ordered his prisoners to file into the jailhouse.

'I don't think they fully believe you, Herr Hauptmann,' Karl Peiper said to Heuzer. 'Or perhaps they think we will kill them.'

'Perhaps they see how close they have come to death already, Karl,' Heuzer replied. He looked at the Delmars again.

'We're not Russians,' Peiper said to his prisoners. 'Now, if we were Ivans you would be dead. Right, Herr Hauptmann?'

'We are doing you a favour,' Heuzer said to Silas Ashton when he was being led away to John Delmar's cells. 'We will stop the Russians for you.' He strolled across to the nearest jeep and picked up the field radio handset.

Karl Peiper led Harry Pellicer and Steve Harris on a final search of Los Muertos for any stragglers left over. They shot another dog and found an old hispanic man dead in a corner of someone's yard.

The sun made a last effort to scatter the cloud as Heuzer came out of the jailhouse into the plaza. Stuart's men were drawn up around their jeeps. Heuzer looked at Stuart for a moment.

'What's the matter, Herr Hauptmann,' Stuart asked. 'Going too smoothly?'

'You sent the second message to Vogl?' Heuzer asked.

'Everythin's ready. I just wish I could leave a more permanent mark. Some day, perhaps.' Stuart looked at one of the small boxes on the floor of Heuzer's jeep. 'Hard to believe such a small thing can be the source of such great power.' He lit a cigarette, then ordered engines started. 'It's gonna rain heavy before dark.'

'Homesick?' Heuzer asked.

'Southerners err on the side of sentimentality,' he said to Heuzer. 'To a fault. Sometimes I cannot answer my own questions.'

'Then don't ask them,' Heuzer said. 'Your men have performed well, Teniente.'

'Let's go, Herr Hauptmann, all this Yankee hospitality is beginnin' to stretch my patience.' Stuart climbed into the passenger seat of a jeep and Billy Watkins started the engine.

Jimmy Mitchell pulled the first jeep out of the plaza, Larry Schwartz sitting beside him. They headed for the railway station. Watkins and Stuart followed, with Race and Kell in the back. They were covered by Harris on the thirty-calibre in the back of the first jeep, while Karl Peiper moved off about twenty seconds later with Pierre and Murphy in the back and Heuzer in the passenger seat, both boxes of plutonium at his feet.

That was when Simon Penny pulled a hard right and skidded up from the Santavista Gap in John Delmar's car. He threw the car right across Stuart's path. Stuart and Heuzer's jeeps stopped.

'It's gone!' Penny said. 'The plane's gone. Dasch and Heinck, too.'

All the anger Thomas Heuzer had ever felt exploded at precisely the same moment Jimmy Mitchell, driving the lead jeep, fell back and then slumped forward over his steering wheel.

Heuzer shouted a warning.

Bullet holes skipped across the window of Mitchell's jeep in a tight pattern. A third burst tore the window apart and killed Jimmy Mitchell, his small chiselled docker's face turning a soft pale shade as the jeep slowed, then built up speed and rolled off the road into a ditch.

The next burst of gunfire hit Simon Penny's car. Penny dived out just before the petrol tank exploded. Bullets punctured Kyle Stuart's right-hand tyres, then smashed his windscreen. Stuart's men fell out of the jeep. And then the firing was solid.

Behind Stuart, Thomas Heuzer shouted at Karl Peiper to reverse. The blond sergeant was already shoving the gear stick into position while Pierre loosed off a burst from his thirty-calibre in the direction he thought the incoming fire had originated. Heuzer watched his windscreen crack and then shatter, and Peiper took a round in the shoulder.

The sergeant pressed his foot down harder on the pedal and the jeep shot back towards the other side of the street. Another round hit Peiper in the leg.

Heuzer saw a head move on the roof of the railway station. He shouted at Pierre and fired himself, and their bullets knocked pieces of the corner off the left of the building but missed whoever was there.

Pierre rolled off the back of the jeep, Albert Murphy took his position on the thirty-calibre and Heuzer grabbed the two plutonium boxes between his legs and pulled Peiper from the driver's seat.

Pierre shot away a lock and kicked a door open and Murphy opened fire on the railway station again. Then Pierre and Heuzer covered Murphy while he unhooked the machine gun from the back of the jeep and gathered up the ammunition belts. Heuzer grabbed a bag of grenades and Pierre rescued a bazooka strapped to the side of the vehicle. Bullets tore lumps out of the jeep. And then its engine exploded.

Directly across the street, Kyle Stuart called for cover from Heuzer and emptied a full magazine from a BAR in the direction of more firing from the overhanging cliffs behind him. Charlie Race and Vernon Kell grabbed all the weaponry and ammunition they could while Billy Watkins covered them from behind Simon Penny's burning car, and Kyle Stuart kicked his way into a house.

Once in, he fired a supporting burst while Race and Kell made their way back from the cover of the jeep, and then three of them broke their way through to the next building, the Los Muertos foodstore, and Billy Watkins covered them from the splintered doorway of the house Stuart had broken into.

With a third storey, the foodstore was the tallest building in Los Muertos. Stuart knocked a hole in the wall of the small house and then passed weapons and ammunition through to Kell and Race, before covering Watkins, who was grazed in the shoulder now and had to be pulled through the hole in the wall.

Then, as suddenly as it had begun, the firing stopped.

22

Every one of Warren Brett's men had wasted the ammunition in their weapons. One of the men next to Brett had caught his finger in his own weapon and taken part of it off.

'Can you see them?' Brett called out to Philip Rand on the radio. Brett was busy reloading a carbine himself and checking the grenades in his pockets, and when he picked up his binoculars, he dropped a grenade at the same time. Two of the men next to him held their breath.

'Three on the foodstore roof, maybe four, but they have cover,' Rand replied. He was in position on the hills south of Los Muertos, between some tall trees and a low trench running along the line of the hills. The hills were brown and the trees splintered the cold evening sunshine.

'What do we do now?' Warren Brett asked. 'Go in after 'em? My God, did you see that? My God ... what's your situation?' He tried to spot Rand across on the higher hills among the trees and the cacti, but the shadows and trenches made it impossible.

'One dead, two wounded,' Rand said. 'One of the wounded is in a bad way ... but don't move, Warren. As long as they can't get out, we're doing our job. Stay put, reload. Try and get some more people down near that railway station. There's four of them down that way, I think, can you see them? And put heavy machine gun fire into that foodstore. But no one else move. Just shoot anything that moves down there.'

Warren Brett pulled out his canteen and watched the New Mexico sun drag itself across the last quarter of the daytime sky. Then there were vultures, ominous blotches on the blue canvas, and Brett felt the terror of thought again.

Below him, Thomas Heuzer picked up a damaged cup from the floor and realised he was in someone's living room. It was small and dark and there were candles on a mantelpiece and various pieces of fruit had fallen from a bowl. The domesticity caused an extension of the silence among the men lying on the carpet among the flakes of baked mud and untreated pine, choking on the cordite and wiping their eyes. Heuzer crawled over to Karl Peiper. Blood ran from Peiper's shoulder wound in a straight line along one of the exposed floorboards to a wall.

'I should ask what happened, Herr Hauptmann. But I'm afraid to.'

Heuzer kept his voice low and spoke in German. 'The gods,' he said to Peiper. 'The gods.'

For a few moments, he seemed paralysed. Then Heuzer noticed all the eyes in the room were riveted on him and Kyle Stuart was calling for directions on the hand radio around Albert Murphy's neck.

The small field next to the ditch where Jimmy Mitchell's jeep had rolled was planted thick with cacti and elephant grass. Larry Schwartz led the survivors of this jeep along the ditch and then up an embankment. 'Teniente, cover!' he yelled to Stuart. Then they made a run for the railway station.

Fire came in from three directions, including the station, forcing Schwartz back down into the ditch. He returned fire, called for cover again, then moved up to the road, this time supported by Harris and Menton. Pellicer went wide of them and he and Schwartz made a run for the train station, splitting the incoming fire. Menton and Harris then turned their weapons on the small yellow hills immediately across the river.

Five engineers jumped up and moved along the crest of the hills, flickers among the thin trees and white scars, firing intermittently. One of them hit Stephen Harris in the shoulder.

But Larry Schwartz made it to the station.

For a moment, it looked like he would be killed, but Brett's two engineers on the station roof came up from their cover to open fire on him. It was a crucial error.

Menton and Pellicer drove them back, Schwartz yelled for cover and Stuart's team across on the foodstore roof killed the two engineers.

Then Schwartz threw a grenade into the train station, shot his way in and climbed on to the roof. Another engineer lay dying on the stairs while Schwartz provided cover for his own men as they ran through the cactus plants and the elephant grass.

Pellicer and Menton made it first, took cover against one of the walls, identified an enemy firing position to the south, and covered Harris. But Harris was hit again, in the leg, from two sides, and Menton had to run out and drag him the last ten yards.

'Jesus, I thought we had it,' Harris said. 'I thought we had it.'

Across the street, Kyle Stuart put his head above the stone parapet of the foodstore roof and tried to spot Brett's engineers, position by position on the north side of the river. 'I need someone to move,' he said.

But no one volunteered.

Thomas Heuzer tried to stem the flow of blood from Peiper's shoulder while issuing commands, but neither the improvised dressing nor the commands were of any use in their situation, and all he could do then was watch the blood pass through Karl Peiper's fingers in ugly uncontrolled spurts and listen to Kyle Stuart's assessment of their position.

'Race has the medical kit,' Peiper said. 'Stupid bastard.'

Heuzer looked at Pierre. 'I need someone to get the medical kit,' he said.

Pierre almost put up a fight, but Heuzer's expression stopped him. If Heuzer had lost anything in the previous few minutes, he was regaining it. And Pierre was his first victim.

Pierre pulled himself out of his cover and shouted at Stuart in Spanish, while Albert Murphy reloaded to provide cover.

Pierre then swore at Heuzer, shook his hand and slipped a magazine into an automatic rifle. 'Wish me luck.'

Heuzer nodded.

Pierre counted, then kicked the door open, shouted for cover, fired left and right, and started running. He was hit from four sides, dropped, pulled himself up, dropped again, rolled over, fired, shouted for support, then tried to raise himself and fell on his face in the middle of the street.

Stuart's shouts at the dead Pierre echoed around the street. And for some minutes after that, there was silence again.

Thomas Heuzer kept staring at the plutonium containers across the floor as if they might give him an answer to all the questions he had. 'I suppose they know what's in them,' he said.

'You will appreciate that what we are attempting to steal is not at the front of my mind, Herr Hauptmann,' Karl Peiper said. 'It's not such a bad feeling, dying, I would have thought it more frightening. However, it offends my sensibilities to die here. Frustrating. That's the problem with death, it's a frustration rather than a fear. I feel very lightheaded. Probably just as well I'm not going home. It's such a mess.'

He closed his eyes just as Simon Penny entered through the back door. Penny was filthy and carrying a carbine and some grenades.

'I thought you were dead . . . or gone,' Heuzer said.

'I tried,' Penny said, smiling.

'Situation?' Heuzer asked.

'We're in a pot and the heat's being turned up,' Penny said. 'They're on both sides, and down at the gas station.'

'So, we can't stay here.' Heuzer put his head above the window, fired a burst at the hills above him and asked Stuart on the roof of the foodstore if he could see what came back. 'We need that medical aid over here, Teniente,' Heuzer said to Stuart then. 'Can you help us?'

'Give us time ... we're watchin' for movement,' Stuart replied.

'I suggest we act now to save ourselves, Herr Hauptmann,' Penny said, 'or start using our cyanide pills. The cavalry will be along in no time, as they say.'

'The jail,' Murphy said, anticipating Penny's next words. 'Thick walls and a bridge over the river behind it.' He fired a burst and ducked while the engineers around him replied in kind. 'And a shitload of Yankee civilians.'

'Remind me to recommend you for a decoration and pay rise,' Heuzer said to Murphy, and when Heuzer smiled, Murphy smiled and the confidence which had started to come from Heuzer again began to rebound on everyone in his presence. 'Clearly, if we stay put, we're finished. And since we cannot move out at them, we have to draw them into us. How long before darkness?'

Philip Rand positioned himself behind a pair of rocks known as Santavista's eyes, the strangest petrified shape he had ever seen, and watched the sun begin to lose interest in the day.

He watched the horizon bend beneath the deepening blue of the sky. Far away, there was white sand and animals that looked like horses.

'There are eighty MPs on the road, Philip,' Brett said. 'Do your hear that? Eighty snowdrops. They say twenty to thirty minutes, Philip.' Warren Brett's voice had a degree of panic which concerned Rand. 'You think we can hold them for twenty minutes, Philip? It's getting damned grey. And the weather's gettin' bad out there.'

'Sure we can hold them for twenty minutes, Warren,' Rand replied.

'What if they start killing civilians?' Brett asked. 'You hear about that. Germans kill civilians.'

'They won't.'

'That sheriff, Philip,' Brett said then. 'I knew he was a bastard, Philip. I knew it. I was coming for you, you know.' The excitement in Brett's voice was threatening to upset the whole engineer position. Every one of his men could hear the fear of their commanding officer.

'Sure you were, Warren.' Philip Rand moved from position to position along the ridge, encouraging his men, checking ammunition levels, examining the wounded, making sure the men drank, moving them around. And when one or two of them asked why they did not attack, Rand shook his head. 'We don't have to,' he said. 'They're rabbits in a hole. We just wait for the ferrets.'

When he had called Master Sergeant Bobby Helm at the gas station, he sat down and wet his mouth and watched the sun die a little more.

23

The long fingers of the evening pointed east along the main street of Los Muertos, bisecting the plaza and cloaking the buildings on the north side of the street in a lazy shade.

The houses on the north side of the main street were all one-storey constructions, tucked into the low hills before the river. The hills on that side went up at shallow angles, but after the river they were suddenly steep, which meant you could not come down from positions above the river without going round by a small road.

Heuzer and Penny picked Peiper up between them and dragged him to the east wall of the house they were in. Penny took a crowbar and went to work on the bricks. When the hole was big enough, Penny went through. Then Heuzer shoved Peiper through and picked up the two plutonium boxes and passed them to Penny before coming through himself.

Albert Murphy left a grenade and tripwire at the front door, then one at the back door, and finally, after he pulled his thirty-calibre machine gun through the hole in the wall, he left a grenade and wire there, too.

They passed through three connected buildings like this and Murphy booby-trapped each one in the same way. Heuzer and Penny widened a final hole in the wall of a building which had once been a post office, and Penny slipped his head out into the evening shadow of a small lane.

The lane provided cover enough for him to slide along the wall to the junction with the main street. Heuzer carried Peiper. Murphy brought up the rear.

As soon as Heuzer moved, Murphy stood up, threw himself around the corner, fired a sustained burst at the ridges to the south of town, caught two engineers out in the open and killed them.

On top of the foodstore Stuart and Kell fired rifle grenades at Warren Brett's positions to the north, and Watkins and Race poured several magazines at Philip Rand's men, while from the roof of the railway station, Larry Schwartz's team fired at both engineer positions in the hills and then rolled off, one by one. Harris had to be held up.

'Tell me my wounds are not serious, Brigada,' he said to Schwartz. 'Like they used to in Russia before a man died.'

Schwartz patted Harris's shoulder. 'I hope you can run,' he said. 'Otherwise we're leavin' you.' The Texan grinned and showed his missing fingers. 'There's soon gonna be more of me lyin' around than on me.'

Then Simon Penny launched a rifle grenade at the engineer positions near the gas station. It exploded in the middle of the street. Heuzer moved from the lane with Karl Peiper on his back and the two plutonium boxes in his hands.

Heuzer made the jailhouse as Penny poured sub-machine gun fire down the street at three of Bobby Helms's men running from the explosion of his second grenade. Murphy supported Penny, then ducked into cover while Stuart's men supported him. Heuzer was already inside the jail when Penny dived through the doorway. And Charlie Race fell from the foodstore.

When Albert Murphy had made it to the plaza, Stuart yelled at Larry Schwartz to move.

The sergeant ran forward, carrying Harris, loosing off short bursts at Philip Rand's men on the south ridges. Then Menton and Pellicer moved. Pellicer got to the middle of the street where

Schwartz had changed direction. Pellicer followed suit but fell. Menton tried to get to him, backed off, then tried again. He was driven back by fire from Warren Brett's men on the north side of the Vibora.

Schwartz and Harris dived through the broken window of Pepper's bar, then shouted at Menton to follow. But the firing from the hills was so intense now even Stuart's men were forced under cover on the foodstore roof. Several more shots hit Pellicer in the middle of the street as Menton was making another attempt to get to him. Menton rolled into the cover of a low arch. He lay on the ground about twenty yards from Harris and Schwartz, picking pieces of wood from his body, trying to reload his weapon. 'Tell the Teniente I resign,' he said.

'What's happening?' Warren Brett called to Philip Rand over the radio. He was trying to help with a wounded man and keep his own men from leaving their positions and moving forward. The reception on the radio was not helping his state of mind.

'They're not moving, Warren,' Rand insisted. 'Just everyone stay where they are. Helm!'

There was a moment of crackle, then the master sergeant came on the radio. 'We've got five down, sir ... three more wounded. We need support.'

'Jesus!' Warren Brett came in. 'Pull out of there, Sergeant.'

'No, don't move!' Rand yelled. 'Warren, get a section down there. And just hold your ground. Warren ...'

Sitting on the stone floor of John Delmar's jailhouse, next to the pine cupboard Rosalyn Delmar had given her husband as a wedding present, Thomas Heuzer stared at the plutonium containers again, until his attention was caught by a low moan from the cells below. Then a child's cry released him. 'I'm expecting them to say something,' he said. 'Those boxes.'

Karl Peiper, slowly slipping out of consciousness, watched

Heuzer, then the boxes. 'As you said, powerful medicine, Herr Hauptmann,' he said. 'Just not the right kind.'

'We have to do something about this,' Albert Murphy said, watching the blood continue to ooze from Peiper's shoulder wound, occasionally picking pieces of splintered bloodied bone from the coagulating hole. 'Tell me they've gone,' he said to Simon Penny.

Simon Penny watched the street. It was a twisted twilight scene, coloured by the moon and a few small fires at the east end of Los Muertos. Then static brought Kyle Stuart's voice on to the hand radio.

'I hate to be the bearer of bad tidings . . .' Kyle Stuart's voice sounded almost amused. '. . . I think the cavalry has arrived.' Three Dodge trucks full of military police were moving behind a halftrack from the Santavista Gap. Kyle Stuart just lay on the roof of the foodstore and watched the vehicles approach. And behind them, the sun was settling down to rest, shimmering on the faint line of the horizon.

24

Warren Brett could not conceal his relief when the mustachioed military police colonel took his hand. Norman Rogers was an old National Guard officer Brett had met at a couple of social functions in Albuquerque. Roger's family owned a ranch near the Arizona border and his own personality seemed to reflect the landscape there somehow. He could not help looking just that bit too long at the black soldiers around the major of engineers.

'You can pull your men back now, Major,' Rogers said when he had studied the small map Brett showed him. 'My boys'll handle it from here.' It was curt and, if Brett had not secretly welcomed it, he might have been offended. Rogers, who called all his men by their first names, then directed two of his officers to begin organising the withdrawal.

Warren Brett thought he should at least put up a protest. He pointed out that his men had handled the situation very professionally, citing individual acts of courage.

'Do you know what they have down there, Major?' Rogers asked with the mannered tones of a large western rancher who is convinced of his own ability. 'Now please begin withdrawin' your men.' He thought for a moment. 'And thank you.'

Brett was going to say something else when a young military policeman, with a helmet that was too big for him, came running up the dry hillside. He saluted the officers and extended his arm. 'White flag, Colonel. Comin' outta the town.'

Norman Rogers turned the field glasses on the lonely sight of Silas Ashton moving up the main street of Los Muertos.

In the jailhouse, Albert Murphy brought Andy Redrow up from the cells. Karl Peiper sat in one corner, while Simon Penny read Iago Santavista's confession with one hand and loaded a magazine with the other.

'Now, before you inform me of the hopelessness of my situation,' Heuzer said to Redrow, 'I am pleased to counter that what I have in those boxes will send everyone within two miles – and I mean everyone – to wherever their fantasies will imagine. And that includes your town.'

'My only concern is the safety of the people down there,' Redrow said. His dignity as he pointed to the cells impressed Heuzer at a moment when the German had hoped to have the upper hand.

'So perhaps we can help each other,' Heuzer said. He turned to his wounded sergeant. 'How are you, Karl?' he asked.

'Not great, Thomas, actually.' Peiper closed his eyes.

'He'll die if he doesn't get to a hospital,' Redrow said. 'You'll all die here.'

'And you?' Heuzer replied. 'Somehow I think the American Government is far more concerned by the loss of several kilos of explosive plutonium than a few cowboys and their families. What do you think, Mr Redrow?'

Redrow sat back, silenced.

'Don't worry, Mayor,' Simon Penny said. 'He'll only kill you if he absolutely has to. Right, Herr Hauptmann?' Penny threw Heuzer a bullet.

Norman Rogers picked fine pieces of grit, accumulated during the journey to Los Muertos, from his moustache while he read the single sheet of paper handed to him by Silas Ashton. Ashton was using his own white handkerchief to clean his face and watching the last of the sun struggle to maintain itself above the mountains to the west.

'Is detonation possible?' Rogers asked Ashton.

Ashton looked back at the pencil outlines of the town. There were two small fires at the east end and their flames broke the monotony every few seconds. 'What they have down there is sub-critical. That means it needs to be forced together at great pressure and speed to increase ...'

'Don't give me the physics,' Rogers interrupted. 'Can he do it?'

'It should not be possible,' Ashton said after some thought. 'They don't appear to have an initiator. That's what sets it all going. But if they do ...'

'You can't guarantee it?' Rogers said. 'Where the hell does this Kraut think he's gonna go to? Every military base from here to the coasts has been alerted by now. There's enough men descending on this place to fight a small war.'

'I am the messenger, Colonel,' Ashton said. 'That's all.'

'Will he do it?' Rogers asked then. He looked at his watch before Ashton could reply. And now his expression was that of a man slipping rapidly out of his depth. 'I need more men,' he said to himself. 'Where the hell are they? Where the hell are those FBI agents I was promised?'

Squatting on the stone floor in John Delmar's jailhouse, Andy Redrow looked at his watch, too. 'That bullet nicked an artery, I'll bet,' he said to Karl Peiper. 'Yeah, that's the truth. An artery. I seen it before. You know what that means?'

'No way,' Peiper said. 'My luck's better than that. I'm a lucky man, right, Herr Hauptmann?'

For once Heuzer did not answer. And Peiper was more distressed by that than by what was happening to him.

'Luckier than Charlie,' Albert Murphy said then. He let his eyes watch a small dog licking at Charlie Race's corpse across the street. Murphy fired at the dog and missed.

'There's movement.' Simon Penny raised himself from the floor. Heuzer crept over to the window. They watched Kyle Stuart make it to the bandstand before the firing started from the hills. Single shots. Stuart crawled the remaining yards, almost burrowing himself into the dirt. He rolled in the door of the jailhouse.

'Sundown service,' he said to Heuzer, panting. 'First aid ... chocolate ... and these.' Stuart passed the first-aid kit to Heuzer, threw three bars of chocolate to Peiper, Penny and Murphy and placed a bag of bazooka rockets under John Delmar's desk. 'No sign of Dr Ashton comin' back,' he said then.

'I expect whoever's in command out there is digesting my threat,' Heuzer said.

'Look, you can't really mean it?' Andy Redrow said to Heuzer. 'For Jesus' sake.'

'You Yankees are lucky,' Albert Murphy said. 'If we didn't have that threat, then they'd kill all of us with a few dive bombers. We're keepin' you alive.'

'Why do you use that term?' Andy Redrow asked him.

'You fly the Yankee flag on your jail,' Stuart said.

'Just who are you?' Andy Redrow asked.

'My friends and I represent the Confederate States of America,' Stuart answered, with a degree of pride in his voice.

Andy Redrow moved forward, pushed Heuzer's pistol aside, then stared at Kyle Stuart in a kind of offended disbelief. 'This ain't *Gone with the Wind*,' Redrow said.

'It's like this,' Stuart said. 'There was this girl in Dresden I was sweet on ...' He grinned at Heuzer. 'My mother would never have approved. You ever ask yourself why you ended up here, Herr Hauptmann?'

'Because I wanted to,' Heuzer said. 'Or it wanted me to. Perhaps it's the same.'

'What you see are the last remnants of the Stonewall Legion,'

Stuart said to Redrow. 'We are the Confederacy. Now, if you'll favour us with your co-operation, I'll see this business is over quickly.'

'Sweet mercy, man,' Andy Redrow said, 'don't you know this town was the last outpost of the Confederacy in New Mexico? Didn't surrender till the late summer of 1865. But that was eighty years ago. The war's over, the Confederacy's gone.'

'With the wind,' Stuart said. 'You think the boss man out there has come to the right decision?' he said to Heuzer.

Heuzer looked at his watch and then at Peiper. 'Time for encouragement,' he said. 'Bring our bartender friend up, Murphy.'

Zach Pepper was brought from the cells and placed kneeling in the middle of the floor.

'What're you gonna do?' Andy Redrow tried to comfort Pepper but his own fear and Heuzer prevented him.

'Now, Mr Mayor, I want you to watch this very closely and report what you see to whoever's in command up there. I'm about to introduce you and your people to the realities of this war. Realities your bombers have been introducing to us for years now.'

Heuzer shoved Zach Pepper to the doorway. For a second or two, everyone in the room was stunned to silence. Then Stuart made a move, as if trying to hang on to something rather than prevent what was coming. 'Heuzer!' His protestation was useless and he knew it.

'You know what'll happen if they catch us?' Heuzer said. 'You tell him,' he said to Penny. Then he turned to Stuart again. 'Gehlen was right. You're chasing something dead eighty years. Welcome to the present, Teniente.'

Stuart lowered his hands and sighed. Something inside him had finally broken.

Pepper was only beginning to realise what was going to happen, and started to cry. He wet himself just before Thomas Heuzer opened the door. 'I always get my men out,' Heuzer said to no one in particular. He kicked the pleading Pepper into the street. Pepper turned once, shouted for everyone to hold fire. Heuzer shot him once in the head and once in the chest. And then there was silence again.

'Now, you go, Mayor Redrow,' Heuzer said then. 'You go up there and tell whoever's up there that's what'll happen if I don't get my way. You make him understand I'm not playing games.'

Andy Redrow did not say a word. The only thing showing on his face was shame.

Fifteen minutes later, as Philip Rand came running towards Norman Rogers, the engineer's excitement made the colonel take a step back, something which startled every officer in his presence. 'Attack?' Rand said, following Rogers. 'You can't attack. That's what he wants, damn it.' He looked at Silas Ashton and Andy Redrow in turn.

'It's gettin' dark,' was all Redrow said. 'That man, Heuzer, will kill everyone down there.'

Rogers regained himself as Rand was drawing breath. Rand came to attention almost as an afterthought. Everybody waited for Rogers. But the colonel virtually ignored Rand. 'I told you to get your men outta here, Major,' Rogers barked at Brett. 'And take this ... officer with you.'

Kyle Stuart made it back to the foodstore during the hiatus on the hills around him. The face he brought back was more subdued than the one he had left with.

'So what's the play?' Schwartz said to him. 'What happened back there?'

'You got that battle flag you always carried in Russia?' Stuart replied. 'I think Heuzer wants Pickett's Charge.'

Schwartz pulled a small stars and bars flag from under his combat jacket. 'I've kept the faith, Teniente,' the Texan said. He looked at his hand then. 'If not my fingers.'

Stuart tried to make out what was happening on the hills around him. He could hear the sound of engines.

The last of Warren Brett's men left their positions in groups of four, covering one another, and were replaced by military policemen who did not acknowledge them or their positional advice.

Philip Rand turned to Warren Brett when the engineers were all gathered around the vehicles designated to take them away. 'You know you could have put up more of a protest.'

Brett shrugged and watched his dead being sorted in the back of a Dodge truck. Their faces were pale in the early moonlight and his face grew red and tight and his muscles seemed to move involuntarily. He slammed his hand against the side of the truck. 'I'm not disappointed,' he said. 'Somewhat sick, Philip, but not disappointed. These boys know the job better. We're engineers. We build things.'

'You think he knows what the hell he's doing?' Rand demanded. 'Tell me, Warren, do you still think I killed Eadie Shaffer?'

But Warren Brett refused to listen now. He was examining the personal effects of his dead.

Around them, more military police assembled in sections of fifteen. Rand scratched his head. 'This is a mistake,' he said.

He lifted his field glasses and watched the military police sections approach the town from either end of the main street, staggered to provide cover from flank attack. But the staggering required positional discipline and a degree of coordination which was easily lost in the confusion of semi-darkness and battle.

In the jailhouse, Kyle Stuart's voice came through the various atmospherics. 'Here they come . . .'

Heuzer drove his fist into his palm and slapped Penny on the back. 'Now, we have them.'

Penny prepared himself and helped Murphy with the bazooka

they had managed to rescue from one of the jeeps. 'Would you kill them all?' he asked Heuzer. 'Down there?'

'You, a Tod man, ask me that? I will get out of this,' Heuzer replied.

25

By now, the whole landscape was a dull shade of grey. Kyle Stuart moved Kell and Watkins into Zach Pepper's bar. Schwartz and Harris took up a ground floor position in the foodstore. Stuart stayed on the roof.

At the plaza, Heuzer, Penny and Murphy left Karl Peiper in the jailhouse and slipped into the shadows behind the building where they could not be seen by the relatively few men Norman Rogers had left on the hills to cover the advance of the main body of his men.

David Menton, who had once survived for three days on his own in a Russian town, fighting his way back to German lines, house by house, crawled into a house across from the foodstore but two buildings down.

Snowflakes reflecting the light of the full moon illuminated the first fifteen military police as they advanced from the railway station. Across the street, and several yards back, another fifteen men moved in snake file, while a halftrack moved up the centre of the street. It stopped at Simon Penny's car.

From the eastern end of town, two more military police sections advanced in staggered formation. Then the halftrack opened fire on the central floor of the foodstore.

Karl Peiper returned fire on the halftrack from the jailhouse. Schwartz and Harris re-occupied the central floor of the foodstore, while Watkins and Kell broke their way out the back of Zach Pepper's bar. Then, when Heuzer announced his own team was in position at the east end of town, Stuart gave Menton the order to fire.

Menton caught the first five military policemen across the street from him with a single burst, killing three of them. Stuart and Schwartz, both armed with Browning Automatic Rifles, took advantage of the surprise and killed two more MPs who had run out into the middle of the street, while Harris used his good arm to throw a bag of grenades into the halftrack. Menton fell back to another building.

At the east end of town, the military police around the gas station began firing in support of men at the foodstore they could no longer see properly. Some of them tried to move forward in their staggered sections and ran into Karl Peiper and a thirty-calibre machine gun. They fell back on the gas station and took cover among the old vehicles there and across the street. The section which was supposed to be supporting them fell back, too.

The gap between the military police sections at this end of town widened just enough for them to be no longer of any useful support to one another. Simon Penny helped Albert Murphy shoulder the bazooka he carried and pulled a rocket out of the backpack he wore. Murphy fired at the gas station. The rocket hit a pump and killed five more MPs outright, setting three others alight. Then the underground fuel tank blew up. Thomas Heuzer and Simon Penny poured sub-machine gun fire into the burning figures running around like giant fireflies in the dusk. And the entire military police attack at that end of town collapsed.

Philip Rand watched the rout. The last intact assault section across the street from the gas station advanced in echelon formation.

Three of Heuzer's positions opened fire on them. Some of the MPs ran further on towards the plaza and tried to take cover at the bandstand, and for a time they looked like they might catch Heuzer's group in a crossfire, but Kell and Watkins had worked their way up the street from the back of their original position and, with Karl Peiper in the jailhouse, they caught the five MPs at the bandstand in a crossfire.

Those MPs not killed tried to retreat dragging their dead. They ran into the men retreating across the street from the gas station. Again, all Heuzer's positions opened up on the same target.

Philip Rand shouted at Brett to intervene.

'With what?' Brett replied. 'With them?' He pointed at his own men. 'With you?'

Beside him, a military police radio operator kept shouting into his handset: 'Red section, come in red section ...' The radio operator turned to Brett. 'I don't know where the colonel is, sir, I don't know where anyone is. I don't know what the hell's goin' on here, Major.'

'I'm pulling out till more reinforcements get here,' Brett said to Rand. 'Yes, I'm pulling out.'

'We can't ...' Rand grabbed Brett and shook him, then slapped him across the face.

'I don't give a shit, Lieutenant. I'm here to build an auxiliary air strip, not fight a war. I'm an engineer, Lieutenant, and you're a fool. Look, Philip, you wanna play crazy, then go ahead and play crazy.' Brett walked away, holding his face.

Rand pulled his pistol and stuck it in Brett's mouth. 'Now I know this constitutes mutiny, and I know I'm likely to be court martialled and shot, but this is how it is, Warren.'

Bobby Helm tried to interfere but Brett brushed the master sergeant aside. 'You stupid bastard, Philip,' he shouted.

The stars had joined the moon to watch.

Kyle Stuart moved across the street at the same time the wind began to fan what was left of the fires around the gas station back to life. Three shots rang out but none of them hit him. He paused at the door of the jailhouse, to look at David Menton's body, before coming through. He had looted several bottles of spirits and sodas and was passing them around. 'Don't tell me you called me over here to inform me you're plannin' some mad Wagnerian Götterdämmerung?' he said to Heuzer.

Heuzer picked up a book from Delmar's desk. 'The Confession of Iago Santavista. Mr Penny, here, has been reading it to me.' Heuzer explained the story to Stuart.

'Do you know how he sent his confession home? Surrounded by Indians, starving, dying of thirst?' Simon Penny asked Kyle Stuart.

'Sheriff John Delmar made a special study of the event,' Heuzer said. 'Now we have it as a bequest.'

'No one knew how one of Santavista's men escaped,' Simon Penny said. 'The man himself never said. And the text has no obvious clues.' Penny took the book and opened it. 'You've gotta look deeper.'

Stuart looked at the text.

'The guide is here,' Penny said. 'The sections of the book are called pledges. It is actually called The Pledges of Iago Santavista. Confessions is an afterthought. Look! Two words every seven pledges. Take them out, put them together and you have the way out. The snake. That's Santavista's sign. They rode the snake ... the Vibora. The river.'

'At the very end of the Santavista Gap, the river splits,' Heuzer said. 'Half of it goes underground. You cannot see it except from the river itself. That's how he got out. That's how we will. Santavista did not die here. He escaped. Just as we will. We'll cover you over here, Kyle.'

Stuart smiled and looked at his watch. 'And how long do you think it's gonna take them to figure what was goin' down? No, Heuzer ... but thanks for the consideration. When we start firin', Herr Hauptmann, you start movin'. And don't stop for anythin'. I'll give you five minutes to get to the river – you think you can carry the stuff?' He looked at the two boxes of plutonium.

'We'll all get out, Kyle.' Heuzer slapped Kyle Stuart on the back. 'I always get my men out.' Both men knew the emptiness of the statement but both needed it at the same time.

Philip Rand was already moving his men into position. Master Sergeant Bobby Helm stood up in the halftrack, gripping the twenty millimetre cannon. Two military policemen, holding Browning Automatic Rifles, covered his flank.

The halftrack began to move up the broken road, followed on the flanks by the shadowy sinews of two lines of men. Twice, Warren Brett looked across the back of the halftrack at Philip Rand, as if to seek reassurance for what they were doing.

The halftrack stopped at the train station. The engineers and military police broke up into groups of four and occupied the buildings nearest the train station. Then Bobby Helm opened fire on the foodstore.

Heuzer looked at the two boxes containing the hemispheres of plutonium and then at Karl Peiper. 'Think you can come along, Karl?' he asked his sergeant.

'I have a good feeling in my belly, sir. I'd salute and the like if I could, but it hurts too much. I probably need a little more time to rest. And I should cover Teniente Stuart, I think. I'll catch up with you, Thomas.'

When Heuzer realised he had asked another man to die for him, he closed his eyes. He packed each plutonium box into a small rucksack, put one on himself and gave the other to Simon Penny. Murphy went into the cells and told everyone to prepare to move.

The Tennessean then pulled the various pieces of John Delmar's office furniture and jailhouse equipment away from the cell doors. 'Right, first cell,' he whispered. 'Everyone up. You're going free.' He opened the first cell door and the ten people in the cell were driven up the staircase into Delmar's office.

Thomas Heuzer then opened the front door, covered the

ten civilians to the opening, then yelled a warning. Then he shoved them out: three women, five men, two children.

Immediately they began screaming. Karl Peiper opened fire over their heads with the thirty-calibre machine gun.

Murphy and Penny shoved the next group out the back door with similar results. The majority of them were women and they screamed when Murphy fired over their heads.

Then there was an explosion from a house further down the street where a section of engineers and military police had tripped another booby trap and Kyle Stuart's position in the foodstore opened fire.

Then a burst of cannon fire hit the jailhouse.

Heuzer shouted into his hand radio. Murphy covered him to the back door. And then Penny covered Murphy.

Karl Peiper managed one more burst. The reply from the approaching halftrack went over his head. It almost cut Murphy in two.

On the steep bank of the Vibora, Thomas Heuzer lay among the spinal scrub and black stones. Around him random shooting and shouting fought for dominance of the night. Simon Penny was first into the water. Heuzer held his arm, then let him slide to a rock. The rock was sharp and Penny cut himself. He held the rock and reached out for Heuzer. Heuzer hesitated before he slipped into the water on his belly.

Both men took their rucksacks off their backs and put them on against their stomachs. They held hands and manoeuvred themselves on submerged rocks until they were in deeper water, supporting each other and the two rucksacks until they reached a place where the water was colder than at the banks.

The current was fast in the centre of the river and the water very dark. It was difficult to hold on to a rock under the water but the figures running along the banks could not see Heuzer and Penny.

Then Heuzer slapped Penny on the back and the two men let go of the rock.

Kyle Stuart watched the military police and engineers move to positions around him. He could feel a sharp pain in his side but very little else. The soldiers running around him seemed to move in slow motion. Larry Schwartz was dying in his arms, holding his stars and bars flag to a huge wound in his chest.

'They're makin' good moves now, sir,' Larry Schwartz said. 'I don't suppose we can run up the stars and bars?'

Stuart smiled. 'Sure, go ahead, Larry, run it up and see if anyone's got a harmonica. We can play "Dixie". You sure you joined the right outfit?'

'Better than bein' with the Yankees.'

Philip Rand shouted a warning at the plaza, then approached Stuart and Schwartz behind the halftrack. Stuart pulled himself up to a sitting position on the grass supporting himself against the bandstand, and reloaded his weapon with an empty magazine.

Very carefully, two of Rand's men and two military policemen took up positions on the flanks of the two remaining Stonewall Legionaries. Then another party of eight men came up behind them. One of them kicked Stuart's weapon from his hand. Stuart tried to reach for it but he was pinned down in position by his sergeant.

Philip Rand touched Stuart with his boot. The eyes caught some moonlight and Rand heard a babbling breath and saw blood coming from the mouth. Rand reached down and touched the stars and bars flag at Schwartz's chest. Stuart's hand prevented him from removing the flag.

'I never thought I'd ever see that flag raised in battle again,' Philip Rand said. He crouched down and examined Schwartz to make sure he was dead. 'I take it you speak English?' he said to Stuart.

'With an accent.'

'You are surrounded.'

'The rest of my boys?' Stuart gestured to the foodstore.

'Dead,' Rand replied. 'You fly this flag. Why?'

'Because I represent the Confederate States of America, established.' Stuart smiled.

'Can you move?' Rand asked.

'Are you offerin' me terms?'

'Only unconditional surrender.'

'Your name is not Grant, by any chance?' Stuart said.

'I don't suppose you will tell me where your captain is?'

'Are all your men coloured?'

Rand went to lift Schwartz but again Stuart stopped him. 'Leave him ... please.'

'You will die,' Rand said.

Stuart smiled and nodded. 'I fully expect to.'

A line of lightning tore the sky and then thunder delivered rain.

As the lightning tore at the fabric of the night, Heuzer and Penny entered a narrow cave, barely able to breathe, blinded, turning in the torrent, ears full of the roar of the water, current crushing them. Once, while he was fighting with the water just beneath the surface, Heuzer was convinced he saw a man on a white horse riding along the gap.

BROKEN KEY

26

Derek Boyd was still busy searching the apartment where Pam Hanny had taken Simon Penny's phone call days earlier when the black car pulled up at the kerb outside. Claude Dansey sent his driver into the building, put his head out the back window of the car and waited for Boyd to come out. 'You're being a bit optimistic, Derek. You won't get anything there. She's gone for good. Hop in.'

'Scene of the crime. Penny might have called,' Boyd countered.

He looked across the street at a window where two more of Dansey's men were looking out. One of them held a cup in his hand.

'I'm thinking of a suitable punishment for those two,' Dansey said. 'And they know it.'

Boyd got into the car. 'You think she's with him?' he asked. They drove out towards Pennsylvania.

'That New York apartment her Russian friends were supposed to have ransacked,' Dansey explained, 'the one she left without a suitcase, it's owned by an old man in a wheelchair. And as far as I know it's always been owned by that same old man. I think she's red, Derek. We have been careless.'

'Any more from New Mexico?' Boyd asked.

'The birds are still free. It's all getting very irritating. Our American cousins are in the process of losing their minds. And my heart's giving me more than the usual trouble. Perhaps I've been at this game too long. Patriotism can be addictive.'

'So you think Penny'll make contact with her?' Boyd asked. 'With Pam?'

'You and I know we can consider that prearranged. Frankly, if he does, I'll blame you for slipping up on his training.' Dansey grinned to relieve his tension. 'But let's assume the love birds cannot resist each other and work from there.'

'I should have been quicker,' Boyd said. 'I should have realised what Simon was. It was all there.'

'No recriminations, Derek,' Dansey said. 'We've all been slow. Anyway, we've a rather bigger problem than apportioning blame. I feel very grubby all of a sudden, you know, Derek.'

'We are grubby that the world remains clean,' Boyd remarked.

Daylight dragged a rain belt across the Rockies. It met a cold front coming down from Canada, and there were floods.

Los Muertos was overcast. Wind from the mountains caused the new leaves on the trees to rustle. The smell of dampened fire hung over the town and the leaves were black. The wind whipped up the sodden ashes from the fires and dropped them on the leaves. Now and then a flock of birds passed in echelon formation. Philip Rand looked up. 'Perhaps they flew away,' he said. Then he looked at Andy Redrow and John Delmar's body.

'He killed himself really.' Andy Redrow closed John Delmar's eyes before the sheriff's body was thrown in the back of the Dodge truck. 'I thought you boys had gone,' he added.

'I didn't kill your daughter,' Philip Rand said to Redrow.

The rain cooled his face and the residual smell of cordite filled his nostrils. He pulled the Confederate stars and bars flag from Kyle Stuart's hand, tearing some of the material on Stuart's nails. 'They should be in the ground,' he said. Then he wiped the rain from his face. 'I was thinking maybe you'd like to have a drink, sir,' Rand said to Redrow then. 'Maybe talk about Eadie.'

Redrow thought about it for a while. 'I don't approve o' mixin' o' the races,' he said. 'Ain't Christian. No offence, son. You're a brave boy.' Redrow walked away, then turned. 'I think my Eadie liked you,' he said.

Jeff Francis reached the Dodge as Redrow disappeared into the gathering crowd. After twelve hours in an aircraft, Francis looked as weary as Philip Rand's men, who were still sitting around Los Muertos in small clusters, waiting to be relieved. Francis took a drink from a water canteen to take the carbon taste from his mouth. 'I think he was trying to make friends,' he said to Rand. Then he introduced himself.

A group of military policemen, trying to extract their halftrack from the jailhouse, were clearing bodies from the porch. Philip Rand ignored Francis's introduction and went over to the bodies. There were ten, all military police and engineers. They were separated by a small gap. 'My major,' Rand said to Jeff Francis. 'Warren Brett. I think he was killed by our own men. He was a brave man. I hope they give him a medal. He deserves a medal.' He glanced at Norman Rogers's corpse but said nothing.

Jeff Francis brushed his hair back in the wind. There were flecks of ash in his hair and he picked them out. He looked back at the Dodge truck containing Kyle Stuart and his men. 'Washington will have a fit,' he said to ease the tension. 'Especially with these guys.' He touched Kyle Stuart's legs. 'We found Delmar's ranchhouse burned to the ground. No sign of his wife, though. You think they killed her, too?'

'What in God's name have those people been doing up at Los Alamos?' Rand asked.

'Very little in His name,' Francis replied. 'I'm going to need your help, Philip. I've ... eh, fixed things with the authorities. Charges against you will be dropped. Hell, you might even get a medal.'

'Don't patronise me, Agent Francis,' Philip Rand said. 'I'll assist you, but don't patronise me.'

Later that day, as he scanned reports of roadblocks prevented by flooding and searches held up by the bad weather, Jeff Francis was distracted by Silas Ashton, now smoking a pipe, who stood beside Philip Rand at a broken window.

'I've told Mr Hoover we'll have them within days,' Francis said. 'And Los Alamos say you are to co-operate, Dr Ashton.'

'I'm impressed by your optimism, Agent Francis,' Ashton said, 'but they've been at large quite a few hours already. What if there's a chance they have slipped through your net?'

'If you had told us what you were planning, Doctor, then all of this might have been prevented,' Francis answered.

'You knew there was a possibility of this?' Ashton asked.

Francis had no answer. Any revelations on his part would undermine the Bureau, he felt. And all the time he could not help feeling he had stepped on the career equivalent of a landmine. So he countered Ashton with the same question Norman Rogers had asked the previous day. 'Can you guarantee they will not attempt a detonation?'

'No, I cannot,' Ashton replied. 'Perhaps with a crude implosion mechanism.'

'Then we should assume they may be intent on detonating the material in a major city in this country,' Jeff Francis said, 'which makes our problem more immediate.' He looked over at Philip Rand with what Manny Rivera often referred to as Francis's inclusivity face.

Philip Rand was about to offer a view when Silas Ashton interrupted him with a rudeness which belied his usual reserve. 'No. They want it for Europe.' Even Ashton felt he should explain himself. 'Something that German captain said to me,' he continued. 'Heuzer.' He walked over to one of the situation maps pinned to the wall at his left. 'The Russians,' he said. 'Here, on the Oder ...' He pointed to Germany. 'It makes sense. Heuzer said he would save us from the Russians. He said that.' Ashton nodded to himself. Rand had the feeling the scientist was waking up to something other than what he was talking about.

'But we're thousands of miles away from Europe,' Jeff Francis said. He stared at the map and then leafed through some papers.

'They must have an aircraft,' Rand said then. 'How the hell else did they get here?'

His aggressiveness unnerved Francis, who while he was not uncomfortable with Rand's rank and contribution, found the situation difficult. He managed to hide his discomfort quickly.

'No aircraft was found,' he replied. 'And nothing took off last night.'

'The Germans have a rocket,' Ashton said then. 'It's called the A10. A huge version of the V2. With a range that can take it across the Atlantic. More if you boost it. Eighty-seven feet high, two stages, two hundred tons . . .' He went back to the table and drew a rough sketch and tossed it to Francis.

'We have photographs at Los Alamos, taken by reconnaissance aircraft over the German port of Kiel last year. They had the rocket riding on one of these.' He started sketching again. 'A Japanese I-400 submarine. We were very interested. And not a little scared. But nothing came of it.'

'Until now,' Philip Rand said.

'And they could fire one of these rockets from this kind of submarine?' Jeff Francis asked.

'Like I said, that's what we were scared of,' Ashton said. 'Their bomb project took in rocketry. Two devastating technologies in their own right.'

'And married together . . .' Jeff Francis touched the sketches. 'So where?' he asked. 'Where is this submarine?'

Philip Rand went over to the map pinned to the wall. 'Pick a spot,' he said.

* * *

Several hundred miles off the coast of Texas, the following morning, Dieter Vogl's submarine broke the diaphragmatic surface of the Gulf of Mexico, just as dawn cast its orange glow on the vast pulsating stretch of blue.

Vogl climbed into the conning tower, took a brief look through his binoculars, and then called Irmgarde Hanke up. When she arrived, Vogl passed Hanke a small glass containing a clear liquid. 'They distil it in the engine room,' he said. 'It will keep you warm while you work.' He thought for a moment. 'I can put you and your people off at a neutral port, Frau Doktor,' he said then. 'If that is what you wish.'

'I think I preferred you when you flirted with me, Dieter. Now you have taken on the appearance of a man who has nowhere else to go, and does not want anywhere else to go. I saw it in that man, Stuart.' She touched her chest. 'I have a future. I believed with this weapon we might have a chance.'

'I never believed we had a chance, Irmgarde.'

Her men came through the deck hatches and went to work on the V2-A10 rocket and its launcher. The submarine had thirty minutes on the surface.

Once, Dieter Vogl saw the small outlines of fishing boats; another time he saw sharks feeding. Each minute on the surface tattooed itself in slow motion on his consciousness. Hanke examined a small round object and made notes.

'Initiator,' she said. 'Encourages a reaction.'

'Agent provocateur,' Vogl said.

Helmut Otto hauled himself on to the bridge and stopped any further conversation between Vogl and Hanke.

'You know, when this war's over I'm going to be a librarian,' Dieter Vogl said to Otto. 'All the moving we do along narrow corridors will give me an advantage.'

'I'll borrow books from you, Kaleu,' Helmut Otto said back. The bearded man scratched his face and winked at Irmgarde Hanke. 'But I'll still be a submariner.' He turned to Vogl. 'They'll murder us, Dieter. And we have no defence.'

That was when Hanke suddenly made her excuses and climbed back into the bowels of the boat. She emerged on the deck some minutes later, and went to work with her men.

'Must be her time of the month,' Otto said.

'I don't like the surface much any more, you know,' Dieter Vogl said. 'It's too beautiful. If Heuzer got picked up or ...'

'Are you going to have the Frau Doktor, Dieter?' Otto asked. 'The boys and I are having bets.'

'What odds are you offering?' Vogl replied.

Otto watched Irmgarde Hanke working on deck and gave his captain the figures.

'You are a man of faith, Helmut,' Dieter Vogl said. 'I suspect you are a Nazi.'

'Of course. The Nazis made me everything I am. I was planning on practising my submariner skills commercially in the future, for whoever paid the most. Nice safe stuff, with reefs all round and beautiful sea creatures to see. And perhaps I will make films.'

'You definitely are a Nazi.'

Otto then waved at Hanke who did not wave back. 'If you don't have her, I will,' Otto said.

'But she's bad luck, Helmut.'

'Do you believe we will ever get back?' Otto asked his captain.

'No. I'll have a hundred marks on me having the Frau Doktor, though.'

'I didn't expect you to be so frank, Dieter. A bit of fanciful thinking might have helped me in our present predicament. I am not averse to the odd white lie and perversion of the truth. You know, sometimes I think of what Germany would look like when I return and what will be left and it scares me to hell. Why don't we just head south and land in Argentina and stay there till this mess is over?'

'Are you saying we cannot save Germany, Helmut?' Vogl asked. He produced a pear from his pocket, took a bite and offered it to Otto. Otto took a bite and called down to Irmgarde Hanke on the deck. She looked around at her men and refused the offer.

'When we lose this war, I will have nothing and nowhere to go,' Otto said. 'And that is a frightening thing.'

'A man who can survive in these boats for as long as you have, Helmut, does not have to worry about civilian life,' Vogl assured him. 'The only thing that will get to you will be the boredom and the endless stories you will have to tell your grandchildren about our exploits. And that will be torture.'

Dieter Vogl scanned the horizon and then looked at his watch. He was sucking the last juice from his pear when a young submariner in oilskins and a dirty string vest came up the ladder to the conning tower. 'Kaleu,' he said. 'This has just come through.'

Vogl read the message, and then burned it. 'We're in business again,' he shouted down to Irmgarde Hanke. 'Clear the decks.'

It was still dull and raining when Simon Penny checked the papers two days after that, then shaved and paid his motel bill. There was a girl standing across the road, reading a diner menu, very thin and sad. The sadness held her and she seemed to float on it. Penny had considered walking over to her and talking to her the night before, but she was with a man who worshipped her. Penny focussed many of his considerations that day on her.

Disguise had changed his appearance in a subtle way: glasses, darker hair, extra weight courtesy of stolen sheets. But if you looked hard, he was still recognisable. He watched the girl across the road move. Her hair fell to the left as she did and she dipped her head and lowered her shoulder. Her breast pressed against the cotton dress as did her hips. And then she turned and looked at him. He smiled but she walked on.

Another woman approached him from the backdrop of a

rainstorm. And anything that could announce it by moving did so.

'We'll have to stop meeting like this.' Pam Hanny showed all her teeth and some of her thoughts and put her arms around him. 'You don't look well, Simon. Was it that bad?'

'I've had it worse,' he said. He struggled to place a hat on his head. The wind was turning up the rim. 'What do you have?'

'Fresh papers. Standby addresses.' She smiled again. 'I'm glad you trusted me.' She hugged him again. 'You know I thought for a while you didn't.' The faith inherent in the statement and the subtext kept Penny frozen while she held him.

He hugged her back all the same and wished for something that he saw as weakness. 'I need you to prepare a safe house,' he said. 'An apartment in Florida. There'll be a guest in three maybe four days. There'll be money and papers to handle. Can you manage?'

'I think I love you, Simon,' she said. She said it to fill a gap, and, like so many things, once said it began to feel true. Perhaps she just missed the intimacy, she thought. 'Do you want to tell me about it?'

He put his hand on her shoulder and kissed her but kept his eye on the young girl he had been looking at since the night before. Only when that girl was gone over a crest in the road did he speak again. 'Look, move on and I'll meet you in Florida at the end of the week. Telephone this number for details.' He handed her a piece of paper. 'You're ready to move?'

'Sure. Where?'

'Wherever.' And now he paused for a long time and let the weakness he feared overtake him. 'And take care of yourself, Pammy.'

'You too, Simon. You could say you loved me. Even for effect.'

'I could.' Penny could not take his eyes off the gathering storm.

27

The cloud seemed to be all backed up in the west and the streetcar shuddered passing the statue of the great General at Lee Circle. The General looked somewhat bored if not embarrassed, and Thomas Heuzer read an advertising board while the green streetcar pulled away and rolled on down St Charles under the shade of skeletal trees while another bell sounded in the distance.

He paused for a moment at the Plattner house. It shook to the roll of the next street car and a faint damp preyed on the white ante-bellum wood, which now had more pretence than reality. Heuzer then walked past the house, stopped and lit a cigarette.

Jenny Plattner stood on the porch, holding a towel and a feather duster. She held a disdain on her features and the moist skin often seen on women from the delta region of Louisiana.

'Be a fine evening if it weren't for the rain coming,' Heuzer said.

'A necessity. Without the rain we will not get the beauty of the flowers, and without that, no fine evenin's.' She gestured to Heuzer to follow her into the house. He took a final look round before doing so.

The remains of the sun pushed through the heavier delta clouds and some wading birds passed overhead on the way to the mud flat feeding grounds further south.

Inside, Heuzer held his breath and placed the soft leather bag he carried in the corner between a coatstand and a period coffee table. He finished his cigarette as he watched Jenny Plattner make coffee with the assurance of a practised hostess. He did not sit down; nor did he take his coat off. 'When were you told?' he asked.

'Oh, last night, I think. Was last night Wednesday? Maybe this mornin'. I get confused in my business. Yes, it must have been this mornin'. I'll ask Jesse, he's my husband. Wonderful timekeeper. Would you like if I made you somethin'? I have a lot of spare food, and I'll bet you haven't eaten good home cookin' in quite a while. How about eggs and cakes and maybe a little spiced fish? That's what my husband has. Of course, he's on a diet. Be down in a little while. Lookin' after some of our girls. We had a long night last night. There was a ship leavin' for Europe. Time off tonight.'

Heuzer finally took off his coat, pulled out an automatic pistol, checked it, and put it back in the coat pocket. He hung the coat on the coatstand and came into the kitchen.

'How should I call you?' he asked.

'How about Ma'am. I do like a gentleman, and there are so few of them left in New Orleans these days. How would you like your eggs?'

'Any way.' Heuzer paused. 'Ma'am.'

Jenny Plattner noticed Heuzer's face had changed since he arrived. She left the kitchen and then came back in with a bowl in one hand and some dirty linen under her arm. 'Yankees been givin' you trouble,' she said, smiling. 'Well, you're safe with us. Have a nice stay here tonight, move on tomorrow.' She pulled a lace curtain and looked out the window. 'And there's the rain again.'

The first thing Thomas Heuzer did after feeding Jenny Plattner's cat the next morning was take another look across the room at the soft leather bag he was carrying. Then he went into the bathroom.

The bathroom was a pot pourri of brass, chipped enamel and Italian tiles, with the usual yellow stains at the water outlets. Heuzer washed. When he had finished, Jenny Plattner was standing at the door. She did not come in.

'I have to go?' Heuzer asked

'Your train's in the evenin',' she said. 'You're up early. I expected you to sleep late.'

There was a gap in the conversation and Jenny Plattner gave him a smile he did not appreciate. 'I don't sleep much,' he said to fill in the gap.

'I do hope none of my girls disturbed you,' Jenny Plattner said then. 'They don't sleep much at night either. Even on rest days.' She walked up to him and kissed him. 'You are somethin' of a beautiful man and I rarely get to kiss beautiful men any more. Jesse sometimes gets to chase the little nymphs, I just get to dream. I'm older than him. Though you wouldn't know it.'

Heuzer pushed past her. 'I have work,' he said.

She sighed, giggled and put a towel over his shoulders. 'Don't turn the light on,' she said. 'I never turn the lights on before eight. I'm fifty-three and I look better in dim light. Do you know how long it has been since I looked good in artificial light at the start of a day? Oh, in the evenin', I look fine. And there's so much to do. I think you would be a wonderful subject for pamperin'. And I would love someone to pamper these days. Jesse doesn't need it so much any more. And we never had any kids. I used to pamper Papa and . . .' She shook her head. 'It's such a nice day.'

'You were going to ask me something else?' Heuzer demanded.

'Oh, I'm botherin' you,' Jenny Plattner replied. 'I'll make you breakfast. But don't tell Jesse, he gets very jealous if I make other men breakfast. And then he has to go to confession. You religious?'

'I was going to be a pastor once,' Heuzer replied. 'It didn't happen.'

'You look disappointed,' she said.

'Determined. I convinced everyone but myself I would be a pastor. So now I have learned to use my determination. Achievement fills in the gaps.'

'It gives me comfort, religion. I do so admire the Virgin Mary. So pure. Who do you admire? No, don't answer. I'll make you breakfast. The soap's over there. It's pre-war, from France. I bet you like John the Baptist. I can always tell.'

'You're a kind woman,' Heuzer said. Both of them knew he did not mean it.

'Oh, what's the world without kindness,' she said.

He smiled to himself, then went to the window again to look outside. When he had checked outside he went to her radio transmitter, in a small room at the top of the house, and sent a short message to Dieter Vogl. It was acknowledged a few minutes later and Heuzer pushed the transmitter back into its case and hid it beneath the floorboards.

Later he asked both Plattners if they had a map of the east coast of the United States.

Jesse Plattner, who was wearing a cream suit and a flower in his lapel, nodded and went to an old oak cabinet in the kitchen and fiddled through a woodwormed drawer. 'I keep maps of everywhere. Father insisted. His father insisted, too. When the Yankees were here they used to hide things in an old store out back. But then the Yankees went and declared such things illegal. I wonder if it still is.'

'I expect not,' Heuzer said. The ease with which he was fitting in made him uncomfortable and it was hard not to believe this was his life and the rest an uncertain memory.

'I do like science, though,' Jesse Plattner said. 'Do you?'

'I want to keep busy,' Heuzer said. We have to keep going, Karl, he thought before he realised Karl Peiper was not there. Behind Heuzer, the structures of his life had all but collapsed. In front of him there was only his determination. He noticed the cat again almost as an afterthought.

*   *   *

Manny Rivera was still rubbing his eyes after four hours watching the Plattner house when Thomas Heuzer came to the window again and took the cat in his arms and fed it milk from a saucer.

'We got somethin', Albie. Get up.'

Albie Rice dragged his overweight body to the window, his grumbling, asthmatic voice almost losing its volume, as he fought to keep himself awake after two hours of intermittent sleep on a hard floor.

'That guy you said came in last evenin'. Is it him?' Rivera demanded.

Rice shrugged, scratched his chin, then his bottom. 'Maybe. Yeah, it looks like him. So what! It ain't Oskar Finger's killer. Nothin' like the description. Probably just a customer.'

'He came in last night, he's still there now,' Rivera said. 'Where's that stuff from Los Muertos?' He reached for a single typed sheet of paper, looked at it long after Heuzer had vanished again, then took his gun out and checked the chamber. 'Get on to Jeff Francis, Albie. Then get as many Bureau people as you can over here. We better take this guy.'

'You sure, kid?' Rice asked. 'If it's just a customer and we blow this, our man won't touch this place.' He grabbed the information Jeff Francis had sent from Los Muertos. 'Jesus, this could be anyone, Manny. Maybe he's a gigolo. Just watch and make notes. Christ, them Plattners have to have some vices themselves. Church socials and women's auxiliary programmes are just too good. Even madams have their interests. I mean, this is New Orleans.'

'Just do what I say, Albie,' Rivera said. 'If we miss this and it turns out to be anythin' so much as black market, then we'll end up watchin' seabirds on the Aleutians.'

Albie Rice, who had still barely woken from his sleep, had never faced a gun-battle with anything but dread. And what made him more frightened now was that Manny Rivera had never faced one at all.

'You're too keen, that's your problem, son,' Rice said. 'Listen, I chased 'em all in my day, and what you gotta have is patience. It all comes eventually. That's statistics. If people knew more about statistics then they wouldn't try to second guess everythin'.'

Rivera, who had sacrificed some balance of thought for his desire to please Jeff Francis, passed the ancient hulk next to him two clips of ammunition. Albie Rice just sighed.

'This is important, Albie. Now we can take him. Are you with me? Because if you're not, I'll go alone.' Rivera checked his gun again and threw a last spare clip to Rice.

'Jesus, you bastard,' Rice said. 'You think crawlin' up Jeff Francis's ass is gonna get you anywhere?'

Rivera was pulling shotgun shells from a leather bag. 'Do what I say, Albie. Now!'

Albie Rice swore, holstered his gun, picked up a piece of bread and some Italian cheese, and ate it all. He went over to a small washbasin and threw water on his face and over his hair. His face bore the signs of his dread. 'I wanna look my best,' he said.

Manny Rivera was already at the door.

The humming of an aircraft engine out of synchronisation forced Jeff Francis to stop what he was doing and look out. The cloud blanket below him was jet black and between the uneven engine and the cloud Francis was held in a hypnotic vice. Philip Rand picked up the small telex lying on the seat beside him.

'We'll be late.'

Francis just nodded. 'You have an annoying habit for awkward truth, Lieutenant,' he said.

'Worried?' Rand asked.

That snapped Francis back from where he was drifting. He took the telex from Rand. 'What do you think?' he said.

'I never killed Eadie Shaffer, you know,' Rand said. 'I just thought I'd remind you of that.'

Jeff Francis nodded and looked at Rand for a few seconds.

There was a degree of sophistry in the lieutenant's eyes, something essentially convincing and very strong, and it caused Francis to jolt before he returned to the window.

28

Despite the best efforts of the sun, a grey pall now blanketed the houses off St Charles Avenue, New Orleans, sucking the colour from the paintwork and flowers and slowing the day. In two of the houses door screens swung on the heavy Gulf wind and then creaked and slammed shut. A pair of caged birds sang in a porch and a girl with porcelain-like skin turned a corner. Then the streetcar bell rang.

Albie Rice loaded a pump shotgun and Manny Rivera took the safety catch off his pistol. Then the older man nodded, moved through the wood and mesh gate and stopped. The spring flowers released a calming odour but Rice still had to breathe deeply before moving on.

He kept the shotgun hidden under his long coat, slipped round to the side of the house, while the sun made another effort to break through the clouds, then held his breath and opened the side gate.

Manny Rivera examined his pistol once again, held it behind his back and walked up the wooden steps to the front door of the Plattner house. He held the screen open and knocked on the door.

Opening the door, Jenny Plattner squinted her eyes, adjusted her dressing gown and hunched her shoulders, so that her neck almost vanished. The tickling steel of what had been dawn made her shiver. Manny Rivera shoved the pistol into her forehead and his identification into her face. 'Not a sound!'

Jenny Plattner stopped breathing and her face reddened. Rivera shoved his palm over her mouth, pushed her back into the hall and held her against the wall. The smell of fried food distracted him somewhat while he checked the hall and the staircase.

At the same time, Albie Rice forced the back door lock, trying to avoid making a click as he manoeuvred the bolt. He managed it but the door had a small bolt and he broke it.

Upstairs, Thomas Heuzer heard the noise as he was examining the contents of his bag. The warmth of the hemisphere he had in his hand and the shine of the plating held him captivated while he made a judgement on the sound he had just heard.

Albie Rice eased his way through to the kitchen.

Directly above him, Thomas Heuzer held his breath. He could hear sounds and his ears broke them up and analysed the parts.

In the living room, Manny Rivera held Jenny Plattner flat on her stomach, bound her with curtain cord, gagged her with a silk scarf and listened for noises from overhead. He heard nothing. He stood up, edged his way to the door, put his gun around, and then his head.

Albie Rice, shotgun in one hand, inched forward from the back door through a passage and into the hall. He could hear water pipes in the basement and birds pecking the roof tiles on an outhouse and soft breezes on curtains in the kitchen and the sound of every organ in his own body.

Then Heuzer made his first move. A step to the left. It put him out of reach of the door. He picked a silenced pistol from the chair beside him and checked the magazine.

Albie Rice stopped. An infinity of small sounds and tiny sensations overwhelmed him. He could smell his own body and hear the house move in the wind. Then Manny Rivera's pistol appeared.

Rivera eased his way around the living room door, and drew breath. It felt like cacti were growing on his tongue. He leaned his head against the wall, saw his partner, checked the staircase again, and gestured to Albie Rice. Before moving himself, he looked back at Jenny Plattner lying on the floor. When he turned back, she broke free.

She screamed and threw herself at him. Rivera jumped back at her and tried to shut her up. Rice hesitated, stepped forward, extended his shotgun, then hesitated again, trying to see what was happening in the living room and covering the stairs at the same time.

Upstairs, Thomas Heuzer opened his bedroom door and stepped out on to the landing. At the same moment, Albie Rice swung his weapon into position, but Heuzer stepped back into the bedroom before Rice could fire. Rice took cover in the doorway of a study across the hall.

'Manny . . .' he whispered.

He stopped himself going to Rivera's aid and edged his way to the staircase, then threw himself against the far wall. He listened again, this time yelling a warning to Rivera, and dashed for the kitchen again. But when he swung himself out the back door and aimed his shotgun at the balcony and bedroom windows, Heuzer wasn't there. Rice shouted to Rivera again.

In the living room, Jenny Plattner bit Manny Rivera, shoved her knee into his groin, and knocked him sideways across the floor. His weapon fell from his hand. Rivera tried to recover his gun, but failed. Jenny Plattner reached his gun first, stood up, cocked the weapon and fired it.

The bullet hit Rivera in the shoulder. He fell back over a chair. Jenny Plattner ran for the door and aimed at Albie Rice, just as Rice reached the staircase again. But the gun failed to fire.

Rice shot her in the stomach and she slammed back into the hall door, struggled a bit and then slumped down.

Manny Rivera crawled from the living room holding his shoulder and his balls. And Rice swore. He picked up the pistol Jenny Plattner had dropped and handed it to Rivera.

'Cover me!'

Then he paused for a moment to check his partner's wound before making for the stairs again.

Albie Rice moved up the stairs, shotgun extended. He looked back once. Jenny Plattner was sitting against the front door, slightly forward, a kind of tepid contempt on her face, as if the woman had never really cared for anything in her life.

Manny Rivera stood at the end of the stairs, reloading the pistol in his good hand, bad hand shaking and blood from the shoulder wound dripping on to the stained floorboards.

Rice reached the top of the stairs, slammed himself against one wall, looked back at Rivera one more time, then began to move along the landing. He kicked at a bedroom door but it would not budge. He stumbled, kicked a second bedroom door. It flew open. Rice shook his head and gestured to Rivera, then waited for the wounded man to reach the top of the stairs before he prepared himself to kick in the next door on that floor. He never got his foot to the door.

Jesse Plattner came out of the room, holding a tray. His operatic face smiled. 'Tea and cakes,' he said. 'Milk and sugar?' He threw the tray at Rice, then pulled a silenced pistol from his velvet dressing gown and shot Rice in the face. Rice fell back through an open door.

Manny Rivera swung round and fired at Jesse Plattner. The rounds caught Plattner in the head and back. Albie Rice fired his shotgun as he fell and caught Jesse Plattner's arm as he was falling. The two victims fell in opposite directions.

Then Heuzer appeared.

Rivera swung round but Heuzer had already fired. He shot Rivera once and the bullet went through him, clipped the bannister and hit one of the china vases on the landing.

Rivera slid down the stairs, holding the bannisters, trying to focus on Heuzer. It was almost a dance, with whoever led the victor. Heuzer fired again. The round caught Rivera in the chest and toppled him back down the stairs. It was a slow freefall and Rivera called Rice's name and some others before darkness began to take over.

Heuzer walked over to him, touched Rivera's torso with his foot, then began to search his pockets.

Rivera heard the breathing. The smell of Heuzer's breath was a fish and egg smell that diminished as Heuzer's breathing slowed. The German examined Rivera's documents with a degree of calm he only experienced in such moments.

Then Rivera raised his legs between Heuzer's, kicked out and sent the German straight back against one wall and into another. The single shot, muffled by the short distance, toppled Heuzer over a small wooden table, splintering its legs.

Manny Rivera tried to raise his head. But the world around him had speeded up and he could not find the gun anymore. Jenny Plattner put the last two rounds in it into him.

'What an unconscionable intrusion,' she said to Heuzer. Then she sank down against the front door again and died.

When Thomas Heuzer regained consciousness, blood was seeping in a small thin trickle from his abdomen. He pulled himself up by a doorhandle, struggling to co-ordinate. Outside, he could hear voices shouting.

29

Walter Schellenberg had just managed to wake up from a drunken sleep when several hundred American bombers came into view on the Berlin evening skyline. The aircraft floated towards the city on a carpet of flak to the anguished howls of the air raid sirens.

'I thought I'd catch you alone.'

The words stopped Schellenberg fastening his tunic and shouting for his secretary.

Reinhard Gehlen stepped into his office. 'Everyone's gone to the shelters,' he said. He closed the door and picked up one of the bottles Schellenberg had been using to relieve his tension. 'Don't worry, the American air force is nothing if not predictable, Walter. You're probably safer here than anywhere else. Sit down.'

'You have news of Heuzer?' Schellenberg asked.

'In a manner of speaking,' Gehlen said. 'I know you told the British about Ground Zero, Walter.'

Schellenberg's mouth dropped and he reached for a drink. At another time, in another place, under different circumstances he would have bluffed it out, turned the tables on Gehlen. But now Schellenberg had nothing left to fight with. He was almost glad to have been discovered.

'I was ordered to,' he said. 'By Reichsführer Himmler.'

'After his last dressing down by the Führer I'm surprised he can order a cup of coffee,' Gehlen said. 'You might ask me how I know.'

'What are you going to do?' Schellenberg asked.

'Heuzer's still at large. He still has the plutonium. The operation proceeds. You will simply accede to any and every request I put to you from here on in, Walter. To all intents and purposes, SD Ausland's days as an autonomous agency are over. You are mine, Walter. And everything you possess. Don't worry, if you are lucky enough to survive this war, I might even hire you after it.'

When Gehlen had left, Schellenberg drank until he collapsed again. And he did not even notice the bombing.

Simon Penny only drank coffee waiting for his train in New Orleans. He read and reread Iago Santavista's Confession. The book was still wet, and as he watched a group of soldiers say goodbye to their women, he peeled the pages apart. The women did not seem as upset as their soldier men were, and the book was still dribbling water across Penny's table.

Penny put on his hat, took out a pencil and wrote a letter to no one in particular. He had hundreds of them, and sometimes he mailed them to addresses he picked out of the telephone book, once or twice asking them to write to some drop address he happened to be using. It was a way of keeping in touch, he told himself. With what, he never said. Occasionally, he got a reply to his letters. Once, he even got a marriage proposal.

The newspaper beside him had a small story about a black American soldier hanged for rape in France. It was about three lines long and Penny had ringed it for a reason he did not know.

Pam Hanny came into the station through a door on his right, and he was still writing when she went up to the ticket desk.

There was a moment when he was tempted to come up behind her and put his hands around her eyes and kiss her. But something more powerful than affection kicked in and he allowed the distance between them to remain. He watched her for a couple of minutes while she talked with an old coloured man behind the ticket counter and then turned on her stilettos and surveyed the station. She did not see Penny. He had placed himself in a corner and was sitting near a water fountain where four of the soldiers saying goodbye to their women were in line for a drink. Pam Hanny read an advertisement for war bonds.

The peace in the station was broken at almost the same moment Simon Penny decided to go over to her. Three uniformed policemen rushed in with their weapons drawn and then five more spread out in a line, and a dozen armed men in overcoats and soft hats arrived. They began to question people in a very random way, letting some go, detaining others for a few moments before letting them go, too, just looking at others and walking on.

Simon Penny folded his letter and placed it in his pocket before picking up his newspaper and heading for the station door. There was a gents room to his right and he went in for a minute while the shouting started and the policemen asked people to stay where they were and the FBI agents with them argued with the policemen about who had jurisdiction.

A single uniformed officer came into the gents and demanded to see identity. There were four men there and only Penny had a driver's licence. But the policeman was not looking for identification. He examined each of the men in turn and merely glanced at Penny's dark hairpiece. Penny walked clear of the station just behind a second batch of plain clothes police and FBI agents.

He walked down the street, found a public telephone and called the Plattner house. The man who answered the phone asked his name. Penny made an excuse and hung up. He was coming back up towards Union Station when Jeff Francis stepped out of a police car.

Francis began shouting orders at the men around him. Philip Rand stood behind him, looking incongruous. He almost turned towards Penny but he was distracted by a man who said something Penny could not hear. Rand grew angry at what the man had said, but Jeff Francis pulled him back. They went into the station, followed by more men with long coats and drawn guns.

Simon Penny waited for five minutes but Pam Hanny did not come out. Then he hailed a cab. As he sat in the cab and gave the driver a destination, two FBI agents passed him. When the cab pulled out, Penny looked into the station one more time. This time he saw Pam Hanny. She and Jeff Francis were embracing. Penny did not watch them kiss, but inside his whole body ached.

Only Thomas Heuzer's head ached. The overly made-up woman beside him had been talking for an hour now, and the soft wetlands threw up a subtle mist while the last of the rain ran red soil in streaks through the grass of the railway embankment. A flock of wading birds bit into an expanse of mud flats and others sang a curious mealtime chorus while all along the horizon fishing boats dragged along the simple line of the inshore horizon.

'Of course, my daughter can't see what a bum he really is,' the woman said to Heuzer. 'I told her that those wings won't count for nothin' when he gets out. Captain ... they'll make anyone a captain these days. Were you in the service? You look too sick. Are you sick?'

'Some,' Heuzer said.

The woman did not pay attention to his answer. She adjusted herself in the seat and looked past him.

'I do love the South,' she continued. ' 'Course you're not from the South, are you? I'd say Philadelphia or one of those New England states, maybe. Definitely a Yankee. We're from Charleston. Family's been there since ... well, since before the war between the states.'

The train attendant, a large expansive man of about fifty with strong features and a singer's voice, announced the next stop. Several soldiers picked up their kit bags and sighed. One or two kissed girls.

'Biloxi!' the woman beside Heuzer said. 'Lot of them boys steppin' off here for Biloxi. Where are you goin'?'

Heuzer did not reply. He was sure he could feel blood seeping from his wound. If he moved and it started to drip, it would give him away, if he didn't move he might bleed to death where he sat. But death did not have the same fear for him as failure. So he held still until the woman stopped talking and he had figured a way to raise himself without putting pressure on his wound.

'Just what am I doing here?' Philip Rand asked Jeff Francis. 'I sit in cars, stand in waiting rooms and have people ask me to take their bags. I notice you never exchange anything with me, Agent Francis. I offer you candy, you refuse. I asked you for a bite of your sandwich, you give me the whole sandwich. Even when we're in a car together, you sit away from me.'

Francis took out a cigarette, lit it and began to smoke. He offered Rand a cigarette. Rand refused it.

'He was my friend,' Francis said. 'Agent Rivera was my friend.'

Rand's manners stopped him saying what he wanted to say, and his intellect fought with his emotions for control before he spoke further. 'I apologise,' he said. 'But I lost men in Los Muertos. And they were my friends.'

'Colonel Rogers was a flawed officer,' Francis said. 'I gave orders for no action.'

'That's not the way it appeared. Who's the lady?'

Francis touched his notebook. 'Someone I used to know. She has family in Georgia.' Francis smiled. 'Don't worry, I have no interest.' He opened his notebook and searched the pages. 'Where the hell did that airplane go to? They must have had an airplane.'

'You haven't answered my question,' Rand replied. 'Why me?'

'North, south, east or west?' Francis said then. 'Which way did he go?'

Rand reached into Francis's packet of cigarettes, fingered a few and then pulled one out. Francis followed every movement.

'You want to know what I think?' Rand asked. He pulled a small map of the United States from Francis's briefcase and stole another cigarette from the packet. 'Here's what I think.'

The weather in the Gulf of Mexico all that afternoon had been dominated by low cloud and depressions. There was nothing flying and very little afloat. But everything that was afloat was military. Dieter Vogl swung his periscope around to the south.

'Contact astern.'

Vogl wiped his brow, downed the periscope, turned to Irmgarde Hanke, shook his head and made his way to the hydrophone operator. Hanke followed without being invited.

'How many does that make?' Hanke asked.

'Five,' Helmut Otto said.

'I'd swear Heuzer has them coming after us to draw them off himself,' Vogl said. 'There was something about him made my perspective uneasy.'

'We could pull out,' Irmgarde Hanke said.

As if to protect his captain, Helmut Otto put his hand on Vogl's shoulder while they listened to the hydrophone echoes from above as the contact came about in a wide sweep.

'Do you think they spotted us?' Hanke asked then. 'Those ships up there.'

Her ears were beginning to betray the pain associated with steep diving to dangerous depths, while the air on board, which smelled like over-stewed halitosis, forced her stomach to perform acrobatics. But since everyone on the boat had these problems too, it did not seem so bad.

'We'll get there, Frau Doktor,' Helmut Otto said. 'Yes, Kaleu?'

'I fear we will, Helmut,' Vogl said.

Otto shrugged and then moved on along the boat.

'I think he resents me,' Hanke said to Vogl.

'He's a homosexual.'

'And you have no problem with that?'

'You know I'm claustrophobic,' Vogl said. 'I hate all this. It makes me want to throw up sometimes.'

'Do you think he will make it, Heuzer?' Irmgarde Hanke asked.

Vogl reached out and put his hand on hers. 'Do you ever question yourself, Frau Doktor?'

'Me? Never,' she grinned.

Claude Dansey had noticed Derek Boyd's sense of his own ability begin to disappear from the moment they lost Pam Hanny. Boyd's character had developed a pause in everything it did, his tall frame seeming to slip with every word or action. Once or twice, Dansey thought he detected a descent into loss of belief in the head of Huntergatherers, which was why he took the sighting of Pam Hanny in New Orleans with such a smile.

'But no Penny,' Boyd said.

'I thought we might have to come clean with our American cousins,' Dansey said. 'Have them sifting through our files and generally disturbing the smooth running of my service. Perhaps Simon Penny knows her colour. Perhaps he knows our Russian friends want to take from the thieves. Nice little number, that, have Jerry take from us, then they take from Jerry. If Penny's on to her, then she's useless. But I live in hope, Derek.'

'I feel responsible for Simon,' Boyd said. 'I'd like to get to him before she kills him.'

'That's always been your problem, Derek, too much of that responsibility nonsense can limit perspective. This game is one big problem, the trick is always to use it to your advantage.'

'How do you propose to do that?' Boyd was joining his fingers in the way Dansey thought brought out the worst of his self-righteousness. Boyd was a man who made modesty a public relations exercise, Dansey felt. And power never seemed to taint him. Dansey wondered if what he was feeling was not just jealousy. Boyd was the future; he the past. The past has so much to envy in the future, while the future has to wait to know what it has missed.

'Let's go,' Dansey said.

30

At Montgomery, Alabama while it was still dark, Jeff Francis and Philip Rand boarded the coast-bound train just before it pulled away from the platform. The train was crowded with people and noise in equal amounts and low harmonica music struggled along the length of the train with the new passengers attempting to find their seats and get baggage into the overhead racks.

Jeff Francis forced his way along the aisles of the train using a combination of good manners and Federal threat. Philip Rand followed in his wake, occasionally touching the tide he was aware could overwhelm him at any moment. Every single eye on the train watched him.

Twice Rand was informed there were seats for coloureds somewhere else on the train; once he was threatened. Francis intervened each time with his FBI identification.

The next carriage up, Rand was punched by a middle-aged man in a broad hat. Rand hit the man back and two train guards, who were both black, hit Rand and were considering throwing him off the moving train when Jeff Francis pulled his gun. The two train guards bowed to the higher authority.

Francis and Rand pushed their way further along the train.

Thomas Heuzer woke to the rocking of the train and the uninterrupted snoring of the woman beside him. He checked his wound. There was no sign of external bleeding overnight. He checked the bag he carried. It had not been disturbed from the rack across the aisle. A girl smelling of lilac stood in the aisle beside him and an old man complained he was feeling faint.

'Would you help me lift him?' the train attendant asked Heuzer. The attendant's pleasant blancmange face and cherry eyes were difficult to resist, and the woman beside Heuzer, who was now awake, kept insisting he help the fainting man. Almost out of habit, Heuzer obliged, and as soon as he lifted the fainting man, who looked healthier than he did, he knew he was bleeding again. He dumped the fainting man in his seat.

'Is that man all right?' the woman next to him asked Heuzer, touching the blood on his armrest and not sure where it had come from. She opened her handbag and took out some bandages and other things. The train appeared to pick up speed.

'Yes,' Heuzer said to her. 'You put that away and I'll call a doctor. Keep my seat.'

The woman went to follow him. He shoved her out of the way. 'I'll be back,' he said. The general movement of those who had to stand and those moving along the aisle pushed him towards the restrooms.

In the toilet, Heuzer opened his shirt and looked at the bleeding wound in the mirror. Then he pulled a bullet out of his pocket, took a screwdriver and pliers and pulled the bullet from the cartridge. Then he emptied the gunpowder from the cartridge on to a small piece of tissue paper. When it was all out, he took the tissue paper and stuffed it into his wound, as far as if would go. When this was done, he struck a match and put the match to the extremities of tissue paper in the bullet wound . . .

He came to, shivering. His hand had been burned and his skin had a long streak of coagulated blood running down to his trousers. His face was white and he found it hard to bring himself up. When he managed to raise himself and examine the wound in the mirror, he found it had sealed at the point of entry but he did not know if there was further bleeding inside and he felt so weak that he thought he might pass out again. He rebuttoned his shirt, then poured water on his face and tried to prepare himself.

The landscape appeared in lines outside the train as Philip Rand stood at a window, lighting a cigarette. The train rushed by darkened low-lying wet grounds where trees were further on in their growth and the shapes were huddled capes and long lines of prostrate figures, grasping at the red soil and holding fast against the heavy breezes and the threat of storms.

Jeff Francis waited for Rand to catch up. They had been through three carriages and were standing at the door of the dining car. In front of them, three waiters in white jackets carried plates of eggs and bacon and fried potatoes, bottles of water and pots of coffee. They were all black and Philip Rand felt he should have been safer here but the black men looked at him with even deeper contempt than the white ones had.

'We might have got it wrong,' Francis said.

Watching the waiters, Rand was going to answer, but his eyes bounced from their familiarity through the dining carriage glass to the next passenger coach and the gradual thinning of the people clogging the aisles. A ticket collector was asking a heavily made-up woman with fiery eyes about the seat next to her.

Something in the way the woman moved her shoulders and looked at the armrest made Rand look at it. Then he pushed past Francis, past the anger of men and women seated for the first breakfast call of the day, through the door and into the passenger coach.

The ticket collector told him he was not welcome in that coach right when three or four of the men in the coach were using stronger language to tell him he was not welcome in any coach that went through Alabama. Two of them were Georgians and Rand pushed past them, focusing on the blood he could now see on the armrest of Thomas Heuzer's empty seat. Jeff

Francis was just coming through the door from the dining car with his FBI identity raised and his left hand on his gun, when Thomas Heuzer opened the toilet door.

He heard the commotion first and then Francis identifying himself and Rand, and then some more shouts from around the carriage. Heuzer pulled his bag from the overhead rack.

The ticket collector began to push Rand out of the carriage, more to prevent a possible riot than because of any real feelings he might have had himself. He was from Philadelphia. Rand was trying to ask the pasty fat man with asthma, who had been sitting in his seat before him and where was he?

Rand searched the train and backed off in the face of the ticket collector and two men who had decided to lend him a hand. Francis pointed his weapon at the two men. That was when Rand saw Heuzer. He shouted a warning at Francis.

Heuzer knocked Jeff Francis off balance and slammed his head into the wall of the carriage, brought the side of his hand down on Francis's neck, took his gun and shot the ticket collector. The man fell back into Philip Rand's arms and Heuzer shot one of the rednecks who were about to beat up Rand. The man's head exploded. Heuzer shot the second redneck in the neck. Then he shot at the lights.

The train shook and the orange juice tipped over as Philip Rand passed the first table in the dining car. A woman sitting at the table tried to catch the pitcher; the man across from her, in a white shirt and suspenders, tried to stop Philip Rand; the man across the aisle from him tried to shout but began choking on a herring bone.

'Get this goddam nigger ...'

Thomas Heuzer turned round, shot out more lights, then swung his weapon at Rand. For a moment, when their eyes met in the struggling light, Heuzer seemed to show a sympathy that fixed Philip Rand. Then Heuzer fired.

The man in the white shirt and suspenders, who was getting up to swing at Rand, got in the way of Heuzer's rounds. They struck the centre of his back and knocked him over the pitcher of orange juice. His wife continued to scream and Philip Rand fired three rounds in the direction of the retreating Heuzer.

Heuzer moved back three carriages, shouting warnings, turning at each door, firing at the lights, reloading as he pushed through the heaps of crowded fabric-covered flesh, curtains of moist smoke and all the sweaty irritation of long-distance confinement. Occasionally, out of a window, he saw a morning star. Once or twice, he shot a man or a woman who got in his way too long. Sometimes he was amazed at the power of his desire to escape. Mostly, it was a mechanical function. And it gave him comfort.

Behind him, Philip Rand struggled to make his way through the panic, fighting off threats and insults and occasionally having to turn his weapon on passengers who figured he was the intruder, no matter what their eyes told them.

Rand reached a buffet car, stopped, looked around at all the faces staring at him, showed them his weapon, picked up a bottle of beer from a small table, drank from it, handed it back to its owner, then shoved his way through two men. But Heuzer was gone.

Five minutes later, Rand pulled himself over several stacks of luggage and mailbags into a long wooden boxcar with barred oblong holes for windows. In the distance, early morning began to shine, and he could see white sand and speckles moving on the horizon. The deep green trees which shaded the damp red soil on the other side of the tracks moved almost together and the sky re-formed in slabs.

The boxcar smelled of lubricant and rotten wood and Rand was busy trying to make out the subsidiary odours when there was a crack, like wood breaking, and then something hit him. Rand came back like an express had hit him, and collapsed in a heap of mailbags.

Thomas Heuzer dived at him, holding a two by four plank, just as Rand cocked his pistol. This time the two by four caught

Rand across the top of the head. Rand fell back again and Heuzer rolled out of the boxcar and swung the plank at Rand again. Rand tripped Heuzer and put a foot into his stomach. And whatever had sealed inside Heuzer opened again.

The two men lay bleeding on the ground, their blood mixing and pushing a trail in the floor of the boxcar. Rand tried to lift himself but could not find the strength. Then Heuzer pulled a knife from a small sheath at his left ankle, dragged himself up and crawled along the boxcar on his belly. He put the knife to Rand's throat. 'We're trying to save you, you know.'

Rand put his gun to Heuzer's head. 'There's nowhere else to go, Captain.'

'There's always somewhere to go,' Heuzer replied, smiling this time. 'It just depends on how much you want to get there.'

It took another two minutes for the train to stumble to a halt, people standing tripping over the bodies of those who had fallen, Jeff Francis scrambling over the bodies, a great surge of individuals squashed into a single expression of angry impotence. Francis had to shove people out of his way to reach the boxcar at the rear.

Rand was lying on his face. Francis put his hand to Rand's throat, turned to a guard behind him and pointed his gun at him. 'How many more carriages?' he asked.

'Ain't no more,' the guard said. 'He dead?'

Francis wiped his mouth and inched his way to the back door. 'No, he's alive,' he said. 'Who else came through?'

'Didn't see no one else,' the guard said.

The sea south of Jacksonville, Florida, made a soft hushing sound on the shore below as Pam Hanny folded the last suit and checked the false documents lying beside the telephone. When she had finished folding the suit, she went to the window to watch the ocean. Only when she had repeated his name did Simon Penny speak.

'Simon ... you're safe,' she said. At least part of her was genuine. 'I thought you'd be caught. There were police and troops all around New Orleans.'

'Tell me about the FBI.'

The pause was so long, Penny thought she had either nothing to say or was busy with an excuse he could tear to pieces. In a way what she said made him respect her.

'You were there.' She picked something up and put it down. 'In the station. Waiting for a train. I asked you a question.'

This pause was even longer. And now all that had been between them was laid bare in a single look. And there was nothing left.

'They asked me to make contact,' she said.

'They? Who are they?' he asked.

'I never told them where you were, Simon.' There was a pleading in her voice, as if she felt she had let herself down.

'Who, Pammy?' he demanded. His voice began to divest itself of any humanity, and the mechanical nature of the syllables frightened her.

'London,' she said. 'I'm London's, Simon. They placed me here as your shadow. I've always been London's.' She adopted a satisfied expression, sure that what she had said would make him step back. But it did not and what she saw in him she had no stomach for. For Penny it was not even an issue now. He was functioning on something she had never seen in the raw. Something that caused him to move about the room like a hunting animal.

'You killed Oskar Finger and Violet Abery?' he said suddenly. It was an odd accusation and the answer was equally unexpected.

'No, Simon,' Pam Hanny insisted. 'I've done everything to protect you, Simon. London knows you're German. Dansey's here. Dansey and Boyd. They're looking for you. They told me to get in touch with the FBI. I tried to tell you before, but I couldn't. His name's Francis, Jeff Francis. There was no love. There is no love. I mean it. I like him, yes, but there is no love. Don't just say nothing, please.'

Now the pause came from Penny's side. And much of the automatic motion was nullified by deep thought. She was having some effect on him, and it pleased her. She almost reached out to him.

'You were to kill me?' he asked.

'I was to try and find you through Francis. I never told them I was still in touch with you. I promise. It's been very difficult, Simon. I've had to do things. I feel dirty.'

She sounded so pathetic he was tempted to put his arm around her.

'I did it for you, Simon.'

'And Tommy and Angel?'

'Moscow. Or Dansey, maybe. I've thought about it. The money you're carrying, it's dirty, Simon, that's how the FBI found that house in New Orleans. I know I should have told you but I have my duty. I didn't ever betray you, Simon. I was trying to help you.'

'So where is Dansey now?' Penny asked. 'Come on, Pammy, tell me. Where is he?'

'I couldn't tell you if I knew. I can still help you, Simon.' She paused before her next sentence. She reached out slowly. 'I need you, Simon.' He fended off her advance.

'I'm going to have to head north,' Penny said. 'This place will be crawling with FBI and police in a couple of days. You should go, too.'

'I don't want to know why you did it, Simon,' she said. 'I don't want to know that, Simon. Just get the plutonium and leave it in a locker, where they can find it. I'll help you. Then we can leave. Just go. The two of us. Just vanish.' She knew what she was saying was ridiculous, but the peculiar thing was that her words seemed to have a bigger effect on him than on herself.

'We're enemies, Pammy,' Penny said. And now he paused for what seemed an eternity. 'Goodbye.'

'Be careful, Simon.'
'I'm always careful. That's why I never cared for you.'
She could tell he did not believe it himself.

31

Three days later, Simon Penny stood his next drink on the Miami bar counter and stared at it for some time before downing it. He had always liked gin, the way he had always liked onions and cheddar cheese and tinned peas, not for their taste but more for the consolation they gave him. The small things that reminded him of himself, he said. He could smell a shoeshine boy's box from where an old man stood at the door. The rain had come again. The old man was debating whether to leave. The shoeshine boy timidly wondering if he could stay.

When the lightning tore the sky for a third time and the thunder echoed against the faded wooden furniture of the bar, Penny went to the telephone. There was a long pause before the man on the other end answered his questions.

When Penny put the phone down he went back to the bar. The old man was still there. The shoeshine boy was gone. Penny ordered a sandwich of onions and a beer.

He downed the beer faster than the gins and swallowed the onion sandwich in three bites. His first wife said he was a pig and his second said he was a dog. He wondered what other animals he had been compared with.

Penny ordered more beer and another sandwich and then left and went for a walk in the rain. He needed the wash.

Claude Dansey was standing across the street beside a car.

✳   ✳   ✳

Many miles further north, Jeff Francis touched Pam Hanny's body with the timidity of a small child whose only living relative had just passed on. Philip Rand stood at the door, still marked by the beating he had received from Thomas Heuzer, rustling the change in his pocket. Behind him, several policemen and FBI agents wandered up and down the corridor. Outside, the sea crashed on the white sands and the wind sprayed the art deco angle of the beach with a bilious spit while a single ship was silhouetted on the black horizon.

'I thought she was in Atlanta,' Jeff Francis said. 'She has family in Atlanta. I have to inform Hoover. I think I should be relieved.'

'You are some bastard, Jeff Francis,' Philip Rand said.

Jeff Francis picked his nose and then tried to pull a cigarette out of a packet he had not used in some time. 'Why the hell are you still alive?' he said to Rand. 'Tell me that.' The Massachusetts angle to his accent, which made everything he said sound like the result of intense thought, was more pronounced when he was upset, and the movements with the cigarettes increased the tension. 'I wanted to love her,' he muttered.

'We have to move, Jeff,' Rand said. 'Navy say that submarine's heading southeast. Weather's turning bad, too. They might lose it. Do we want it intercepted?'

Francis shook his head and examined Pam Hanny's personal effects laid out on the bed, and began fingering a small sea shell, examining the colours, feeling the texture of it between his fingers. 'The Keys,' he said. 'Has to be the Keys.'

As Dieter Vogl's submarine surfaced in rough seas about fifty miles from the Florida Keys, the night was a combination of pitch and swell, and the rain drove horizontally from the west.

Vogl stood in his oilskins, breathing fresh air with the enthusiasm of one for whom it is a luxury.

Everything below was wet and the cooped up smells of weeks

underwater seemed to combine in a great push to get out into the night.

'How close do we get?' he asked Helmut Otto.

'The charts say we can move through this channel and arrange a meeting here.' His number one pointed a torch at the relevant spot. 'We're moving into a bottleneck, Dieter,' he added. 'I'd hate to have to try and get out quickly.'

Vogl nodded. 'Rotate everyone up here for fresh air,' he said. 'Do you think we should run, Helmut?'

'I want to say yes, Dieter. What about the sewage?'

'Keep it. I don't want anything to hint at us being here.'

'It's making life down there very toxic, Dieter,' Otto said.

'I don't like repeating myself!'

When they were down in the control room again, Vogl turned to Otto. 'We'll give Heuzer twenty-four hours.'

'And then?'

Vogl smiled and raised his eyebrows. 'And then we'll give him another twenty-four hours. Do you expect to survive this war, Helmut?'

'Of course, Kaleu. Would I come to sea otherwise? I have faith in you, I have faith in me, I have faith in this boat. We will return. And when I am really in a good mood, I have faith in the Führer and Germany. Is that what you wish to hear?'

'I wish to hear the truth.'

'That is no longer on offer.'

'Dive, if you please, Helmut. Set a course for Broken Key. And get me something to eat. I've decided not to seduce the Frau Doktor. I just don't like her any more. I think she's too much like Heuzer.'

Broken Key is about fifteen miles northwest of Key West, and about half the size. In 1945, the village on the south side of the island was a main street affectionately known as The Hinge because of the way it bent, and this ran as far as the trees. Beyond the trees there was a cemetery with strange epitaphs like:

Even the Devil was Good Once. Then there were more trees, and some cane fields and swamps. The swamps covered the coastline. There were several settlements along this coast and the sea often made them inaccessible except by boat.

Thomas Heuzer reached a beach on the northeast side of the key that Friday morning after the weather had forced him to beach his boat in the mangrove swamps. He sat down on a log and eased his bare feet in the sand. The figure of a wiry woman, shaped by pressure, approached in a thin dress and cardigan. 'You made it.'

Rosalyn Delmar put out her hand.

32

The first floor room where Thomas Heuzer sat up in a metal bed that afternoon had a latticed shutter banging in the wind and a rainbow hanging across the window to the balcony. There were three wicker chairs and a metal table on the balcony. And there were leaves.

Rosalyn Delmar went over to a conch and picked it up. 'You should rest, Captain,' she said. 'I'll do what needs doin'.'

'I think I'm leaking again,' Heuzer said. 'Where's my bag?'

'Under the bed,' she said. 'Keeping you warm.'

Rosalyn Delmar listened to the conch and put it to Heuzer's ear. 'My husband gave it to me,' she said. 'I listen to it every mornin'.' She put it down in a corner and came back to Heuzer. 'My husband was a weak man,' she said as she examined Thomas Heuzer's wound. 'Tried to be strong. You're right. You're bleedin' again, inside. And I think you're infected.'

Heuzer looked over her shoulder. Outside, the leaves rustled in the wind and the rainbow deepened its hues as the day made a last attempt to brighten up. 'I'm very cold,' he said.

'You have a fever. I'll have to get you somethin'. Otherwise you won't make it.'

'I'll make it,' he said. He tapped his skull, as if the words themselves were enough.

She stood up and went to the window. 'Could be a bad storm,' she said then. 'Lots of things come in before a storm.'

She pointed to various things in the room: netting, floats, pieces of wood. 'I think I'll go beachcombin'.'

She looked at Heuzer as if she was making measurements.

'Eadie Shaffer liked to beachcomb,' she said. 'That was her husband brought you here. Mikey. My cousin. Came to visit us, married Eadie. So maybe I'm to blame for your trouble.'

'I have no trouble,' Heuzer said, smiling. 'Please accept my regrets on the death of your husband and son.'

She shook her head. 'Not my son. John's. By his first wife. She ran off with ... well, she ran off. They both loved Eadie so, John and Gus. John just couldn't let go. And Gus, well, Gus was his father's son. This is my family home. The one I keep in here.' She touched her head. 'Been here for centuries, we have. You heard of Iago Santavista?'

Heuzer nodded and smiled so that his teeth showed. He used the moment to take in air. Lightheadedness was beginning to overwhelm him. 'Let's say I've followed her career closely.'

'There's a legend that Iago Santavista came here lookin' for another route to the City of the Sun,' Rosalyn Delmar said. 'Yeah. Years after Los Muertos. But I don't believe in legends the way John did. Too much white blood in him. I'm part Seminole.' She touched her forehead. 'Seminole are smart. I thought it was for the best. Killin' her, I mean. Eadie just couldn't help bein' trouble.'

But Heuzer was not interested in what she was saying any more. He did not need to be. He kept staring past her at the sea. 'Do what you can for me,' he said.'

She came back to the bed, touched Heuzer's forehead and went over to a washbasin. She took a cloth and wet it and came back to the bed. Then she took a bottle from the floor and began to clean Heuzer's wound. She took one more look outside.

'I'll go into the village,' she said. 'Get some things for you. You've given the submarine a time?'

Heuzer winced as she forced the cloth into his wound. 'Tonight,' he said. 'My signal.'

A US naval seaplane touched down on the water at Broken Key two hours later and disgorged Jeff Francis, Philip Rand and five more FBI agents. Rand was the last into the little boat that brought them ashore. He and Francis were barely talking. The FBI agent seemed to be on a personal quest now. And they had reached the last stop.

At the jetty, Francis took his hat off and offered cigarettes to everyone. A fresh breeze laced with the smell of fish and very small, very warm drops of rain blew in from the west. Philip Rand watched an ancient pickup filled with lobster pots crawl between potholes towards the harbour.

Mike Shaffer woke in the back of the pickup, soaked and shivering, wishing the warmth of the remaining sun on his cheeks would spread further down his body. He scraped the sand from his face, stood up and jumped from the back of the truck. He walked down to the water's edge. There was a silver sheen on the sea and the waves had settled into a lapping motion. On the shorelines it was slow, almost laborious.

'Don't suppose you could spare a dime?' Mike Shaffer asked Francis. Philip Rand reached into his pocket and pulled out ten cents.

'Don't want nothin' from you,' Shaffer said.

Jeff Francis shoved his FBI identification in Shaffer's face. 'Get lost,' he said. 'You're drunk.'

'Get lost ... get lost. Who you lookin' for?' Shaffer shook his head. 'Never mind, forget it. I musta downed a heap last night. Yep, and now I don't got a boat any-more. You see what drinkin' does for a man? No more mine. His.'

'Whose?' Philip Rand asked, trying to make friends as much as interrogate. He was still examining the island and trying to second-guess Francis.

Shaffer walked off, shaking his head and waving Rand off. But Rand continued to follow him. There was nothing else to do.

Not long after that Rosalyn Delmar stepped off her small boat at Broken Key harbour with her back to the possibilities of another storm. Behind her, small black clouds gathered in hunting packs and the sea blanched before the small clouds became one and the water went grey in preparation for the main event. She tethered her boat to the newly painted jetty, glanced at the naval seaplane to her left, then said hello to a trio of fishermen who had been watching the storm building to the northwest for an hour and had decided not to risk it. Then she walked up The Hinge and turned right to the small drug store. Before she went in, she looked at the sky one more time.

After buying what she thought she needed, she went to the post office, bought a few stamps and a war bond, then walked back towards the harbour by a small track which ran parallel to The Hinge.

Three old men came hobbling along the street and seemed to take an age to cross the road. The man behind them was white and much younger. And dressed in an expensive suit.

'Could I trouble you, ma'am?' Jeff Francis raised his hat.

'Do I know you?' Rosalyn Delmar asked him.

'No, ma'am. But I'm with these gentlemen.' Francis pointed to the other FBI agents. 'We're looking for a man . . .'

Strange shadows were beginning to form around the harbour, and when Rosalyn Delmar looked up she saw that the clouds were now almost black again. And they lay like lazy animals across the sky.

'FBI takin' darkies,' Rosalyn Delmar said, nodding up The Hinge at Philip Rand, who was talking to Mike Shaffer. He had his back turned to her.

'He's not FBI,' Francis said. Then he explained what they were looking for. 'And you are . . .?' he asked.

She gave a false name. 'I haven't seen anyone I haven't seen before,' she said. 'Look, there's another storm comin' and I have to go, or I won't get back.' She left Francis considering his next move and continued on down the street.

'Nice talkin' to you,' he said after her. 'Thank you for your help.'

'You can have a statement any time you like,' she shouted back then.

Jeff Francis kept watching her until she stepped on to her boat and started the engine. The boat bounced between the rising waves while the swell pulled her across the water at an angle and the dark clouds seemed to sink and she was afraid for a moment that the whole sky would cave in. She had disappeared around a headland when Philip Rand shouted to Jeff Francis.

Thomas Heuzer had just managed to pull himself out of bed and across to the balcony when Rosalyn Delmar's boat reappeared. He watched her approach the smell jetty, through the swelling waves and the small sea birds perched on the tops of tree stumps. It was still calm and the sea lapped a calm rhythm on the pebbled shoreline, touching an old net and a heap of seaweed and the skeleton of a shark. Part of its jaw was missing.

'You came back, then?' Heuzer asked, leaning over the balcony. His face was so pale he might have been dead, Rosalyn felt.

She paused and looked back at the sea. 'There's G-men on the island,' she said. 'They're in the village. We have to go to the swamps now.'

Fifty miles off out to sea, one hundred metres down on a shelf, Helmut Otto handed Dieter Vogl a slip of paper. Vogl was writing in the logbook and drinking from a bottle of schnapps. His body was irritated by a salt rash and his hair had lice. Several of the crew had lice and no amount of effort to get rid of them had worked. Otto stood back.

'He's there,' he said.

Vogl read the message, then made another entry in his logbook. 'Get Frau Doktor Hanke down here, Helmut, would you.'

'I'm here already,' Irmgarde Hanke said.

She stood at the entrance to Vogl's quarters but did not enter.

Vogl handed her the message and Hanke read it. 'You're about to get a chance to test your science. Unfortunately, once we surface, if anything other than our man is there, we're dead.'

'Our date,' she said.

33

Rosalyn Delmar stopped dead at the top of the stairs. In the candlelight of her house, you might be forgiven for believing the small snub-nosed revolver Jeff Francis pointed at her was some kind of offering. Rosalyn Delmar smiled irritably.

'I would like you to drop the bag and put your hands on the rails,' Francis said to her. 'Then come down the stairs. You resemble your son, you know.'

Francis stood to one side while Rosalyn Delmar came down the stairs. 'He was not my son. Gus,' she said. 'Never my son.'

Francis pushed her against a wall flaking paint, frisked her, then led her to an armchair. 'Where are they?'

The baseball bat caught him across the bridge of the nose, then in the stomach and then in the back below the ribcage. He staggered, feet deserting him, trying to find the leather bag he had dropped, trying to make sense of the figure in front of him.

Thomas Heuzer swung the baseball bat one more time, and Francis fell back. Heuzer almost collapsed, too, from the effort.

'Get down to my boat,' Rosalyn Delmar said to him. 'Go on, I'll deal with this.'

When he reached the jetty, Thomas Heuzer sat down beside Rosalyn Delmar's boat and watched the first heavy rain belt of the night wrap itself around Broken Key. The rain was soft against his face and the clouds appeared to be standing on the sea.

He rubbed his face, shone a small torch at a compass, then looked at his wound again. A trace of pink and yellow fluid seeped through the bandage. About twenty feet away, the tidal water lapped at the reeds and a frog croaked in the water.

The water was a strange viscous liquid, shot through with motor oil and the remains of rotting fish carcasses and the muddy flats that the wading birds used at low tide.

Heuzer reached down and scooped some water for his face, then opened the bag he was carrying.

He heard two shots from the house.

The shots caused Philip Rand's feet to sink into the sand. He pulled them free with difficulty, extended his gun hand and attempted to part the darkness with his other hand, occasionally falling over submerged roots and pieces of old boats and various shipboard items.

Away from him, in the trees, the crescent moon moved slowly in and out of vision, and the smell of the sea was strong on the night air. Voices shouted for directions and Rand answered them.

Clear of the mud and other flotsam, he started running.

Jeff Francis caught Thomas Heuzer at the edge of the mangrove swamp. The water cooled Francis' burning head as he slid in, but the sand gave way and then the water swallowed him. It took him some time to surface.

Heuzer was sitting on the sand when Francis reached him, blood from his stomach running through his fingers in the smallest streaks and the strong rain watering down the streaks still further, making them fan out between the hairs on the back of his hands.

'There was another man,' Francis said. He described Simon

Penny. The blood flowing from his own head wound fell to the sand in drops that looked like flower petals. 'Where is he?'

Heuzer tried to laugh but his fatigue prevented it. 'Just pull the trigger. I have nothing to give you.' He squinted. 'I speak five languages, you know, and I'm still a captain.'

Francis almost felt sympathy.

Philip Rand leaned down and shone his torch in Rosalyn Delmar's face. She had been shot once. 'Spread out. Ten-yard intervals. No one stray out of sight of anyone else. Let the dogs go.' None of the FBI agents or local men questioned his commands now and the dogs were unleashed.

The dogs thrashed around in the undergrowth trying for a scent, before heading for the shoreline, barking into the blackness. Reluctantly, the men behind them followed.

Francis pulled the gun he held away from Heuzer's head. 'I want you to get up and start moving. Over that way.' He pointed to the trees again. 'And take your time. Otherwise I will blow your brains out.'

Heuzer laughed some more, then coughed up blood, then laughed again. 'Okay, okay, you win . . . I think I'm contaminated by that shit I'm carrying. Do you know about it?' He pulled himself up from where he sat and put his hand out for Francis to shake. 'If you shoot me, it will have no effect. I am beyond death. Go on, shoot me, you'll see. I won't bother explaining.'

As Heuzer began to stumble through the mangroves, the moon found a way through the clouds as the wind picked up until a low moan stopped everything for a moment. Heuzer turned to see Jeff Francis dropping his hand to his side and sinking to his knees. The Bostonian started to vomit.

'You better come out of there,' Philip Rand shouted into the mangroves. 'I'll empty this whole damn thing into you if you don't come out.' He reloaded his shotgun, took in the sounds of the dogs changing direction and the shorthand of voices screaming orders and warnings in the deep darkness beyond the trees.

The figure moved, then stumbled, then said something incoherent, then fell to its knees. An attempt to speak was muffled by the wind.

Rand approached a little more, shotgun outstretched. He was sweating and there was a stream of mucus coming from his nose. The figure ahead of him moved again. Then it swore, turned and began moving away.

Philip Rand aimed the shotgun and thought for a moment. Someone called his name and a torchlight shone through the trees and swamp roots. Rand shouted at the figure ahead of him to stop, crouched and slid into the water and told everyone to hold their fire. Voices joined in long lines and asked positions over the angry barking of dogs, while the various artificial lights crisscrossed one another in the swamp.

'Don't shoot!' someone cried.

Rand put his hand to his mouth and listened. Another voice shouted a warning, a third asked for directions. Then there was a shot and another shot, and then everyone opened fire.

Out of the water, with the moonlight for a carpet, Philip Rand approached the body lying in the shallows. He examined the face of the dead man in whatever light the moon provided. The mask was white and fixed and almost smiling, and the moon then blinked through the clouds and the smile froze and the pale features of the face seemed to be fixed in time as if that was now Jeff Francis forever, and only he knew the joke.

34

Dawn came with a protest, slow, long, uneasy and shivering, and the storm which had come up the night before had not blown itself out yet. The sea was still high and the clouds had cleared revealing a blue in the sky which appeared cold to the touch. Philip Rand opened a shutter and watched as two FBI agents poured themselves juice in Rosalyn Delmar's kitchen.

'Anything?' one of them asked Rand.

He shook his head.

On board Dieter Vogl's submarine, the men were wondering what had happened to Heuzer, too, and the air had begun to taste like the contents of a bilge. Vogl kept looking at his watch, and Helmut Otto.

'What do you think has happened?' Otto asked.

'We have to surface,' Vogl said. He turned to Irmgarde Hanke. 'Are you ready?'

Hanke was sure she could see the markings on the bone beneath Vogl's skin, and the veins in the skin were pronounced like wire mesh inside glass. Vogl's eyes were a glassy pink and frozen in a fixed stare which spoke of fear. He had sores on his skin from the sea and from not washing, and his hair was greasy and speckled.

'Just say so and we'll just slip away,' Vogl said to Hanke then.

'We cannot wait, Kaleu, not any more,' Helmut Otto said.

'If we must move, Dieter,' Irmgarde Hanke insisted, 'then we must move.' She held out her hand.

Thomas Heuzer pulled out a pair of field glasses and watched the shoreline. He was lying in tall reeds. There were wading birds and kingfishers in the area. Rosalyn Delmar's small motor boat was still moored to the jetty in front of her house. The FBI had not touched it and there were no guards around it.

Heuzer touched his wound. The bleeding had stopped but his hand was shaking and his strength was almost gone. The only thing powering him now was a dream.

Two hundred yards away, Philip Rand put down the cup of coffee he had in his hand and looked out the window. The men around him were scratching themselves and pulling on clothes.

The FBI agents moved around Rosalyn Delmar's house in small steps, as if to conserve energy and warmth; two went outside and took a leak into what passed for flowerbeds. The radio crackled slowly into life.

The man struggling along the jetty appeared to be a small animal at first, and then, gradually, his features began to take shape and he developed into the image of Thomas Heuzer Philip Rand now carried in his head. Rand opened the door and drew his gun while looking at the figure on the jetty and listening to the radio announce that allied troops had crossed the Rhine.

Thomas Heuzer hauled himself into Rosalyn Delmar's boat in a semi-haze, barely aware of what was around him. For a few seconds he passed out. Then he was talking to himself. About a father who had always had hope on his face; about a mother who worried she would become someone else; about a wife who only ever saw herself. He had been brought up on flat land with no trees, where they said you could see yourself on a clear day, educated with the discipline usually reserved for monastic orders, for purposes that could not be fulfilled. He had spent all his life breaking the fetters. Now he was loose but everything was obscured.

Then the waves began to part.

Philip Rand fired at Heuzer, then watched Dieter Vogl's submarine begin to surface with a mixture of awe and fear, then fired several shots in its direction and then at Thomas Heuzer again.

Heuzer fell back in the boat and watched the engineer officer waste his ammunition. When Rand had stopped firing, Heuzer picked himself up and emptied his own gun.

Rand resumed firing. He was joined by two FBI agents. None of their bullets hit Heuzer.

Heuzer focused whatever was left of himself on the huge boat that had pushed its way to the surface of the green carpet that was the early morning sea. Birds and other sounds sang him on his way. He smiled.

Philip Rand and the agents beside him just watched.

The huge submarine shook, roared, let out a moan, and then settled, half in, half out of the water, slowly pulling the rest of its bulk to the surface. From the north, two American destroyers appeared on the horizon, and overhead, three navy submarine hunters approached in a wide arc.

Thomas Heuzer circled in his boat half a mile from his objective. Dead.

The same day Oliver Dasch was found floating in the Vibora, Peter Heinck drank champagne in the Zocalo in Mexico City and Claude Dansey showed Derek Boyd a single sheet of paper.

'It's a copy of a report sent to you by one of your people at Malmo station,' Dansey said. 'A warning of sorts, received from Walter Schellenberg, it would appear. Not much, is it? It seems I went looking for Simon Penny and I found you, Derek.'

Boyd closed his eyes. 'The Russians really are awfully close to Berlin, Claude,' he said. 'Awfully close to us. You've said so yourself many times. Look at Pam Hanny, look at the damage she could have caused.'

'I liked her, you know,' Dansey said.

'I suppose I'll swing for this,' Boyd said. 'My conscience is clear.'

'Damn your bloody conscience,' Dansey replied. 'It was never going to succeed, you know.'

'No plutonium?' Boyd asked. 'I'll bet you know Reinhard Gehlen personally.'

'We should talk, you know,' Dansey said.